OGLALA CHALLENGE

"Nobody goes!" No Nose shouted, motioning to his three Oglala companions to block the door of the dimly lit hut. "You come here to steal land!"

"Land's everyone's, ain't it?" Tom said, resting one hand on the table in front of him and showing off the pistol he held in the other. I'd already drawn my pistol, but No Nose hadn't noticed.

"Maybe we have some fun," No Nose said, and his brown face broke into a smile. "Maybe we cut some hair from these *wasicuns!*" He turned and spit a torrent of Lakota words at the other Indians who howled their approval. Then he turned back to us. "You will both die," he promised bitterly.

"Everybody does it sometime," Tom said, grinning as he cocked the hammer of his pistol. "Your move, No Nose. Show these brave hearts what a big chief you are. See if you can find your knife, 'fore I cut you in two!"

PRESCOTT'S CHALLENGE
G. CLIFTON WISLER

ZEBRA BOOKS
KENSINGTON PUBLISHING CORP.

for Craig

ZEBRA BOOKS

are published by

Kensington Publishing Corp.
475 Park Avenue South
New York, NY 10016

First printing: December, 1990

Printed in the United States of America

Chapter One

Summer in the Laramie Mountains was a season of promise. Wildflowers in a thousand shades decorated the hillsides that had been smothered by winter snows. Down below, a dozen streams fed the swelling North Platte and sent it churning relentlessly eastward, toward the Missouri and civilization. Civilization! Farms and towns and churches . . . people who played out their lives by rules, accepting hardships as preparation for eternal rewards.

Papa was such a person. Mama, too. I guess maybe I was like that myself once, back in Illinois when I was a scrawny farm boy yet to grow his first chin whiskers. But once Papa loaded us onto a wagon and headed westward, I knew I'd left more behind than kinfolk and memories. The civilized Darby Prescott stayed there, too.

Me, I never took a backward glance, for what others saw as hazard and peril, whispered in my ear of adventure. And if death had haunted my path, well, it was as much a part of life as birth, after all.

So Tom Shea said, and ever since that crusty old scout first kept my wayward soul out of trouble when I was a fourteen-year-old tenderfoot, I'd grown to take his words for gospel. He was rarely wrong, and when he was, he didn't admit it. The past four years he'd been a second father, though he didn't tolerate the notion when others spoke of it. Now I was twenty, an age he deemed past the need of a guiding hand.

"You've got yourself grown, haven't you, Darby?" he asked, running his fingers through the considerable growth of beard flowing from his chin and cheeks. "Been a long time since you were in need of a mother's milk or a daddy's hand."

I thought on it some, and he was right as usual. Mama and Papa had done a whole lot more'n that, to be sure, but ole Tom'd never admit to it. And if I spoke of the time he rubbed life back into my half-frozen carcass, or shielded my foolhardy hide from a Sioux charge, he'd mutter to himself and walk away, unable to come to terms with gratitude.

Yeah, that was Tom, all right. Eager to help, but red-faced embarrassed if anyone expressed thanks. He wasn't really at home when there were more than a handful of folks around, unless they were Crows or Shoshonis, who took things for what they were and didn't waste words on yesterdays or tomorrows. And he was at his best roaming the mountains west of Scott's Bluff and east of the Willamette, shooting game to feed and clothe us, and worrying nobody alive with our comings and goings.

Me, I wanted company now and again. After all, there were other things than mountains and rivers a young man thought to explore. When the howling north wind sent icy daggers through my ribs, I couldn't help remembering the inviting eyes and sharp tongue of Laveda Borden, the Fort Laramie trader's daughter.

"I expect you back through here 'fore long," she'd said when Tom and I'd visited the post that spring, hunting up some work for idle hands. Three moons had come and gone, and we weren't at Laramie yet. We had found some purpose to our wanderings, though. The American Fur Company had set up trading posts here and there along the Oregon and California trails, swapping powder, shot, trade blankets, and trinkets to the plains tribes for buffalo hides and such beaver or fox pelts as could be bartered. Traders brought in a fine profit restocking the westbound emigrant trains, too. Tom Shea and I'd agreed to haul pelts and hides east from Green River to the American company's post at

6

Fort Laramie, with the promise of wages and fresh supplies at trail's end.

"Not a bad use for a pair o' ole mountain goats like us, eh, Darby?" Tom had declared.

"Not half-bad," I'd answered, and the matter'd been settled then and there. To be truthful, I'd rather been scouting for a wagon train, bringing folks west to a new beginning. But Tom couldn't stomach pilgrims two years running, and this way we would get back to Laramie and Laveda after a fashion.

So there we were, camped in the high country overlooking the North Platte River, with wildflowers and songbirds keeping us company. Through the faint morning mist, I could almost see wagons rolling beside the sluggish river, flanked by companies of women and children full of hope and burdened by weariness. Or maybe a party of Sioux would gallop by, barechested boys eager to raid horses from their Crow enemies, or brightly painted warriors out to find a brave heart fight. The whining wind told me it was all imagined, for the sounds of laughter or galloping ponies were absent from the silent horizon.

I tossed a pair of oatcakes into my skillet, and listened to the goose grease crackle as breakfast cooked. We were as alone as before, ole Tom and me. And he was snoring like an old grizzly in midwinter, dead to the world. The horses, hobbled so they wouldn't stray, munched buffalo grass nearby. Their nostrils took in the scent of the oatcakes, and they lifted their heads and stared at me a moment. Tom slept on.

Oh, well, I thought as I flipped the oatcakes. He's entitled to a sound sleep now and then. I'd known him six years, and he'd known little enough peace in that time. I pulled the oatcakes out of the skillet and set them on a tin plate. As I threw two other cakes into the bubbling grease, Tom rolled onto his side and cracked open one eye.

" 'Bout time," I told him. "Bound to sleep away the morning, and with us just two days shy of the fort."

"Got that trader's gal on your mind, do you?" he asked as

he shivered away a morning chill and hurriedly dressed. "Things bein' as they are, I best find my shears. You've got a shaggy look to you, Master Prescott."

I frowned as I passed him the plate of oatcakes. Judging from Tom's appearance, it was probably so. The old scout's beard stretched down his chin halfway to his breastbone, and it was a wonder how he stuffed food into his bewhiskered mouth. I also took note of the white streaks that were invading his beard. Men grew old early in the high country. Tom had, anyway. So had I.

After I scrubbed up the breakfast plates and tossed the crumbs off for the ground squirrels and birds to devour, Tom began packing up our belongings. I drew out Papa's old razor and headed for a nearby pond. For a moment I stared at the reflection of my face forming on the smooth surface of the water. My cheeks and chin were inhabited by thin, sandy brown hairs, and I couldn't help feeling older than my twenty years. Opening up my shirt, I gazed at the thin white scars left by a dying grizzly all those years ago in the Blue Mountains of eastern Oregon. I'd come to be a man in all the ways that mattered in the high country.

It's a hard thing, discovering you've gone and grown up, I thought as I rubbed shaving powder in my moist hands, then dabbed lather onto my face. It wasn't but yesterday that I was a skinny tenderfoot afraid of his own shadow. My, those folks who'd gone west with Papa's train back in '48 would've been surprised to learn that Darby Prescott had come to be tall and straight. He'd wintered in the high country, too, and fought Sioux Indians!

"Best hurry up there, Darby," Tom called as he took out his tarnished shears and honed them on a razor strap. "Got clippin' to do, you'll recall."

"Sure, Tom," I answered, pushing my long mane away from my ears so I could cut away the last of the whiskers. I washed away the soap and waited for Tom to start the clipping. He soon appeared, and I sadly watched a season's growth fall onto my shoulders. My ears and neck felt naked without that hair, and I began to miss the old me straightaway. Laveda would grin, though. She preferred her visitors to come civilized.

"You look to've been Sioux-scalped," Tom observed when he finished.

"No, I've got all my skin, no thanks to you," I said, dabbing a piece of cloth to the nicks in my ears. "Sioux'd do a thorough job of it, I'm guessing."

"Always have," Tom quickly agreed. "Take some doin' though, catchin' you in one place long 'nough to do any cuttin'."

"Got the itch to stop a while?"

"Me?" he asked, laughing. "Never once."

"Even so, I'll bet you wouldn't mind passing along these hides to the American Company's agent. I feel hobbled like a prairie pony, with all these packhorses and mules to guard."

"Does bind a man, don't it?"

We stashed the last of our belongings and began collecting the animals. It wasn't hard to load the pelts and hides. Tom tied each securely. The trail ahead was rocky, and the loads had a bad habit of shifting with each jarring step that the pack animals took. It wouldn't do to have half a winter's profits for the American Fur Company break loose and roll down the mountainside.

There was little chance of mishap, though. Tom and I were old hands at making our way across rivers and mountains. As for working with stock, I sometimes thought I must be half-horse. I got along with four-legged creatures much better'n I did with most of the two-legged kind. Even so, it sometimes took a fair amount of blasphemy and an occasional slap on the rump to move the mules and horses along toward the river.

Once we reached the North Platte, an eerie silence fell over us. I read the haunted gaze in Tom's eyes and knew he was remembering other times. In a few weeks that rutted trail would be full of wagons rolling west. Hadn't I envisioned the same that very morning myself? Well, the two of us had shared some high times on that trail, and buried friends and family. It was only natural to see a ghost or two.

Phantoms couldn't hurt you, and I kept the stock to a good pace as Tom wandered to the river and back again. Then his eyes spotted something on the hillside ahead, and he waved for me to halt.

"What's got into you?" I asked. "If we keep at it, we'll be in sight of the fort by nightfall."

"Not this day," he declared, pointing at a thin column of horsemen making their way down the hillside just ahead. The sun danced across their bare shoulders, giving them a shiny bronze appearance. Their pinto horses managed the descent with ease. I helped Tom control the pack animals, then examined the approaching riders. Their buffalo hump shields were painted with horses or buffalo or elk. I recognized two of those shields. They were Oglala Sioux.

I breathed a bit easier when I saw that the tails of the horses hung loose, not pinched and braided as those belonging to a war party. The men's faces bore no traces of paint, either. Still these were Sioux. Tom and I'd run across 'em before, and I had a fair-sized scar on my elbow left by one of 'em a year or so back. They weren't showing any inclination toward being friendly, and when they fanned out into a half-circle, I counted twelve.

"*Hau!*" Tom called. It was a greeting. He spoke a fair amount of Shoshoni and Crow talk, but he'd never had much business with Sioux. Me, all I knew was to stay out of the way when Oglala riders appeared.

Tom also held up his right hand to show he meant no harm. A tall, rather youthful-looking man emerged from the Indians and matched Tom's motion. He then babbled out a dozen words, but they were beyond our understanding. Tom made signs then, telling the Oglalas he didn't understand their words and that we came in peace. I made the peace sign, too, though I kept to the animals. The Sioux leader motioned for a boy of about sixteen to come forward.

"I'm called Two Nations," the young man said, his back stiff and straight as a lone pine. "My father is called Elisha Brown. From him I learn English."

"They call me Tom Shea, and that there's my partner, Darby Prescott," Tom explained. "We ride the Platte River Road, as the treaty says we're allowed, and we bring hides to the trading post at Fort Laramie."

The young Sioux translated, and I read the darkening brow of the leader. He spoke loud and harshly at the boy, who then turned to Tom.

"The white men cut Mother Earth with their wagons," Two Nations said angrily. "Look how even in summer the grasses won't grow. Where are the deer and buffalo that once roamed here? Gone! Many killed. When our people come to trade with the wagons, we are shot at! Now you come!"

"I've been through here often!" Tom answered.

"Three Fingers, the Miniconjou call you," Two Nations said with a grim face. "You kill our people when we ride against the Crows."

"Long time past," Tom argued. "Not now."

"We know your heart," the boy went on. "Spotted Elk says the Crows sing of the many Lakotas you have killed. You put on the bad face for us. Maybe we kill you now."

"He tell you all that?" Tom asked, turning toward Spotted Elk with menacing eyes. "Tell him he's welcome to try. Only I'm on a road guaranteed to me by treaty, and if he breaks it, he'll have the army to answer. As for me, I won't be all that easy to kill. Sioux've tried before."

Two Nations translated, and Spotted Elk glared. He then spoke to his companions, and they replied with wary glances. Two Nations hurried back to his companions, and the Oglalas turned and rode away without saying another word.

"None too friendly, this bunch," I said to Tom when we resumed our journey.

"Can't much blame 'em, I suppose. Wagon trains *have* cleared out the game, and more whites west of the Mississippi mean the end'll come faster for the tribes. Isn't only Oregon's got good grazing land and plenty of water, you know."

11

I did know, and I nodded glumly.

"Maybe your papa was right," Tom went on to say. "You might've been a whole lot better off to learn the farmin' trade and stay on that place with your sister. Not much left for a wayfarin' man to do. Haulin' hides ain't much of a life."

"Better'n plowing fields," I told him. "Besides, if we took to farming, who'd bring the trains west? Who'd keep the greenhorn kids from getting snakebit or Sioux shot? Who'd show the women how to cook on buffalo chips or the best way to pluck a prairie hen? As for the men, they'd be sure to follow the first huckster on some fool cutoff and wind up eating each other in the Sierra passes!"

"Figure it so, do you?" Tom asked, a grin spreading across his face.

"Know it so," I assured him. "Isn't just anybody could've got Darby Prescott to Oregon in one piece."

"Didn't get everybody there, though. Buried some."

"Mama," I whispered. "Still, she chose to come, and she told me she always dreamed of seeing the Rockies. Now she's up on that mountainside like she wanted."

"Sure," Tom muttered. I knew he was recalling other faces buried along the way. Funny how it's always the ones that don't make it that you remember. The hundreds who survived, well, maybe they didn't need remembering.

As we continued our journey along the south bank of the North Platte, an eerie quiet again settled over us. Except for an eagle turning slow circles in the heavens high overhead, we were utterly alone. I thought back to the first time I'd ridden out ahead of the company with Tom Shea, scouting the trail for trouble and shooting game when we had the chance. What a tall fellow I'd felt, my bony fourteen-year-old shoulders flung back so that my chin jutted in front of my face. By day's end I'd hung over my saddle like a deer carcass, the life ridden out of me. I'd been so sore I could hardly sit down. I slept that night on my belly — much to Papa's amusement, as he later admitted.

Now life had again set a lonely trail in front of us, and I

12

felt more than ever a need to hear singing, to feel the soft touch of a comforting hand or an adoring cheek. I drew a mouth organ out of my pocket and took up a mournful tune.

"Got a long face for a man 'bout to see trail's end," Tom observed. "Feelin' the lonelies, are you?"

"Feels like a month of Sundays since I didn't feel 'em."

"That li'l trader's gal might be waitin' for you at the fort, I suppose. You caught her eye when we were through there in April. Likely she's hungry to see you again."

"Oh, she's got a world of work to do," I said, trying to convince myself as much as anyone else of it. "And there's a fort full of soldiers to draw her eye."

"Mostly old drunks and pups hardly used to wearin' long pants. Not but a couple o' dozen, either, as I recall. Was a young lieutenant there, though, might catch her eye."

"Only one I remember was a captain, and he had a wife and a wagonful o' kids."

"Not the one I remember," Tom said, grinning at the wrinkles appearing on my brow. "Was a New York dandy, too, with shiny brass buttons and a silver watch. Course I pity the soldiers who'd follow him into a tangle with Sioux or Cheyenne warriors, but he's bound to give you a run for that trader's gal."

"Her name's Laveda," I complained.

"Yeah, I remember it now. Got hair as yellow as Iowa corn, and she's built to take a January wind. Yes, sir, she'd be a fair gal to take to your cabin, assumin' you undertook such a foolish notion."

"You had a wife, Tom."

"For a time," he said, frowning. "Fair time, too, I'll admit. But this life never offered much to a woman. And I never knew anything else'd keep me content."

"There are worse things than running a trading post. Look at Jonas Redding. He's done well enough. Jed Burkett's done even better at Green River."

"Oh, it's good enough for a man that doesn't mind walls, Darby. Me, I need the open country, the high skies."

"You never get weary of moving from place to place all the time? Never hunger to plant your feet in one place, take a woman, and make a home?"

"Had a woman. A boy, too," he said, staring strangely northward. "But the spirits didn't figure me for that sort o' life, and they nudged me in another direction."

"Others've lost family," I argued. "They tried again."

"Maybe the knife didn't cut 'em as deep," Tom said, flexing his maimed hand. "Maybe the memories passed."

I frowned. I'd never forgotten Mama or Papa or even my brother Matthew, who'd only been three when he closed his eyes on the world. Tom'd been the one to tell me life goes on, that you've got to lift your chin, spit at the wind, and ride on. But I don't guess there'd been anyone to give him that advice. The Crows cut fingers to mourn the dead, and Tom'd cut a digit for his wife and another for his son, leaving him but three on his left hand. Sure, the Sioux remembered him. They'd been the ones to kill Tom's family. He wasn't a man to trifle with anytime, and he must've been death riding the wind the summer he cut those fingers!

Darkness found us still miles from the fort, and we made camp on a nearby hillside where a bubbling spring promised fresh water. There were bones and arrowheads half-buried in the sandy soil, and I took it for a favored Indian camp. I asked Tom about it, but he only cut himself a bit of jerked buffalo meat and took to chewing on it.

I saw the horses tended and the goods protected from dew and rain. Then, as I pulled off my trousers and took to my blankets, I gazed overhead at the moon. It hovered there, almost smothered by a cloud. Tom followed my eyes upward, then sighed.

"A weeping moon," he whispered. "Wearin' a veil. Seems fittin' what with so much sad talk on the trail this day."

"We'll be at Fort Laramie tomorrow," I reminded him. "Once we're shed of all those hides, we'll feel lighter on our feet."

"Once you take that gal on your arm and lead her around a dance floor, you mean," Tom said, laughing.

14

"I'd settle for a walk along the river. And some good talk."

"My talk gone stale, has it?"

"Worse'n moldy biscuit," I said, laughing at his pretended anger. "Kind of like those corncakes the Shoshoni boys dry and skip across Wind River."

"Not so bad as that," he said. "I know buffalo dung's got a better flavor'n that."

"Me, I never tasted either."

"Well, you're young yet," Tom said, laughing. "Take up such cross words with your elders, you might get the chance."

He pounced on me and wrestled me to the ground. There'd been a time when the fight would have been over that instant, but years in the high country and riding the plains had lent iron to my muscles. I squirmed out of his grasp, then flipped him over my thigh so that he was now pinned. That lasted less than a moment, for he drew me against his knees, then threw me over his head and into the piled hides.

"Lord, you never taught me that one, Tom," I complained as I rubbed my sore hips.

"Ought always to save somethin' back, son," he advised. "In particular when you've got yourself a good man to teach."

"You figure I'm one?" I asked as I set my blankets in order and returned to them.

"Only the best," he said as he turned on his side. "Best partner I ever came across. Good as my own boy would've been."

I thought to reply, but he grunted and groaned, and I knew he'd spoken more than he thought fitting. It wasn't his way, after all, to talk of closeness. But I knew later on there'd come a time when I'd wish I had spoken.

Chapter Two

We were up with the sun that next morning, and by mid-morning we'd covered the eight or nine miles to the fort. Actually, there wasn't anything very military-looking about the place. Fort John, the old adobe-walled structure, lay to one side of a collection of structures that the army had built upon taking over the place. There were trading posts and a grog shop as well. Only the frayed banner flying atop its pine pole at the head of the parade ground seemed to belong.

The strangest sight of all was the sprawling encampment of Sioux surrounding the fort. Summer was annuity season, and the Indians broke away from the buffalo hunt long enough to accept the treaty goods guaranteed by the government. There was no reckoning when the goods would appear, and the soldiers weren't any too careful about who got what. Some Sioux and Cheyenne bands had appeared after the giveaway and found every last blanket and powder cartridge had been meted out in their absence. Now no one dared miss the annual handouts.

"Like a bunch o' kid's waitin' outside a St. Louis candy shop," Tom remarked. "Lord help us if they was ever to turn angry. Must be a couple thousand."

"They could cause a lot of mischief," I agreed. "Don't figure 'em to turn on the fort, do you?"

"I fought the Sioux a few times, Darby, and I never found 'em short on courage. Nor brains, either. As things are, they get a wagon train o' trade goods each year for keepin' the peace. And they mostly get left alone, too. No point to upsettin' that kind o' arrangement."

"No, I guess not," I said, not finding much comfort in Tom's arguments.

We passed the Sioux encampments without lingering. No point in riding past an army of empty pockets with a small fortune in pelts and hides! Myself, I thought it would have been nice to turn over the goods to Doyle Marcus over at the American Company's place, but it lay on the far side of the Oglalas, and Tom appeared eager to give Spotted Elk time to forget about yesterday.

So we rode instead to the fort. That was fine by me, for scarcely had we gotten within sight of the trading post than young Laurence Borden, Laveda's scrawny sixteen-year-old brother, announced our arrival.

"Sis, looks like that buzzard-bait Prescott fellow's back," Laurence hollered.

"Lock up the silver!" Jesse Borden, their father, shouted. "Ole Tom Shea's bound to be along."

I was pretty used to such talk, and I only laughed and hurled my own insults at the Borden men. Then, as I rolled off my horse, a couple of bluecoats rushed over and leveled their muskets toward my belly.

"Hold it right there!" a young lieutenant ordered as he hurried over toward the trading post, buckling a sword onto his hip.

"Keep mighty still, mister," a fuzzy-cheeked soldier who couldn't have been any older than me commanded. "Lieutenant's orders."

"Lieutenant be hanged," I barked. "I've done nothing to deserve such treatment."

I then saw that another pair of bluecoats held Tom in check. I'd seen a hundred strange things in my life, but never in all my days did I dream Tom and I'd find ourselves at odds with the Laramie garrison!

"Now, Mr. Borden, what is it these men have taken from you?" the lieutenant asked, turning to the trader. "I heard

17

mention of silver. It looks as if they've taken hides off somebody, too."

"Taken?" Tom stormed. "You West Point pup, do you think a Green River road agent'd ride right up to your fort with his loot? Fool, how long you been out here? Three days!"

"A good deal longer," the lieutenant answered. "Mr. Borden, I asked a question."

"Well, ole Tom here wouldn't take a thing 'cept in trade. Might be a bit of larceny in that, but not as the law'd see it. Now Darby over there's after my one true gem, namely daughter Laveda. That right, Darby?"

"If it is, I'll never own up to it," I said, trying to grin my way out from under the sights of those soldiers' muskets.

"I don't believe I understand," the lieutenant said, frowning. "I swear you spoke of thieving."

"Was all a jest, Lt. Grattan," Laurence explained. "It's by way of greeting these old-timers."

"Old-timers?" I asked, staring over at Laurence. He wasn't but four years younger, after all.

Laveda appeared then, took in the situation, and laughed.

"John," she said to the lieutenant, "do you plan on shooting them? Or would you rather come inside for a cup of coffee and a visit?"

"Lieutenant?" a weary-armed soldier asked.

"Seems there's no danger after all," the officer said, putting his men at ease. He then dismissed them to their posts and accompanied us inside the Borden trading post.

We sat together for a time, catching Laveda and her family up on our wanderings. Lt. Grattan asked a few questions about our encounter with Spotted Elk. Then another officer entered the store.

Lt. Hugh Fleming commanded the garrison at Fort Laramie. The army had cut back the command of late, and the dwindling number of soldiers left the post with a pair of junior lieutenants in command. Fleming was a quiet, studious type, in stark contrast to the fiery-tongued Grattan.

18

"Some'd feel a bit uncomfortable in command of a fort and forty men surrounded by a few thousand Sioux," Laveda commented. "Hugh says it's enough to keep the peace."

"Or start a war," I grumbled, not at all happy about the way Laveda addressed these soldiers by name.

"Won't come to war," Grattan argued. "Long as the army's here to show these Indian's the narrow path they're to walk. Old Lucien August had some cattle run off. I had 'em rounded up and back in a week."

"Oh, and I thought Conquering Bear tended to that," Fleming added. "Was a family matter anyway. August married a Sioux girl, you know. Now he spends more time drinking than trading with them. We pay him to interpret sometimes, when we can find him."

"Oh, he's married to one, all right," Grattan admitted. "Got no great love for the people, though. We've talked on it some, and he says this country's perfect for grazing land, if only the Sioux were under control. A few hundred hunt buffalo in a country big enough for ten thousand whites!"

"Land's theirs by treaty," I pointed out. "And they'll hold it by force of arms."

"Hold it against the army?" Grattan asked, shaking his head. "No, sir. Give me yon howitzer and a twelve-pounder, and I'll ride down every red-faced devil on the plains. Me and thirty men's all it'd take."

"Sure," I said, thinking to myself it was all it would take to start a war that would paint the Platte red with emigrant blood.

The soldiers didn't tarry. They had their duties, and we had our animals to tend. Besides, Laveda and I had some visiting to get done, and it wasn't apt to happen with a bunch of bluecoats as an audience.

It's strange how things turn out. I'd often thought about what I'd say to Laveda when I got back to the fort, but once we were alone, my mind went hollow-log empty. I sat there staring at my toes, trying to get my tongue to working, and she turned her little half-circles and placed her hands on her hips.

"Well, don't you have any words for me, Darby Prescott?" she finally asked.

"I, uh, well , I was . . ."

"Got yourself tongue-tied, eh?"

"Guess so," I admitted. "And, well, I was just . . ."

"Yes?"

"I was thinking, well, maybe if we took a walk . . ."

"You've ridden halfway across the territory," she complained. "Been gone months doing it. If that wouldn't loosen up your tongue, I don't know what would."

"Isn't my tongue's the problem," I said, taking off my hat and scratching my head. "Gone and got brainless, I guess."

"I'm not so sure you had a brain to begin with!"

"Did once," I said, taking a deep breath. "Back when I was a normal human being and not a Rocky Mountain wayfarer. I don't know, Laveda. Guess it's just I'm not used to be being around civilized folk anymore. Last year and a half all I've had to converse with's been pine trees, ground squirrels, the wind, and Tom Shea."

"One's about the same as another, too," she said, grinning. "Darby, Papa's been doing a lot of thinking lately. He says there's a good trade out on the plains, swapping supplies with the Indian's. He's talked of taking Laurence with him, hiring Lucien August to interpret, and leaving me to tend the store. I'd need help."

"I wouldn't hire August," I warned. "There's lots of talk about his drinking. He's none too friendly toward the Crows, having a Sioux wife and all. What's more, he doesn't treat the girl any too good, and that puts him in poor stead with her family."

"Maybe Shea would hire on. Especially if you lent me a hand with the store."

"Better if Laurence stayed," I suggested. "He's young for the kind of hard life the plains brings."

"He's gotten taller. You'd notice if you took the time to stay now and then."

"Likely would."

"Darby, would you consider staying a bit?"

"Still got a job to do right now," I pointed out. "And there's Tom. He's been a father to me, and I wouldn't run out on him."

"You're not a child needs someone to show you the way," she argued.

"No, it's *him* needs *me* now, I'd say. Like your papa needs you. Strange how the world turns on its head sometimes, Laveda, but it does. You run up debts growing up, and you pay 'em as you can."

"You're right, of course. There's still the interpreting."

"You'd trade with the Sioux, though, and Tom's not too welcome amongst 'em. Next spring we'll likely take another train to Oregon, too."

"That's how you want it, Darby? Always riding here and there, never settling down."

"Not altogether, Laveda. But I guess you wake up one day and find out who you are. Man can't shed his skin like a snake, you know. I got to be me."

"Sure," she muttered. "You'll stay awhile, though, won't you?"

"Got to get our pelts and hides to the American Company. Afterward we'll have some time."

"No colonel's lady to host dances now, Darby, but the piano's still in the big house. We've had dances with Corporal Jones playing, but he's got a talent for abusing the keys."

"That how you got to be on such good terms with those lieutenants?"

"Didn't expect me to hunt up a nunnery, did you? I wouldn't have to go looking for dance partners if you'd stay put!"

"Can't hold you to blame. There was this little Shoshoni gal up on Wind River with the prettiest hair, and she . . ."

"I deserved that, I suppose!" she said, punching me lightly on the arm. "I had to loosen your tongue, didn't I? Enough! Let's take that walk."

As we ambled along the banks of the Laramie River, we gazed at the distant Indian camps. Once, not so very long ago, the Sioux, Cheyennes, Shoshonis, and Crows had roamed the plains as masters. But now, I couldn't escape the sense that they were playing out a losing hand. Soon the rumbling wagons would again roll west from Independence, bringing civilization closer and closer each season. The Sioux would not long stand in their way.

"Gone thoughtful on me, have you?" Laveda whispered.

"Bad habit of mine. Can't help seeing what I look at."

"Try looking at me," she suggested.

I grinned and gripped her hand tightly. Then we returned to the trading post.

That night Laveda baked a pork pie, and Tom and I ate our full. Strangers would have guessed us starving men, to see us stuff our mouths so.

"You ought to see what she can do with fresh venison," Laurence declared. "Bring us a deer or two, Darby. She'll show you."

"That's a bargain," I answered.

"Are you of a mind to stay a bit, son?" Borden asked. "Could be I'd have some work needed doing."

"Just got to deliver those goods to the American Company tomorrow," Tom answered. "Then he's free of obligation."

I exchanged a nervous glance with Laveda. We'd both noticed how Tom spoke only of me. As to obligations, there were all kinds, weren't there?

Tom and I passed the night in the Borden storehouse, stretched out on blankets set atop beds of fresh-cut buffalo grass. I slept like a small child, long and sound. Only when I awoke did I note what a restless, labored slumber Tom had endured.

Laveda fixed us up some breakfast, and she and Laurence rode out to the American Fur Company trading post with us afterward. Doyle Marcus met us with a worried look on his face. The Oglala camp wasn't but a mile away, and a band of Sioux boy's sat on his fence, watching his stock.

"Can't take delivery here, friends," Marcus announced. "Look at 'em! I've had more company than's comfortable, especially if a man cares to keep his hair. The annuity goods've been due in here a week or more, and there's been nary a sign. Get along to Scott's Bluff. Jonas Redding can take the hides and give you payment. While you're there, see what you can find out about the annuity wagons. They get too late, we're apt to have a hard time with these Sioux. There's some already not any too friendly."

"Told Jed Burkett at Green River we'd bring the goods this far," Tom argued. "That was our agreement."

"Well, I didn't agree to it!" Marcus shouted.

"It's all right, Tom," I said, knowing Tom himself relished the ride to Scott's Bluff. "Looks like it'll be another week, Laveda."

She frowned, and I read disappointment in her eyes. But we were used to such happenings. Laveda, in fact, had brought along a bag of provisions for us.

"Papa said Doyle Marcus wasn't enough of a fool to take those hides off your hands," she explained. "Watch yourself, Darby. Sioux Indians aren't the only trouble you're apt to meet on the North Platte."

"Oh?" I asked.

"Got some mighty handsome women on some of those wagon trains coming west. You take any to heart, I'll borrow Papa's shotgun."

I laughed at her joke, then helped Tom pull the pack animals into line. Soon we were back on the North Platte riding eastward.

Always before when we'd headed out from Fort Laramie, I'd felt a sense of adventure rising in my chest. I knew from the first that this time was different. Tom's eyes possessed a wariness, and I grew cautious myself. We hadn't ridden five miles when he slowed the pace. As he shortened the interval between the packhorses and bunched the mule's between us, I drew out my rifle and rested it on one knee. Moments later a dozen Oglalas emerged from a ravine and blocked the trail.

"Ah, trader's," a burly Sioux called out. His yellowing teeth formed a cackle of sorts as he spoke to his comrade's.

But it was his nose that best identified him. It was nearly gone, as if a large animal had chewed it to the bone.

This was No Nose. I'd heard enough talk to know he wasn't a man to trifle with. He often visited the wagon trains, spending his summers extorting coffee, sugar, and blankets instead of hunting buffalo. He was a celebrated horse thief who'd learned English while spending a year and a half as a prisoner of the Hudson Bay Company.

"You got much hides," No Nose observed as he brought his men closer. "You trade maybe guns, maybe powder."

"We've got all the hides we can carry," Tom answered. "And we need our guns. Can't ever tell when we might have to shoot a skunk or two."

"You got nothing," No Nose said angrily. "All this is mine. This is my trail, my mountains. Nobody cross unless I say."

"Seems to me the army might take issue with that," Tom said. " 'Course that'd be after I got through with you, so it shouldn't concern you much. You'll be crowbait by then."

"Big talk," No Nose said, reaching out to snatch a hide. I turned the barrel of my rifle and slammed it down hard, mashing his fingers. He howled and reached for a knife. Tom pulled a pistol and shot the blade from the Sioux's fingers.

The horses stomped and bucked nervously, and I readied myself for the fight I judged would come. Tom glared at the Indians then and shouted at them angrily, making signs to match his words. Then he turned to No Nose.

"You touch my property again, won't be just a nose you'll be missin'," Tom warned. "Hear me?"

"I hear," No Nose said, drawing his group back from the trail. "Is long trail, trader. Long trail. We meet again maybe."

"That'd be your bad luck," Tom declared, motioning for me to start the animals along. "Last bad luck you'll ever have, and that's my promise."

"Long trail," No Nose repeated. "Very long."

I didn't need Tom Shea to tell me we'd meet No Nose and

24

his friends again. Was only a matter of when and where, and that was the sort of problem ole Tom could solve quick as lightning. He kept us near the river, away from ravines and hillsides that could hide a raiding party. And toward nightfall we made camp on a sandbar surrounded on three sides by boggy quicksand. After hobbling the horses, Tom built up a buffalo chip fire and set me to digging a shallow trench across the neck of the bar.

It was as close to a fort as a man could build in a few hours, and it offered as much protection as a man could hope for in that open country. We gobbled a bit of smoked bacon and cold beans from Laveda's provision bag, then made our beds.

"I'll take first watch," Tom told me. "Sleep sound while you can, son. I'd guess they'll come a bit shy of dawn."

I nodded my agreement. Sioux were wonders at using the sun as a screen to their movements. And we were sure to be tired after waiting out an anxious night.

As it happened, though, No Nose came around midnight. There was a fair moon up, and if the sounds of their horses splashing through the shallows of the river hadn't attracted our attention, their shadowy forms creeping through the moonlight would have done the trick. Anyway, Tom roused me, and we waited with rifles at the ready for the Oglala charge.

There were four of 'em came, all young. I figured they might be twelve, maybe fourteen, but hardly any older. Out on a horse raid, eager to win a name, those boys weren't fit targets for a pistol ball or a rifle bullet. Tom's eyes betrayed the same feelings, and I grinned. Stripping my shirt and kicking off my boots, I waded into the shallow water, taking care not to step into the quicksand. I quickly swam around behind them. Then, howling like the devil, I emerged from the water, my white skin ghostlike in the moonlight.

The Oglala boys, surprised and unnerved, scattered. I clubbed one with a length of wood and wrestled a second to the ground. A third had run afoul of our trench, and Tom had him roped and bound like a prize pig.

"What do we do with 'em?" I asked, dragging along my two terrified prisoners.

"Have some fun," Tom said, taking out his knife and running it along the ribs of his captive. Then he slipped the blade beneath the boy's belt and sliced it clean in two. That young Oglala stared in terror as Tom, wild-eyed and fearless, stood over him with that knife. I suspect he feared the worst sort of carving would follow. In the end, we tied 'em up proper and hung 'em naked from a nearby willow tree.

"That ought to earn 'em a name, all right," Tom declared when we strapped the goods atop the pack animals that morning. "Won't be many youngsters eager to join ole No Nose's next raid. A chief sees to his men, you know. Only a coward leaves 'em to undergo such a shamin' as havin' their hides bared before the enemy."

"We the enemy, Tom?" I asked.

"Always have been," he said, giving me a reassuring slap on the shoulder. "Some are beginnin' to see that."

"You mean No Nose?"

"Oh, he's mostly wind and thunder, Darby. But when the good ones, the warriors, turn to war's trail, then we'd best find a high mountain to hide. Won't be a good place for a white man to ride. No, sir."

Chapter Three

We had no other visitors on the dusty trail to Scott's Bluff. The towering bluff seemed to welcome us as it emerged from the distant haze. And when we reached the American Fur Company's post run by Jonas Redding, we were surprised to find a caravan of wagons formed beside the North Platte.

"Well, how do you figure this?" Redding asked, as Tom and I left our animals to drink at river's edge and started toward the storehouse. "You fellows bringing in hides from Laramie?"

"Mostly from Green River," I answered.

"Had in mind to leave 'em with Marcus at the fort, but he was nervous on account of the annuity goods comin' late," Tom explained. "Now, you'd be happy to take 'em off our hands, wouldn't you?"

"Got wagons full of trade goods to send west," Redding said, nodding toward them. "I'll turn the teamsters around and send them back to St. Louis with the hides. You can take the supplies back."

"Never agreed to such a labor," Tom said. "Was promised pay for what we already done."

"I'll tend to that," Redding readily agreed. "But as long as you're headed west, you could . . ."

"Don't believe I said what we were plannin' to do," Tom barked. "Now, that money'd sure be nice to feel in my hands."

Redding nodded, then led the way to his trading post. Once inside, he supplied us with the remains of a buffalo stew, washed down by cold cider. It burned like coal oil, and I half-choked to death. Tom just laughed and downed a second cup.

"Boy's never taken to hard liquor," Tom explained. "Tried to get him used to Green River corn back in May, but ole Darby's too sensible to lose his head over a jug."

"Me, I don't see how a man can get by in this lonesome, windswept land without a nip to rouse his juices," Redding declared. "Now, you likely got some sort of accounting from Jed Burkett." Tom handed the requested papers over, and Redding nodded. "I'll add on for the haul to Scott's Bluff," the trader announced. "Double the sum if you'd haul the supplies back."

"Seem awful eager to talk us into it," I observed. "Haven't you got teamsters hired for the job?"

"Oh, three went and quit. They hear tales of Indians and such. Another got himself shot over a hand of cards, and there's a fool boy in the storehouse broke his leg down at the river. I'm shorthanded, you see, and there's the annuity train coming along any day now."

"That's apt to be good news for the folks at Fort Laramie," Tom observed. "Ole Marcus was mighty touchy 'bout those goods arrivin' late. Sioux's growin' restless."

"Well, I never knew the government to make a thing easy when it could make it hard," Redding grumbled. "If you took the trade goods along, you'd have a cavalry escort to Fort Laramie, and you could go west with the first wagon train."

"We really don't have much else to do," I confessed, turning to Tom. "I'm sure the American Company would be generous . . . in advance."

Redding reluctantly nodded, and Tom finally muttered his approval. We then accepted a handful of greenbacks and such supplies as we asked for. Afterward I lent the traders a hand shifting their goods to a storehouse and loading pelts and hides into the wagon beds. Late that afternoon teamsters drove three wagons east while we awaited the arrival of the annuity caravan. We'd accompany them to the fort.

The annuity wagons were half a week in reaching Scott's Bluff. I couldn't remember a time when Tom was so restless. He paced around the trading post, muttering to himself, or else climbed atop his horse and rode off alone. I couldn't imagine what it was had him so out of sorts. Finally I asked him.

"Don't know I'm anxious 'bout anything, Darby," he answered.

"Well, you've near worn out a year's shoe leather stomping about this place, and I don't remember you riding off alone in Sioux country before."

"I don't know there's words to explain it all," he said, glancing away. I came closer and waited patiently. He gripped my shoulders and turned toward the river. "Darby, I got myself a feeling just now. Nothin' good'll come o' this trip, and plenty bad could happen."

"Did you have a dream?" I asked. More than once I'd dreamed of spirits or had hints of what might happen. Ole Tom, he was more prone to bringing about the end he chose. Just now, though, his face was pale as a summer moon, and I sensed a strange foreboding.

"It's just a feelin'," he said, "but I only had one the likes o' this twice before."

"And?"

"First time was when my sister died."

"The second?"

"Someone died then, too," he whispered.

I knew by the dead look in his eyes and the way he touched his mutilated hand, that his wife and son had been the victims. Now I understood. He'd never be fearful for his own sake. It was me that worried him.

"Sioux wouldn't find me easy to kill," I assured him. "And the annuity train won't take forever."

"Seems it has already," he declared angrily. "Treaty makes an Indian a promise and then breaks it straight away. Nothin's half so dangerous as a Sioux who's been cheated."

I nodded my agreement, and we set off to scare up some fresh game for the supper table.

When the wagons with the promised goods finally arrived, they were hardly escorted by an army. Instead a patrol of ten cavalrymen, led by yet another youthful lieutenant, trailed the wagons. And Tom and I noticed with not a little concern that a shadowing band of Sioux appeared on the far bank of the river.

Jonas Redding greeted the soldiers warmly, and while he and the lieutenant swapped stories over a jug, Tom and I brought the pack animals in where they wouldn't tempt the eager fingers of the younger Indians. It hadn't been so long ago that No Nose's band had launched its raid, and we knew there was little chance of repeating our earlier success.

While we worked with the stock, the soldiers tended their animals. I spoke to a corporal named Stocks, but he kept mum about the journey west.

"Just wanted to know something about your lieutenant," I explained. "Tom Shea and I're bound to travel to Fort Laramie with you, and we've seen Indians. Wanted to know whether we could count on much help if it came to a fight."

"My boys'll do all right," the corporal assured me. "Rawley and Hardin are fair shots, and the rest'll make noise. Not but a pair o' old ones on yon hill and some boys. Shoot, they's just curious's all."

"So they'll spread the word we're coming," I said, frowning. "You'll find there's some up ahead can do a good deal more. Spirits run high regarding the annuity. Some say it's awful late coming. They speak for war. Bad blood among some of the Oglalas, I hear."

"Pity," Stocks said, spitting tobacco juice past his toes. "'Cause that Lt. Malter's green as turnips. Come a fight, he'll get somebody kilt."

It wasn't a warming thought, and I dreaded telling Tom. He already knew, though. I found him arguing with Malter over the formation of our train.

"I brought my share o' trains through to Oregon with nary a scrape, Lieutenant," Tom complained. "You keep your

30

horse soldiers all bunched up in the van, and any Indian takes the notion'll have us scalped and the goods miles away 'fore you know what's happened. Use your men as flankers. That'll give an impression of strength. Your way's an invitation to get killed."

"He's right, Lieutenant," I said, joining the discussion.

"What would a boy know about it?" Malter asked, looking down the length of his pointed nose at me. "I've been trained by the best soldiers in the nation, and I'll do the deciding. A good officer never splits his force."

"You ain't got much to split," Tom declared. "Less still if Darby and I take off on our own. I've a mind to do just that, too."

"Better stay with the annuity goods," Redding argued. "They are the company's responsibility, too."

"You mean for me to wetnurse this young jay?" Tom asked. "You didn't pay me enough, Redding. Isn't that much cash in the territory. Come on, Darby. Let's ready our goods. With or without young Napoleon here, we're off early tomorrow."

I nodded, then made half a bow to the lieutenant and hurried toward the storehouse. There was, indeed, plenty to do, and only me and Tom there to get it done.

We left a hair after dawn that next morning. Tom led the way, and I nudged our packhorses and mules along the trail. We hoped the Sioux watchers would wait for the soldiers, but they were with us from the start. A couple of youngsters rode by, jumping on and off their horses and shouting taunts. We ignored them.

By midday Corporal Stocks and a pair of privates caught up with us.

"Lieutenant's pretty hot 'bout you all headin' out on your own," the corporal informed us. "Truth is, he said he might put the both o' you in leg irons. Ain't your fault the fool teamsters take all day gettin' started, but it'd surely be better if we rode as one bunch."

"You mean it'd be best if we were sittin' in the rear for the Sioux to grab instead o' your wagons," Tom responded.

"No, thanks."

"Spoke to the lieutenant about his dispositions, explainin' how the Indians have a likin' for pickin' off the tail end of a train. He wasn't too excited 'bout hearin' this, as he said you said pretty much the same thing yesterday. Anyhow, he said I could take three men and bring up the rear, so I guess it's me playin' Sioux bait. Chose Hardin and Rawley, my best shots, and young Hayes, who can ride like thunder for help. That make things better?"

"Whole lot better," I told him. "Unless the Sioux come in strength."

"Won't," Tom declared. "The chiefs swore to keep the peace. Danger's some young fire-eaters out to make himself a name. He might prove dangerous, but once he's dropped, the others'll lose stomach for a fight. Just like those boys followin' No Nose, eh, Darby?"

I laughed, then related the tale to the corporal. He, too, chuckled at the story. Then he pulled up short and waited for the caravan to catch up. Tom stopped as well, and I knew we'd rejoin the others shortly.

Thereafter we were part of a gradual movement westward. I wished we'd been ahead of the wagons, as their dust was enough to choke a cloud. The soldiers in the vanguard had it easiest, but Tom vowed a little dust was all right, so long as he could keep that greenhorn lieutenant out of his hair.

It looked like Malter was just as eager to avoid us. First night out he camped with the teamsters, leaving us to the corporal's attention. Tom and I took a turn at guard duty, but the Sioux had vanished that afternoon, and we had no trouble.

The second day our only problem was avoiding a bog where the river had flooded. We came across a big herd of buffalo a short time later, and the soldiers joined in the hunt. I dropped a big bull, and the bluecoats shot a pair of smaller ones. We stripped the carcasses and butchered the meat. As I worked on my bull's hide, I saw a small company of Brules approach. They gazed on with sour faces and spoke among themselves. Next morning our red shadows returned, and I worried an attack might come at any moment. That night I watched Tom load every gun he had.

"Trouble coming?" I asked.

"I smell it," he replied. "Might walk over and warn the corporal. He seems a fair man. Shame they're never the ones to call the tune. Brave ones end up dead or lamed."

"Not all of them," I said, grinning. "Some live to see their white whisker days."

"Not many," he muttered.

"Only the best," I said as I trotted off to tell the corporal.

It was hard to find a sound sleep once the sun sank into the western horizon. Little sounds drew my attention. A snapping twig or a hoot owl's cry spoke of approaching Sioux, and I fretted over Tom's dream. If only he had shared it, I might not have been so nervous. I'd fought Sioux before, and they didn't scare me so much. I understood them and knew how to defend myself. The unknown offered no like chance.

Tom was the first to hear the Indians approach the wagons. He crawled from his blankets like a phantom, and I followed. We both had a pair of pistols in our belts and rifles in our arms. In the end, we used only our wits and our voices. The Sioux were trying to make a surround, and they announced their progress with three owl hoots. However, Tom had us creeping through the ravines past the fringe of camp, and we soon began making owl hoots of our own. Our calls soon had the attackers addled, and I managed to set one frail-shouldered young man to flight when I pelted his head with a buffalo chip. Tom caught another young one and gave him a good wallop on the backside with his rifle butt.

Three of the raiders did make a quick charge, during which they managed to steal the lieutenant's chestnut mare and a big black that was so much trouble it broke loose and returned to its wagon.

All in all, I considered it the best kind of victory. Nobody got killed, and except for losing a horse, we made out just fine. Lt. Malter looked on things differently, and he made a point of speaking harshly to his command.

"Fool soldiers," Tom remarked. "Sure is a good thing we're not at war."

"Always good to find a bit of peace."

"Guess that's so," Tom said, yawning. "Sioux would sure make short work o' such a greenhorn bunch o' soldiers, and that lieutenant'd get his whole command cut to pieces first try."

"He might do all right. He stood up and directed his men well enough. Mighty good way to catch a bullet, and not a little brave."

"Don't confuse brave and stupid," Tom grumbled. "Dead man don't do anybody much good."

That was true enough. Even so, I had more respect for the soldiers. If they were inexperienced, well, so was I once. Fate is a good teacher, and if the west gave leave for the newcomers to learn, I wagered they might do just fine.

We didn't sleep any too well, and morning came early. As we rode along, often flanked by long lines of Sioux warriors, I drifted in and out of a light slumber. The landscape was featureless and plain, with only the ravines out of which our enemies emerged now and then offering proof of the peril we faced.

Toward midday the lieutenant formed his wagons in a circle, and Tom and I drove our stock within. The Sioux approached so that we could note both bands. There was a Brule bunch and a larger collection of Oglalas. All looked longingly at the annuity wagons and their precious cargo.

"So it's come to this, has it?" Tom asked as we walked out and stared at the Sioux. Here was a people long defiant, determined to maintain their way of life forever. Already the determination was waning, even as the weeping moon shrank nightly.

"Time's passin' us by, son," Tom remarked sadly. "Wonder if the wagon trains won't stop next summer."

"Always folks in need of a fresh start and new land," I told him. "They'll not stop."

"Then a big fight's sure to come, Darby, and I pray I'm

elsewhere. Won't be a pleasant fight, with rules of a sort. No, this is apt to turn vicious."

"We made it this time," I told him. "Will next, too."

"Will you?" he asked. "Be hard."

"We'll talk more of it tonight, when we've turned the trade goods over to Marcus."

"We will, you figure?"

"Sure," I whispered. "Always have."

Chapter Four

We did, indeed, reach the storehouses of the American Fur Company that night, and we eagerly turned over our trade goods. Lt. Malter was nearly as eager to pass on the annuity goods, and he said so. Then the lieutenant formed his men and rode toward the east without even bothering to report to the post commandant. It surprised me some, but then Tom said there was likely no mention of reporting to Lt. Fleming in Malter's orders. That young lieutenant wasn't one to stray much from the book.

"You fellows aim to take the trade goods along to Burkett after a time?" Doyle Marcus asked Tom.

"Got 'em this far," Tom answered. "Word from Redding was they'd go out with the first train headed west."

"I'd sure feel easier if you took 'em along," Marcus said, nervously rubbing his hands together. "I've got a world of goods in the storehouse already. The annuity goods and all. It's enough to tempt anybody, and there's the whole Sioux nation out here. If they steal the annuity, well, it was theirs anyhow the way I see it. But the company supplies . . ."

"I've got little use for the Sioux," Tom said, bitterly staring at his maimed hand. "But I never knew 'em to break a promise once they touched the pen to a treaty paper. The giveaway's late, but there they sit, patiently waiting. I wouldn't fret over the Sioux."

"You're not out here on the plain, surrounded by 'em," Marcus pointed out. "I'd see you were well-paid. Well, what do you say, Shea? Take the boy and ride out to Burkett?"

"Darby?" Tom asked, turning to me.

"If there's danger of a raid on the storehouses," I pointed out, "it'd be twice as bad for two men riding alone along the Platte River road. Better to wait for a train. We could do it then, if you like. Or if the Sioux get busy hunting buffalo. I don't know I'd care to tangle with No Nose again, not in open country."

"He's right," Tom said, tipping my hat back away from my eyes. "Besides, I'm tired of the trail just now. Got to get a rest before I think on anything."

"Be best to leave tonight, before the Sioux know the annuity goods are here," Marcus complained.

"Oh, they know," I said, pointing to the shadowy figures a hundred yards away. "Isn't likely any Indian — much less a Sioux — would miss what's happening on his doorstep."

Marcus frowned. Tom motioned toward our horses, and we mounted up and rode along to the fort. I was eager to rest on a soft mattress in Laveda's storeroom, and I had money to spend as well.

We were received warmly at the fort. Jesse Borden welcomed us inside his store, and Laurence fetched us cool glasses of sassafras tea. Laveda pretended anger, accusing us of delaying our return to Fort Laramie in order to alarm our friends, but she couldn't maintain it long.

"Thought we'd been scalped by Sioux, did you?" Tom asked, grinning. "Can't imagine a young one with a comely figure like yours cryin' over ole Tom Shea, so you must have the eye for young Darby."

"She does," Laurence quickly volunteered.

"Guess I could warn you that he's little more than traildust and buffalo hair, and he snores to boot, but you wouldn't pay it no mind," Tom said, laughing. "Was young once myself, you know, and I wouldn't've listened to any three-fingered reprobate told me such a thing."

"Well, I'll keep in mind he snores, if I come to need such a warning," she replied, giving me a nudge in the ribs. "I could use a hand shelving blankets and flour. Darby, if the Indian's didn't chop off *your* fingers, you might come along."

"Better go," Laurence advised with a grin. "Hasn't let Papa or me within ten feet of those flour sacks. Saving 'em for you."

"If I'm not back by morning, send for the cavalry," I told Tom as Laveda dragged me along.

"Anybody didn't know better'd guess you were out of sorts," I said when we began heaving the flour sacks off the floor and cradling them up to the bare shelf where they belonged.

"Expect me to be happy with you two days later getting back than you said?"

"I expect you to figure I wouldn't be controlling when I got back or even how. You're not joking about this, are you?" I asked, noticing my words didn't raise a grin on her face. "You were worried. That's a waste of breath, you know. Tom and I've gotten through all manner of trouble through the better half of this country. Nothing's coming along we can't deal with."

"I've seen these Sioux myself," she said, resting her head on my shoulder. "There are some with scalps hanging from their belt. They're proud of it."

"I've lived with Crows and Shoshonis who were just as proud of the Sioux they killed."

"Darby, there was a young man in last week with three scalps on his belt. They were all blond. I thought some of the soldiers might hang him, and they might have if Lt. Fleming hadn't taken charge. All I could think for a week was how those scalps were a family, like Papa and Laurence . . . and me."

"You're safe here."

"Oh, sure, there are sometimes twenty or thirty soldiers. Only that idiot Johnny Grattan thinks they can control that mob of Indians out there."

"They don't have to," I pointed out. "The chiefs don't want war. They'll keep the young men in check. If there's trouble, it won't get started by Indians."

"Does it matter how it starts? Will that make me any

38

safer?"

"No, I guess not," I confessed, easing her along to a nearby chair. "I'm no friend of these Sioux, Laveda, but I know 'em some. They wouldn't bother your papa's place or you, either. You trade 'em powder and guns which they need. They can't get 'em on their own. They go killing traders, it'll scare others away. They won't do it. Makes more sense to fight the soldiers, or even a wagon train."

"I'd sure feel better if you'd stay close till these Indians move their camps away from the fort."

"We've got to take some goods out to Jed Burkett at Green River," I explained. "Be gone a month at the outset. But we won't go till the first train gets here. Meanwhile I plan to scare up a deer so you can cook it up."

"Use the hide for some new moccasins," she advised. "Your old ones are wearing thin, and shoes come dear. I do have some cloth around somewhere that would make a nice new shirt and some trousers. Those are growing mighty thin, too."

I examined my clothes and agreed. The trail was tough on britches, and I never had been any good at keeping the elbows in my shirts. Only buckskin lasted long.

"Some new clothes would be a rare kindness," I told her. "If a dance comes along, I could hardly take you wrapped in a buffalo robe."

"Oh, you could," she argued. "Would make waltzing a bit trying, though."

"I've got some money for the cloth."

"I didn't ask for any," she barked. "You wouldn't take money for the venison."

"Not if you're cooking it."

"Nor otherwise. I know you, Darby Prescott. Now help me get the blankets stowed away. Then I'll find you some jerked beef to keep your stomach from rumbling all the night."

"Yes, ma'am," I answered, hurrying to where the blankets lay.

I did as instructed, and after gobbling the dried beef, I

joined Tom in the storehouse. He was already tossing in his blankets, and I undressed hurriedly and scrambled into my bed.

The next morning we chopped some wood to pay for our lodging and the fine breakfast Laveda put together. Then I saddled my horse and prepared to scare up a deer in the hills beyond the Laramie River.

"Wasn't plannin' on leavin' me behind, was you?" Tom asked, tossing a ragged saddle blanket over his big buckskin. "You know better'n to go ridin' alone in Sioux country."

"Was planning you'd come along," I told him. "Know a good place to begin?"

"Sure do," he said, saddling his horse. When both saddles were in place and we were atop our animals, Tom led the way toward the river. Soon we were hunting deer tracks in the hills beyond the fort.

Stalking deer wasn't a task best accomplished on horseback. As soon as we spotted tracks in the sandy soil, I scanned the hillside for a good place to leave our ponies. Not too far away a small creek cut through a stand of cottonwoods, and we tied the horses securely and left them to drink and graze. Tom and I drew out our rifles and set off through the underbrush. It was good deer country, full of sign. But I also detected moccasin tracks. The Sioux encamped nearby hadn't neglected those hills in their search for food.

Tom always said half the skill of tracking was being patient enough to wait out your prey.

"The hawk knows that," he explained once, when I was still a mop-haired farm boy setting off for Oregon. "He knows ole rabbit's down there, so he circles 'round till rabbit thinks it's safe to leave his hole. Then, whoosh, hawk's got his supper."

So it was that we read the pattern of deer tracks and came to the same conclusion. Deer came to the stream for a midmorning drink. We simply hid ourselves in the underbrush, taking care to let the wind hit our faces. The deer would now come on us unawares, and our rifles would do the rest.

I don't know how long we waited there. It seemed an eternity. Frogs down at the creek croaked or splashed in the shallows, and a coyote gave us a good sniff before departing for less dangerous surroundings. Overhead some jays chased a crow out of the cottonwoods, and a squirrel chattered away to its mate. It was almost midday before the deer came, and then there were just two of them. The buck was fair-sized, but the doe was small. We both took note, and I motioned for Tom to take his shot. He shook his head and pointed toward the buck.

Sure, I know, I told myself. Leave the doe for a harder day. I raised my rifle, drew back the hammer, and waited for the buck to fill my sights. Then I locked the trigger and squeezed. The air exploded. Sulfrous powder stung my eyes and obscured the scene for a moment. The doe took instantly to flight. As the smoke dispersed, and the wind revived my strangled throat, I saw the buck lying lifeless on the hillside before me.

"He's not so big as that giant you dropped upriver, but he'll do," Tom observed as he started toward the animal. "Make some good moccasins out of that tough ole hide. Maybe a new shirt, too. You keep growin' plum out o' the things you had last winter."

"People grow," I told him. "Laveda's promised to do some sewing for me, too."

"That gal's set her cap, all right, Darby. Course a man could do worse. She's comely, and a good worker to boot. Won't cost you ponies like a Shoshoni or a Crow gal would."

"She'd expect me to help with the trading post, Tom, to settle in not just for the winter, but for always."

"Would that be so hard?"

"Would it for you?"

"Not me we're talkin' 'bout, son. Don't you have any trace o' your papa's settlin' feet in you?"

"Never was much like him," I said, frowning. "He knew it. You did, too. It's why you offered to take me with you. I'd made a poor farmer, always looking to the next hill, wondering what it would look like. Too much of the wayfarer in

41

me."

"Man gets older, he has an urge to nest sometimes."

"I admit I feel it. But I can't see Darby Prescott old and gray, tending a counter or loading shelves."

"More likely off chasin' grizzlies and runnin' ponies, eh?" Tom asked, laughing.

"Chasing you, you old buzzard," I said, drawing my knife and stepping to the buck. As I skinned the deer, Tom and I traded jests or friendly taunts. Then we butchered the meat and prepared to return to the fort. We collected our horses, tied the meat behind our saddles, and mounted up.

A strange silence fell over the hillside, and we froze. Words weren't necessary. Both Tom and I knew something was dreadfully wrong. The sounds were all wrong. The ground was disturbed. Then I saw a flash of color to my right and began loading my rifle. In seconds a guttural warble flooded the air, and we found ourselves surrounded by a dozen young Brules.

"Just come to hunt," I explained, pointing to the deer carcass.

"Hau," Tom called. "Kolas. Friends."

"No kola," a young man said, stepping up so that I could see his face. He had been among No Nose's Oglala raiders. I saw the rope marks on his wrists and cringed.

"We mean you no harm," I insisted, making the appropriate signs again and again. Tom sat atop his horse, rifle at the ready, and waited for the Sioux to push the action or let us go about our business.

"You take . . . clothes," the raider said, glaring at me with rare hatred. "I take . . . yours."

"No," I answered. "You tried stealing my horse, but I caught you. Some white men'd killed you. Was you brought it on yourself. You!" I shouted, pointed to him. "Just like now, I'd be happy to ride along, bothering nobody. You keep at this, somebody's sure to get shot."

Tom made signs to echo my words, and I did my best to do the same. The Sioux eyed us angrily. They had the numbers, but their bows wouldn't do half the damage my rifle and pistols would. There'd be a lot of dying. That was for sure.

"You go," said a tall young man with the hair on each side of his head shaved above the ears. Likely he'd just undergone the trial of membership in some warrior society, and he was asserting his position among the other young Brules.

"Go!" others shouted, shaking their bows and lances.

"It's time," Tom told me, and he led the way past the Indians and off toward the Laramie River and the fort. Behind us the young Brules shouted taunts and insults, which rolled off my back like rain from a midsummer thundershower. It would take more to bring me to fight them.

Back at the fort, we brought Laveda the venison and set to work chopping stove wood to make a proper cook fire. As I trimmed branches from a willow, a pair of Brule boys rode past, babbling at me and baring their backsides. Laveda stared in disbelief, and when I laughed, she insisted on an explanation.

"Oh, we ran across 'em hunting," I told her. "Just boys having a spot of fun."

"You sure?" she asked.

"Well, if they'd wanted, they could've shot me full of arrows. Didn't, so I'd say it was sport."

Lieutenant Grattan, who'd also witnessed the event, thought differently. He had a bugler summon soldiers, and he might have led the whole command after the two pranksters had Tom and I not argued him out of it.

"Just boys gamin', as they have out here since the first sunrise," Tom argued. "Were three of 'em made a try at our horses out on the Platte, and we nabbed 'em, tied 'em naked to a tree, and now their cousins want to make a show of how it was nothin'. All right with me. I didn't aim to kill nobody, and I still don't."

"Let it pass, Lieutenant," I pleaded. "It's nothing."

"I won't have the ladies of this post subjected to such offensive behavior," Grattan complained.

"Only lady saw 'em was Laveda," I pointed out. "I expect she's seen her share o' backsides bathing in the river when the wagon trains pull in."

"I have," Laveda said, forcing a grin onto her face. "Don't let it trouble you, Johnny."

"I swear one day I'll teach those Indians some respect," the soldier muttered.

"What could you teach 'em?" Tom asked. "They only know one thing. If they've got an enemy, they'll kill him. Use every trick you ever imagined to do it, too. Good, hard fighters, these Sioux. I've killed some, but it took a fair bit of work. They can be fierce as mountain cats in a fight, and there's lots of 'em."

"If I had thirty men . . ." Grattan began.

"You could get 'em kilt easy headin' after Sioux," Tom declared. "Best fighters on the plains, save the Crows. Say your prayers it never comes to a fight, Lieutenant. Lots o' graves to dig then."

We spent a week at the fort, helping out the Bordens at the trading post and doing a little hunting. Laveda finished my new shirt and trousers. I fashioned the moccasins myself, and Tom and I exchanged some of our cash for such shot and powder as we thought we'd need in the coming months. I also outfitted myself with some good wool blankets and two pair of union drawers.

"Old ones were holier'n a church steeple," I told Tom. The remainder of my share of the money went into a new Sharps rifle, a model 1852, that put the old Hawkens to shame. It was a much admired gun, and I think I could have swapped it to the Oglalas for any girl in the tribe.

"That's as fine a buffalo gun as I've come upon," Tom remarked after trying the rifle himself. Straight away he bought its twin from Jesse Borden.

"Seems to me that money might have found better uses," Laveda scolded as I helped her stack tins of peaches on the shelves. "You might have used it to start your own trading post, maybe at the Sweetwater Crossing, or up near South Pass."

"Those are lonely places," I told her. "Emigrant trains rarely need resupply between here and Burkett's place at

44

Green River. Snake River country'd be best, though I don't care to winter there."

"Maybe you'd prefer town life."

"Tom doesn't take to people much," I reminded her.

"You won't be with him forever, will you? I thought we might plan a future together."

"Plan?" I asked. "First train'll be along soon, and I'll be off to Green River. No point planning past the next moonrise, Laveda. Something just comes along to change everything."

She scowled and stalked off to be by herself. I knew she wanted, expected more from me, but it just wasn't possible. Not then anyhow.

I guess it was only natural we'd have other run-ins with the Sioux. What with the government reluctant to pass out the annuity goods, and the thousands of Indians camped so close by, there was bound to be some kind of trouble. Feelings ran high, and us not understanding the other made things worse. Old Conquering Bear thought a bit of foolishness might put some of the hard feelings to rest, so he sent some of his people to the fort with an invite to a bit of feasting.

Only a couple of soldiers went, but a fair number of the civilians accepted. I guess it was mostly curiosity sent Laveda and her family. Me, I was reluctantly dragged along.

The Brules put on a fine show of horsemanship to get things started. I'll never forget the boy who stood upside down on the back of a racing stallion. Those Sioux rode on top, underneath, even sideways on their horses. A few ran alongside, hopping on and off. What a show!

There was food aplenty, for the warriors had found a herd of buffalo, and great thick hump roasts and savory steaks were there for all. After eating, the old men swapped stories through translators, and the boys joined in for a bit of wrestling and gambling.

I wasn't much for making wagers as a rule, but when some of the Sioux started racing horses, I could not hold back. I had a sleek spotted Appaloosa raised by Nez Perce

45

off in Oregon, and I swear that horse had wings on his feet. I didn't ride him regular on the trail, as his nature was to gallop, and mountains didn't suit him. Still, Pepper, as I called him, was a money winner.

The Sioux had eyes for speedy horses, and when they saw Pepper, some of them backed out. In the end, only five riders chose to race, and the chief challenge was bound to be a tall young man called Maga Inyan, which Two Nations explained meant Stone Goose. Maggie Indian, the people at the fort called him. The Goose just smiled real big and glared with his icy cold eyes. I don't think he had much use for white people.

The older Brules set up the course, and it was mostly circles leading up and down the banks of the Laramie River. I didn't care too much for all those river crossings, as they sapped your speed, but it was their feast, after all, and they let me walk over the route.

"Seems fair enough," I told Tom. "Don't see any tricks."

"It's the ones you don't see that'll trip you," he warned.

Was he ever right on the mark! If I'd had any sense, I'd hung back on Stone Goose's hip and let him reveal the secrets of the trail. But Pepper hadn't had a real run in days, and the horse took off like an arrow shot from a limber bow. I surged ahead, feeling the crisp wind on my face, tearing at my cheeks and bare forearms. The Sioux were close behind as we splashed in and out of the river. Then as we approached the final crossing, they hung back. I saw the Goose swing around to my right, but before I could figure out why, Pepper plunged into the grandaddy of all buffalo wallows.

The crowd on the far hillside exploded with laughter as Pepper lunged forward suddenly, pitching me into a sea of mud and buffalo dung. I sank in that muck up to my eyeballs, covered from nose to toes. But instead of accepting my fate and giving up the race, I sloshed over to Pepper, managed to mount the poor animal, and got going again.

The crowd hollered again, but this time they were urging Stone Goose to close the distance. After all, once I got through the bog, I was across the finish line. The others, going around, had lost considerable time. It was a real battle, seeing if I could nudge Pepper through the wallow before the Sioux racers could catch up. For a few minutes it looked hopeless. Then Pepper bolted out of the muck, and we rushed forward.

I could hear Stone Goose screaming as he slapped his pony into extra effort. I had the edge, though, and I didn't give it away. I crossed the line, rolled off my lathered horse, and collapsed to the ground, spitting mud from my mouth and fighting to catch my breath.

Silence fell over the crowd, for their disappointment was great. Tom and Laurence collected on wagers they'd made, and I took my share of goods as well. Then Two Nations appeared with the Goose. The defeated racer muttered something, and Two Nations translated.

"He says you ride good . . . for a white man," the young mixed-blood said.

"White?" I asked, scraping muck from my face. "Mostly brown just now."

Two Nations explained to the others, and they roared with laughter. Even Stone Goose laughed. He then held up my hand and slapped my back.

Conquering Bear greeted us both, and though I didn't understand his words, I read a fair degree of friendship in his wise old eyes. Here was a man, I thought, who would have fought you to the last arrow, but he respected you just the same. A man was lucky to come by an enemy like that, one who'd give you a good, fair fight.

"I won," I announced when Laveda walked over.

"Won yourself a good scrub, I'd say," she declared, backing away. "Best visit the river, Darby Prescott. You stink!"

I had to confess it was true, so I led Pepper downstream and began washing the muck and sweat from us both. A fair-sized party of Sioux youngsters were already there, ridding themselves of dust and mud accumulated during their wrestling matches. Two Nations appeared shortly, bringing along the other racers. As we splashed each other or traded jokes, I found the hard feelings I'd once held for the Sioux fading, replaced by the seeds of understanding. It wasn't like those boys were friends, but they were, after all, not so different.

I think it was the same for them. Seeing me in that river, naked, with bear claw scars on my chest and the old arrow wound on my elbow, I was more familiar than strange. Their curiosity was sated as they tugged at my chin whiskers and wondered at the little hairs sprouting from my chest.

"Stone Goose says you must come and hunt with us," Two Nations declared. "We've seen you shoot. You have the true aim."

"Thank him," I answered. "Soon I go to Green River with some trade goods, but I'll be back. Maybe we can hunt buffalo when they put on their winter coats."

"*Hau!*" Two Nations howled. He translated my words for the others, and they readily agreed it was a fine notion. My toes were beginning to get soggy, so I gave my clothes a final dip in the river, then climbed onto the bank and spread them out to dry. The others swam a bit in the river, then joined me.

We didn't talk much, just chewed some dried buffalo meat the Goose had brought along and observed the smaller children splashing about nearby.

"My brothers," Two Nations said proudly, pointing to two light-skinned boys near a tall willow. "You have brothers?"

"Yes," I said. "Far away. In Illinois."

The words meant nothing to him, but he seemed sad. He then spoke of his family, of the Sioux cousins he rode with, of camp life that wasn't all that different from the Crows and Shoshonis and Nez Perce. Finally my clothes were dry, and I dressed myself. We parted with a wave, a nod, and a promise to hunt the buffalo. I rode back to the fort alone, but feeling less wary of the sprawling encampments nearby.

Chapter Five

The arrival of the first emigrant company at Fort Laramie brought on a celebration of sorts. The cavalry fired off their mountain howitzer, and the women and children turned out to welcome the wide-eyed pilgrims to the foothills of the Rockies. Traders like Jesse Borden welcomed the flock of travelers to his door, then sold them everything they needed, or rather that they could afford. Laveda undertook the organization of a welcoming dance, and I found myself enlisted as musician.

The assembled Sioux viewed the arrival of the wagon train with consternation.

"When will the soldiers hold the promised giveaway?" they asked. Conquering Bear rode up with a small delegation of Brules to demand that the goods be handed out so that the people could get on with their summer hunting. Other headmen arrived to say the same thing.

"Later," Lt. Fleming answered. "Have patience."

I suspect it wasn't the first time a soldier had said that to an Indian. The frowning Sioux faces testified to it.

I didn't much bother myself with the cavalry's troubles though, nor with the Sioux, either. Laveda had me pounding out tunes on the piano left by a departed colonel's lady. If I wasn't stocking shelves, tending Pepper, or hunting with Tom Shea, I'd be at that piano, doing my best to bring a harmonious tune to the high plains.

"I don't understand it," Laveda remarked. "You used to play so wonderfully!"

"Well, this outfit would be better off with a less accomplished musician and a better hand with a tuning fork," I told her. "Grit and sand and Lord knows what else's got into its workings. Be lucky if it doesn't sound like a chorus o' lovesick coyotes."

Judging by the applause of the emigrants, I'd say it wasn't that bad. Didn't hurt to have a fair fiddler and a couple of horn players blending their notes.

Tom didn't spend more'n a few minutes at the dance. Mostly he just went around, greeting this lady and that, tasting a pie or munching a biscuit. He devoted his time to swapping tales with the train's scout, a willowy fellow named George Trace. The two of them sat off to one side, emptying one of Jesse Borden's jugs, and before you knew it, Tom had arranged for us to haul the American Company's trade goods along when the wagon train pulled out.

"Couldn't you just turn over the supplies to Trace and trust him to get them delivered?" Laveda asked when I began packing up my gear.

"If Tom doesn't trust the man enough to suggest it, who am I to raise the point?" I asked. "And asking a wagon scout to haul flour and powder, when his own company's apt to be in need, is a bit like asking a hungry wolf to watch your baby chickens."

"You'll be away two months!" she grumbled. "Summer'll be near gone when you return."

"Oh, be a lot of summer left," I argued. "Besides, with trains coming through here all the time, you'll be busy yourself. Hardly know I'm gone."

"I'll know," she said, clasping my hands. "I'll miss you."

"Well," I said, trying to avoid her probing eyes, "I'll miss you some, too."

Next morning Tom and I loaded up five mules with trade goods and joined Trace's westbound train. I rode atop Pepper, and Tom sat atop a sleek brown mare he'd ridden most of the way from Oregon to the Rockies a year ago last spring. We brought along a pair of spares, too, giving us a small herd of animals to nudge along the trail.

Trace seemed glad to have us along, for there wasn't any surplus of men in the company. Back in the old days, I recalled brothers of grandpa's setting off with an Oregon or California-bound family, and there were grown sons, too. This batch was mostly young families, with plenty of little ones, but nary a toad-sized boy to aim a rifle or help drive his wagon. As a result, the scout put us back with the tail-end wagons, and we half-choked on trail dust.

"Can't help feeling like I'm eating myself west," I grumbled to Tom the second day out. "I got grit in my armpits, up my nose, between my toes, and in other less comfortable places."

He laughed, then pointed to a gaggle of children up ahead, who were walking backward to avoid the gray cloud thrown up by the lead wagons.

"Likely get themselves snakebit or horse-stomped," I declared.

"Know you'd rather be up ahead, showin' the way, Darby," Tom said, shaking his head sadly. "Next year we'll have our own company to take west. This time 'round, we've only got to stomach it till Green River. Three weeks, maybe less. Not so long, you know."

"No," I agreed. But it didn't make the dust any easier to digest.

That first week and a half, we made good progress. There was plenty of grass for the horses, and the water in the North Platte ran swift and clean. Some afternoons I splashed around in the shallows with the emigrants, and at night I'd take out my mouth organ and offer up a tune or two. Tom and I took some of the men out after buffalo, whenever our trail crossed the path of a herd. My new Sharps put an awful big hole in anything, and it proved fearful when turned against a buff. The pilgrims didn't hit much, but they were there to help drag back the carcasses, and the adventure called to the younger ones.

Other summers I might have taken those folks to heart, made a bond with a few of the little ones, but knowing in a week our paths would split kept me at a distance. Tom thought it just as well.

"Ole George seems a little bothered to have folks turn to us for advice," Tom explained. "We're not goin' all the way, after all, and when the tough days come in the high country, they'll be needin' to have his words, not ours."

I nodded my agreement. Actually the trail was straight and clear, and there wasn't much to say anyway.

Next day, though, we came off the North Platte and began crossing the Sweetwater, so as to get over on the southern bank. The river was wider than normal, and getting everybody across took most of a day. Afterward, everybody and everything was wet, so the folks spread their goods out to dry. Women took the opportunity to do some washing. Both clothes and youngsters got a fair scrubbing, after which the older ones got in some swimming and more than a few pranks. Late in the afternoon a band of Oglala Sioux appeared, led by our old friend No Nose. But the Nose appeared nothing if not friendly, and Trace organized a bit of trading, a few wrestling bouts, and a horse race or two.

A big-shouldered Iowan named Gus Powers produced a jug, and the Oglalas joined in a round of drinking. No Nose provided a pair of dice, and soon a half-dozen emigrants joined the Oglalas in an animated round of gambling.

I kept away from those Indians. I'd had my run-in with 'em already, and Tom and I worried over the trade goods. All went well till supper. Then there was a fierce shout, and a pair of Oglala boys raced off from the camp, jumped atop their ponies, and fled as if someone'd taken a brand to their backsides.

Tom saw the animals securely hobbled, then started for the crowd that was gathering just ahead. I grabbed my Sharps and followed. We were still twenty feet away when we heard the shouting. A rifle exploded, and silence crept over the scene. By the time Tom and I arrived, No Nose and three companions were backing away from Powers. The Iowan held a Kentucky rifle in his hands.

"I'll put a ball through the rest o' you heathens, too, if you try such a trick!" Powers threatened. "I won't be cheated, I tell you!"

The rest of the wagon people stared in horror at the blood-spattered corpse of a young Oglala. Trace did his best to calm Powers, as did the big Iowan's wife and older daughter. Two small boys clung to the wheel of their wagon and watched the retreating Indians.

"Lord, you've gone and done it, haven't you, Powers?" Trace said as he finally pried the rifle from the big man's hands. "Never should've allowed you that jug. You've kilt a man, and a Sioux to boot!"

"He cheated me!" Powers argued. "I won't allow no redskin to take my silver. No, sir!"

"Didn't have to kill him, Gus," Mrs. Powers said. "We're all of us God's creatures, after all."

Powers turned toward his wife and read the fear in her eyes. By that time I reached the corpse. Turning him over, I saw it was Younger Elk who had been killed. The Elks were a powerful band among the Oglalas, and I'd seen the whole bunch often at Fort Laramie, riding in to complain about the delayed giveaway.

"Best bury the boy," Trace announced. "And keep a double guard. We could be visited tonight."

"Don't bury him," I advised. "His people will come for him. I saw a brother among the younger ones that ran off."

"He's right," Tom agreed. "We've seen these ones before. Not with No Nose, though. He's a bad one."

"Well, it was a misunderstanding, pure and clear," Trace said, eyeing Powers coldly. "Best thing to do is round up our goods and prepare to head out early. Sioux'll mourn three days. By then we'll be well west o' here."

That was all true, and the people cheered some hearing Trace take command. Work overwhelmed their worries, but I felt certain with No Nose and the Elks nearby, we hadn't seen the last of trouble.

That proved right enough. Within an hour No Nose rode up to the train with Spotted Elk, the slain Oglala's uncle, and close to fifty others. Their faces were painted, and they'd tied up the tails of their ponies.

"War party!" someone called out.

"Get out your rifles!" another said. "Hurry!"

I found my Sharps and followed Tom toward where the Oglalas were formed up in front of the camp. Trace was already out there, signing with the angry Spotted Elk. I exchanged nervous glances with Tom.

"Likely they'll want the body," John Johnson, a schoolmaster from Ohio, mentioned. "Maybe we should bring it to 'em."

"Tom?" I asked.

"Figure the two of us can carry it?" he asked in turn.

"I can," I answered, handing him my rifle. "Cover me."

"Son?"

"You're the best shot," I told him as I approached the blanket-covered corpse. "And they don't remember me as a brother to the Crows."

He nodded soberly, and I turned to my grim task. I dropped to my knees and eased my hands beneath the cold body of Younger Elk. Then I drew the body close to my chest. Carrying it as gently as I could, I started toward the restless horsemen. Trace saw, explained why I was joining the parley, and waited for me to set my lifeless bundle at the feet of the Oglalas.

For myself, I saw little of the anger etched in the faces of those Indians. The body I carried was light, frail almost. Often the blanket fell away from his face, and I read youth and hope in the silent eyes. I'd carried dead boys to their graves before, all too often. It was part of life on the trail, I knew, but each time the grief and pain came fresh.

"Here he is," I said when I gently laid the corpse on the ground. I then signed the same words, adding gestures saying that our brother was dead.

"He's not your brother!" No Nose shouted harshly. "Give us the one who did this! We'll show you death!"

Spotted Elk was in charge, though. He made many signs to express his grief, then dismounted and examined the body of his fallen nephew. Only the bullet wound that had killed him marred the frozen form of the youth, and Spotted Elk seemed comforted there were no other marks on the body. Then he spoke to his companions, and three of them climbed down and took the corpse away.

Spotted Elk now demanded that the killer be punished.

"Was a bad business, Chief," Trace said, turning to No Nose so that the words might be translated. "You had people there.

54

A man had a bit too much whiskey, and there might have been some tricks played with the dice. A gun was fired, and a man is dead."

Spotted Elk listened to the translation, then angrily shouted his response.

"Give us the man," No Nose demanded.

"Can't do that," Trace argued. "We've got a treaty. It's for the authorities to punish, and we're better'n a week from Fort Laramie. We'll hold our own trial, I promise. The man'll be punished."

Again No Nose explained to Spotted Elk. The Elk turned to his companions and waved angrily toward the nearby wagon train. Instantly warriors rode off. They reappeared here and there, and in no time the company was surrounded.

"We can make a trade," Trace pleaded. "No need for anybody else to be hurt. We've got many blankets, much powder."

No Nose didn't bother translating. Instead, he barked, "We trade, white man. You give us killer. We give you many lives. You don't give, we kill everybody."

"Maybe," I said, swallowing hard as I gazed at the remaining Oglalas. "There are many good guns in that camp, and it wouldn't be just white men did the dying. You kill these people, and the treaty's broken. You want that?"

I didn't wait for a translation. I made signs to explain my words, and Spotted Elk watched with cold eyes as my fingers made the words come to life.

Spotted Elk signed his own reply. "You called my blood your brother. Inside my heart is torn. I must be whole again. Give me this killer of the people. He must die."

I was the one to translate, for Trace hadn't caught all the meaning. But he was the one to answer. Then, frowning heavily, he led me back to the camp.

"What do they say?" a chorus of emigrants asked. "What's to be?"

"They ask for Powers," Trace explained. "It's him or us."

"No!" Mrs. Power's screamed. "You can't mean to turn Gus over to those bloodthirsty savages."

"Wasn't them shed blood," Trace replied. "We turn him

55

over, or they attack. Need I tell you who's likely to die then? How many women and children'll pay the price for a drunken man's amusement? Got to be, folks!"

"No!" Gus Powers shouted, heading for his wagon. A pair of men blocked the way, and George Trace managed to pin one arm behind the Iowan's back and force him to turn.

"Got to be this way," Trace announced to the reluctant emigrants. "Better one man kilt than the all of us."

"And my wife and young ones?" Powers asked.

"We'll see 'em safe to trail's end," Trace promised. "After, they'll have to look after 'emselves, as the rest of us will. Now come along."

"Jeremy, get my rifle," Powers shouted as he broke loose from Trace's grasp. The scout never hesitated. He drew his pistol, aimed, and fired. A ball exploded through Powers's forehead, and the big man fell in a heap a dozen yards from where a startled Jeremy Powers cradled the weathered Kentucky rifle.

"It's done now," Trace said, wiping the sweat from his forehead. "I'll take 'em what they came for. The rest o' you keep your guard up."

"No," Mrs. Powers pleaded. "Give my poor Gus a Christian burial at least."

But Trace was determined to meet Spotted Elk's demands, and the Oglalas took charge of the corpse.

"What'll they do with my Gus?" Mrs. Powers asked. She searched the faces of her friends, then turned toward Tom and myself. She begged Trace to tell her. Those who knew wouldn't say. It would have brought her no comfort to know.

I spent a restless night, rolling from side to side, tossing off my blankets so that the cold penetrated my bones. I saw a hundred shadows in my dreams, but always the hollow face of Mrs. Powers and her four terrified children brought me shivering into consciousness.

"Can't take 'em to heart, Darby," Tom advised when he shook me awake next morning.

"Them?" I asked, rubbing the sleep from my eyes.

"Heard you callin' out," he explained. "No need mournin' a

56

fellow like that Powers. He killed a boy sure as daylight, and he wound up payin' the price."

"Would you have handed him over, Tom?"

"Would've kept that corn liquor away from the Indians," he grumbled. "And I'd never thrown dice. Bound to be hard feelin's, and shootin' has a habit o' followin' such."

"Figure it's over now? I don't rest too easy knowing No Nose is anywhere nearby."

"Don't figure he stands in much favor with the young men," Tom declared. "Got those three tied up goin' after our horses, and he got Younger Elk kilt this last time. Spotted Elk'll have his people mournin' three days. No, I'd say we're safe enough on that quarter."

"Good, because I've swallowed all the trail dust I can stomach for a bit. I thought we might break away today, make camp out by Devil's Gate."

"Oh?" he asked. "Ain't likely you'll find much peace in that haunted place."

"Thought you might care to visit your sister," I explained. "As for peace, well, I've found it there before."

"Guess it wouldn't hurt much. Haven't seen any buffs to hunt. Be a job keepin' the stock all together with just the two of us to watch 'em at night."

"Done it before, Tom."

"Well, I admit we have. I'll go have a word with Trace."

I don't know what Tom said to George Trace, but the sound of the scout's voice could be heard a mile away. Likely the Oglalas had stirred him up. Or maybe shooting Powers had taken a toll. Whatever it was, neither Trace nor the emigrants was happy to see us ride off that morning. Devil's Gate wasn't far off the trail, and we'd rejoin the others the next day. Still, I watched the wary eyes of our companions and hoped they wouldn't suffer in our absence.

It wasn't a long ride to Devil's Gate, and we were there a little shy of noon. There was no mistaking the place. There was a gap in the rock ridge north of the Sweetwater, like the notch you'd put in a log. The Shoshonis told how it was put there by a monster demon, and they feared going there. The burial

57

scaffolds of some tribe or another clung to the steep sides of the gap, and the wind whistled through there, singing a haunting tune that set the hairs on your head on end.

We had to cross the Sweetwater to reach the gate itself, and there were easier things than getting four stubborn horses and a like number of mules into and out of the swollen stream. Still, we had reasons for making the effort. On the rock wall of the gap was etched the name of Tom Shea's young sister, dead of fever long before I'd ever heard of Oregon. We gathered up wildflowers to set on her grave, and I played a hymn on my mouth organ.

"Seems more and more it's graves we visit on our way through this country," Tom observed as we made camp beside the river. "My sister's. Your mama's. Young Jamie, who walked the trail with you back in '48. Crows and Shoshonis. World o' grief, this road's brought."

"And lots of beginnings," I reminded him.

"Been west to Oregon half a dozen times now," he muttered. "With you, twice now."

"Be three times next year."

"Still got scout fever, do you?" he asked, laughing. "Me, I thought maybe you might take that Borden girl and make a home for yourself. You could do worse, Darby Prescott."

"Guess so," I admitted. "But I've got the wayfaring itch. I don't know that I could get to be a sit-around-the-fireplace kind of man. It's a long trail to Oregon, Tom, but a man feels good helping others to find their way."

"Know that," he said, grinning. "Done it a few times, haven't I? But I never heard of a scout had himself a wife. Least not a white one."

"Plenty of emigrants married and on the trail."

"True enough, Darby, but a scout's got to have his eyes on the trail and his nose to the wind. Needs to smell out trouble. And he's the one folks look to as a leader come hard times. A man gets wed, he's got other worries 'sides his company."

"I could always come back to Fort Laramie at trail's end."

"Be a hard winter's journey," he pointed out. "Askin' a lot for a woman to wait a year to see you, then wave good-bye come first thaw."

"Guess it would," I confessed.

I thought no more of it that night. Again my dreams were full of hollow-cheeked children, only this time they resembled Laveda Borden. All seemed bewildered, wondering when their papa would come home, and the haunting sensation that he wouldn't seemed to etch itself across their mother's brow.

I awoke early and set to work readying the animals. Tom rose early as well, and we had our weary mules splashing across the Sweetwater and chasing the Trace train right away. We caught them an hour short of noon, and for the first time in the ten days we'd been part of that company, I felt welcome. A couple of boys even raced out to beg a ride, and that night I shared the tale of my battle with a grizzly in the Absaroka country to the north.

It was another ten days to Green River Ferry, and I lowered my walls and let the people steal their way into my heart. I carried little Cynthia Bassett around on my shoulder one day, and I led the older boys off down a hollow to shoot rabbits the next. I found a few moments to talk to Jeremy Powers, too.

"You say you saw 'em put Pa up on a mountaintop?" he asked.

"Like a respected enemy," I lied. "Sure he's resting in peace, like you all will at trail's end."

Tom pulled me aside afterward and slapped me on the back.

"Words o' comfort, those," he said. "Course I never recall the peace I ever found at trail's end."

"Maybe you never stopped long enough to give it a chance," I suggested.

"Maybe not," he admitted. "Could be we'll find it when we unload those danged mules at Burkett's place and get back to Laramie. Be August maybe, but I figure there's good huntin' still waitin' for us."

"Better be," I replied. "Got a fine rifle now. I plan to put it to use."

Chapter Six

It was drizzling the day we reached the Green River ferry, and it took every ounce of skill for us to get our skittish mules aboard that narrow flatbed of a ferry barge. I swam the horses across to avoid the toll, and Jed Burkett met us on the far bank with a broad smile.

"Figured you two'd end up bringin' my supplies," he said, laughing. "Been waitin' on you a week. Got a jug unplugged and some good company ready to rob you at the card table."

"Don't know we'll stay long," Tom spoke up. "This boy's all hot and lathered to get back to Laramie. Has a gal waitin'."

"Darby?" Burkett asked, grinning. "Why, I figured you'd been wild so long as to've forgot what's important in life. She ain't too pretty, is she?"

"Never heard there was such a thing," I answered.

Burkett laughed, and Tom slapped me across the back. The two of them took charge of the mules and led them along to the company storehouse. Me, I hobbled the horses and left them to graze beside the river. I said a few good-byes to the train folk, then walked off a ways and stretched out alone on a hillside. Here it was, the middle of July now, and we were maybe two weeks hard traveling from Fort Laramie. Laveda'd been right. Summer'd mostly be gone when we returned.

That night Trace's emigrants and a handful of trappers joined together for a bit of dancing and drinking at the trading post, and I again played my mouth organ and spun a few tales. The melody was sadder this time though, and I couldn't muster any enthusiasm for my story.

Tom noticed.

"Always the hardest part, takin' a fork in the road," he told me. "Sayin' farewell and headin' out. Got cash money in our pockets for a change though, and I haven't worn through the seat o' my britches. How 'bout you?"

"In fair shape," I answered. "Could use a new pair of boots, though. Next buff we drop, I'll scrape off the hide hair and make a pair."

"Might keep a sharp eye out for a fox or two as well. I don't figure that gal o' yours'd have cross words for you if you brought her a nice soft coat."

"Elk robe'd be as warm."

"Different kinds o' warm," Tom said, grinning. "Take it from a man who'd know."

"Who'd that be?"

"Ole Tom Shea," he said, planting his thumb in his chest. "Wasn't always a crusty ole mountain goat, you know."

"I do know. There was the Crow woman. And the boy."

"Sure," he said, gazing at his feet. "But 'fore that I knew how to spin a dollar so it'd catch the ladies' eyes. Why, once in St. Louis I had three of 'em on my elbow the same night. One was a theatrical gal, all feathers and smiles. Well, that was a time, I tell you."

"Do tell me," I pleaded.

"Well," he began, "I wasn't but twenty-five, and these gals were . . ."

A pair of wagon youngsters popped their heads up then, and Tom laughed. He shook his head, laughed even louder, and waved me off toward the hill where I'd spread our blankets. It was there he completed the tale. As he talked, his eyes brightened, and I couldn't help thinking he was coming alive for the first time in years. But the story was too quickly concluded, and the sun was long gone. We took to our blankets and let sleep swallow our worries.

A half hour after dawn the next morning, we started across Green River. Behind us Burkett was rousing trappers from his porch, and the emigrants were wearily stirring to life. I didn't look back. I'd learned better than to prolong a parting.

For the next two days we were carefree wayfarers, and the trail was all our own. Except for soaring hawks and curious ground squirrels, the sandy, treeless plain ascending into the South Pass was ours. We were utterly and completely alone. I couldn't help thinking that this was how the world must have appeared to Adam, or perhaps to old Noah setting his boat down after the long journey. Only Adam soon had Eve, and Noah, well, he had more company than he likely cared for.

We soon had visitors, too. To begin with, a party of Shoshonis stopped by to trade. They didn't get much more'n a stick of tobacco and a hunting knife, and they left us a good pair of elk hides already chewed soft as goose down. Then toward dusk the sound of creaking wagon wheels brought the horses whining in protest. I climbed a boulder and beheld a ragged company plodding up the pass, its haggard people showing the agony brought on by months of toil. For a moment I stared hard. Men, women, even children were pulling and pushing two-wheeled carts up the trail. They had no stock!

"Pushcart company," Tom announced. "Saints."

"Mormons?" I asked. "Hauling everything by hand?"

"Not altogether a bad notion," Tom explained. "See, they've no worry over grass to feed animals. There's no hitchin' and waterin' to worry with. And they travel light from the start, unlike some folks I've known."

"They look half-dead," I observed. "Look there at those little girls helping their brother keep that cart going! Be a miracle if the young ones don't all die of exertion."

"Trail's always hard on the little ones," Tom grumbled. I saw his eyes darken and knew he was thinking of his sister. Well, it *was* hard, and it wouldn't help to have an eighty-pound boy hauling a full-grown man's loaded cart.

"Look there," I said, pointing at where a girl of twelve or so prodded a half-dozen cows along. "Seems like *they* could pull a cart."

"Dairy cows," Tom pointed out. "For milk. Not much fat on 'em as is."

"Nor on the children, either," I said as they grew near. I

62

stared in wonder at the ghostlike skeletons marching along. They were badly sunburned, the lot, with hair almost yellow-white. They weren't dressed like most saints, in plain home-spun blue and brown cotton or wool. No, these folks wore short britches and long socks, most of 'em. The men's shirts were odd-fitting, and the women's skirts were fuller than most emigrants wore.

The sight of our cook fire brought on a wild charge of the younger ones. The men shouted orders in a strange, German-sounding language, full of rounded sounds that didn't belong on that harsh, windswept trail.

"They're Swedes," Tom declared as the children drew to a halt beside our fire. One or two, spotting my deadly Sharps, backed up a step. They jabbered and pointed at the two rabbits turning over the coals.

"They are hungry," a slender, red-faced young woman explained as she parted the crowd and stepped to the fire. "We have been long on this journey. Our hams are gone, and we have eaten the chickens."

I gazed at Tom, and he nodded. The rabbits wouldn't go far, but neither of us was much for seeing a child go hungry.

"You're welcome to the rabbits," I told the Mormon girl. "If you can take a gift from a pair of scoundrels like us."

"You are not of our faith?" she asked. "We were told soon we would meet others who followed the way of Brother Brigham Young."

"Some run the ferry at Green River," Tom told her. "More settlin' here and there as you take the south fork o' the trail down toward Salt Lake."

A trio of older men then appeared, and the girl shared our offer. There was a bit of discussion, and one of the men nodded.

"Gunther says we can accept," she said, smiling. "It must be God set you in our path."

"Yes, ma'am," I said, taking the first rabbit from the spit and offering it to the crowd. One of the elders took the food and began parcelling it out so that there would be some for all. I passed over the second rabbit, and he did the same.

"What of you?" the young woman asked.

"Oh, we eat regular enough," Tom assured her. "We'll scare up somethin' later on."

"You hunt?" she asked, gazing hungrily at the small portion of rabbit in her hands.

"When the rabbits won't jump in the stewpot o' their own accord," Tom said, laughing. "Get elk and buffs sometimes. That'd feed you proper."

"You will shoot one for us?" she asked.

"Got to be movin' along," Tom muttered. "Got business elsewhere. You'll be along in Green River soon, with your own people to see to your needs."

"Yes," she said, sadly sitting beside the fire and drawing a frail boy to her side. Her eyes revealed doubts. As I glanced among the weary, nigh-starved company, I had no confidence a one of them would see Salt Lake. Already some of the younger ones were sleeping on the bare ground. Others threw a blanket out beneath a pine and sprawled there.

"Maybe we could find you a buffalo," I said, staring at the hollow eyes of our uninvited companions. "Tom?"

"Layin' over a day wouldn't hurt so bad," he agreed. "It's you was in a hurry, Darby?"

"Bless you both," the girl said. "I'm called Marta. This is my brother Edvard."

The small boy huddled at her side looked up and managed a faint grin. She stroked his hair and hummed a soft, comforting song.

"This'll never do," Tom grumbled then. "Don't you pilgrim's know how to make a proper pine bed? Here, gather round. Let me show you," he said, lifting Edvard off the cold ground and carrying him on one shoulder toward the nearby pines. In no time Tom kicked a bed of pine needles together and laid the boy on it. A willowy woman of forty or so covered the child with a blanket, and the other children hurried to build their own nests.

"*Dank u,* thank you," Marta told us. "You are much kind."

"Hear that, Tom?" I asked, grinning. "Much kind."

"Nothin' at all, ma'am," Tom said shyly. "Let's get our own

beds made, Darby," he mumbled. "Mornin's certain to come early."

And so it was. No sooner did my head touch the blanket than Tom was shaking me to life.

"Sun's up," he announced. "Game's waitin'."

I shook the cobwebs out of my head and blinked my eyes into focus. Then I hurriedly got dressed, saddled Pepper, and followed Tom down the mountainside.

Summer was a time to spot buffalo in South Pass, but elk frequented that country year 'round. There wouldn't be near as much meat, but a couple of elk would fill those starving bellies and get them along to Green River. The Mormon ferrymen could take charge of the company there.

"What is it moves people like that onto this plain?" I asked Tom when we dismounted near a small spring-fed lake. "They head out without a scout, into country they don't know, with only the certainty of hardship and danger to accompany them. Lucky the whole bunch doesn't die!"

"It's faith of a sort, I suppose," Tom replied. "You believe in a thing enough, it seems like it happens. Take those buffalo dreams you had when we were travellin' with the Shoshonis that year. You couldn't know there'd be buffs out there, but your dream said they'd be there. Happened, didn't it?"

"Figure Marta and her people had a dream?"

"Had words to believe, anyway. I sometime's envy folk who got that kind o' belief. Even if they get 'emselves chewed up by Sioux, or starved or carried off by fever, they stomach it and come out stronger at trail's end."

"You always tell me a wise man uses caution," I reminded him.

"You're fed well enough, ain't you? Not too many holes in your hide. I'd still say it's good advice."

I nodded my head. Then we concentrated on the task at hand. It wasn't long before we located tracks—fresh ones— and after carefully threading our way in and out of the pines and cottonwoods, we spied a small band of elk not a hundred yards from the lake. They were on their way there for a morning drink, and Tom and I waited for them. I loaded and steadied my Sharps, then motioned for Tom to pick out his target first. He held up two fingers, and I gazed to my left at a large, broad-shouldered buck. I selected a younger buck standing respectfully ten yards from the larger animals.

Tom nodded, cocked his rifle, and fired. I did likewise, and in a sudden explosion of sound, the two elk fell as if struck by lightning. The other animals scrambled away into the safety of the trees, and we started down the slope to make the throat cuts and skin the elk.

It wasn't particularly joyful work, butchering meat. I'd never had a stomach for it back on the Illinois farm where I'd been born. There were other brothers to do it there. Now I did what was needed myself. A man learns self-reliance in the high country, or he dies early.

By midday we had the meat packed inside the hides. We then tied our life-giving cargo behind our saddles and headed back to the pass. I don't think I've ever felt so welcome as when Tom led the way among those Swedes. When we opened up the hides and revealed the fresh meat, there were cries aplenty. Children gazed eagerly at rumps and shoulders and ribs.

"Bless you," Marta called, and the others mimicked her words. Tom then organized a walk to a nearby stream for a bit of nut-gathering and a wash, while I took the now unneeded hides and stripped the flesh while the Mormon's built up cooking fires.

It wasn't the flames warmed me that afternoon. The sun was bright and high, and the wind blew calmly out of the west. It was as bright a day as I recalled, but it didn't hold a candle to the glow on the faces of those young Swedes when they chewed their first elk steak. Later on Tom helped them fashion fishing line from vines, and he gave away two dozen hooks. I don't suppose there was a trout left for five miles around by nightfall. Those little ones didn't know the land, and they were tenderfeet where making up a trail bed was concerned. But I'd say they were natural born fishermen, if ever such a thing existed.

That night Tom and I moved our camp off a ways, into a stand of cottonwoods. Even so, we could hear singing around the crackling fires of the Mormons. There was fresh spirit in those tired, thin faces, and new strength in arms and legs.

"Figure they'll make it, Tom?" I asked as I climbed between my blankets.

"To Green River anyhow," he answered. "After that, who knows? I wouldn't wager they wouldn't, though. Those kids got backbone, even if they're nigh as tall as a Rocky Mountain locust."

"Some of those are as big as your leg," I said, laughing.

"Tomorrow we'll be back on the trail," he said, sighing so that I knew he, too, would miss the laughter of those Swedes.

"Yes," I answered. "And a week and a half hard traveling to Fort Laramie."

"Might not be as hard as you think, Darby. Be others along the trail now."

I nodded. But it wasn't like Tom to share camps with wagon trains. And we did, after all, have some miles to make.

We left early that next morning, but not so early the Mormons didn't notice. Marta and a small delegation of elders greeted us as we saddled our horses.

"We have much thanks for you," she said, nodding to the elders. "You bring back to life the children. Never we can thank you, but I bring you this."

She took a small, shiny brass object from her mother and passed it into my hands. I opened the lid, and a delicate tune whispered its notes across the hillside.

"A music box," I said, handing it over to Tom. "No, I can't accept this. It's precious, and surely a keepsake of your family."

"Take it," Marta pleaded. "Is part of the old life. We go to find better."

"But . . ." I started to argue.

"It's a gift," Tom said, placing it again into my hands. "Don't shame 'em, son. It'll bring you joy, hearin' a tune on lonely nights. Thank her."

"Thank you," I said, making a bow toward Marta and her mother both. "I wish you every good fortune on your journey."

"*Dank u,*" she replied. "Bless you both."

The Mormons then turned and started toward their carts. The children peered down at us from the hill, waving their hands as Tom had no doubt taught them. We returned the gesture, then climbed atop our horses and set off eastward. I looked back but once, and I was immediately sorry. So many of the faces watching our departure were sad and hollow again. Better I'd recalled the smiles and the waves.

Chapter Seven

Tom and I returned to Fort Laramie the first day of August. We must've passed twenty wagon trains along the way, trudging along in spite of July's fierce midday heat and cool, windy nights. Most of those companies were in good stead, for now there were a hundred capable scouts eager to earn their living showing tenderfeet the way to California or Oregon. A few of the trains were ragged, quarrelsome bunches, terrified by their own shadows and eager to shoot at anything that moved. Twice, just passing such bands on the road, I had to duck under a rifle shot. If they'd been better at aiming, I might have been punctured a time or two.

"Now that'd been somethin' to explain to ole St. Pete," Tom declared. "Gettin' yourself pilgrim-shot!"

Worse, the startled Indiana farmer who pulled the trigger said he'd mistook me for an Indian. Me! Here it was, midsummer, and the sun turned my hair near enough to butternut for me to've been one of those Mormon Swedes. And who ever saw a Cheyenne or a Sioux with whiskers on his chin?

Things being what they were, I wasn't a little happy to reach the Fort Laramie outbuildings. The soldiers were drilling, as it seemed they did every day. Lt. Grattan had them at it hard. Laveda's papa said it was West Point turned soldiers' heads, made 'em believe in browbeating their men. Well, I never saw a Crow drill, but I wouldn't want to face a handful of 'em coming at me on horseback.

I didn't bother with the bluecoats, though. Instead I turned my horses over to Tom and hurried to the Bordens' store. Laveda was busy restocking shelves, and she didn't notice me slide inside the doorway. I motioned for Laurence to keep mum, then sneaked around behind her.

"Howdy!" I howled as I popped out at her.

"Ayyy!" she screamed, reaching for a handy frying pan. It was a good thing she recognized my face before she swung that skillet. That would've been even harder to explain at the Pearly Gates.

"Don't you ever do such a thing to me again, Darby Prescott!" Laveda scolded. "Close to scared me out of my skin!"

"Was a sight!" Laurence hollered. "Sis, I never knew you could jump so high."

"So, you were in on this, too, were you?" she said, her face growing redder by the moment. "I'll be getting even for it, Laurence. You bank on that. As for our wild Indian here," she added, turning toward me, "I'll have to figure out something for you as well."

"Just thought to surprise you," I said, painting my face with pretended gloom. "Gone all these weeks, and not even a word of welcome."

"Welcome home," Laurence said, grinning.

"Wasn't from you I was expecting it," I grumbled. "Laveda?"

She pretended anger, but I placed the Swedish music box on the counter and lifted its lid. As a gentle tune filled the air, she brightened.

"Welcome home," she said begrudgingly. "Almost got a frying pan on that pointed head of yours. That would have been a fine greeting."

" 'Bout like gettin' Sioux-shot," Tom said, joining us. "Darby, we got camp to make. Good to see you youngsters."

"Glad you're back, Mr. Shea," Laurence said, shaking Tom's hand. "As for making camp, the storeroom's still handy if you're none too particular."

"It'd be your Papa's place to offer it," Tom replied. "He handy?"

"Papa's made no secret you're welcome there," Laveda an-

70

swered. "He's gone out to visit the Oglalas. He'll be back soon."

"They still here?" I asked. "Thought they'd scatter sure after the giveaway."

"Likely will," Laveda said, gazing nervously out the door. "Hasn't happened yet, either thing. Army says they're expecting someone out from Washington to oversee things, but I don't know. We've sure got a lot of edgy Indians."

"I imagine," I muttered. "Guess they're used to broken promises, though. Should be. There've been enough of 'em."

"Not where the Sioux's concerned," Tom said, scratching his head. "I hate to think how they'll act if they think the treaty's a trick. Be a lot of yellow hair danglin' from scalp belts."

"Tom!" I scolded, observing the sour looks from the Bordens. Both were blond as autumn wheat.

"Don't mind me," Tom apologized. "My tongue takes to waggin' when I get 'round people, after so much time in the wilds."

"Wasn't a word of it untrue, Mr. Shea," Laveda remarked. "If it was up to me, I'd see the goods distributed tomorrow. Papa's done his very best to cut down his profits and keep the camps supplied, but we've got the wagon trade to see after. That's why we're here, after all. And they pay cash money."

"Sure," I said. "And maybe that Washington fellow'll come along with the next company to pass through."

"Maybe," Laveda mumbled. I could tell she didn't believe it.

Jesse Borden returned from his journey to the Oglala camp in time for supper. Laveda mixed some vegetables and the shoulder roast from an emigrant ox into a tasty stew, and Tom and I joined the Bordens in stuffing ourselves. I'd lived six weeks on fresh game and wild turnips, and those carrots and potatoes were a true delight.

"Never had a meal to top it," I announced as I helped Laurence clear away the plates. "Thanks, Laveda, Mr. Borden."

"If you want to thank us proper, you won't go running off on American Fur Company business this time," he answered. "And call me Jesse. Too many misters around this post to suit a

71

plain man as it is."

"Papa, why not ask him?" Laveda suggested.

"Ask what?" I questioned. "Need some help?"

"We do," Borden confessed. "And it'd be a good opportunity for you two as well."

"Go on," Tom said, waving me back from the counter. "Spell it out."

"I've done a fair bit of trade with the Indians camped nearby," Borden explained. "But things being what they are, I can't get out there but one day in five. You two could make the swing every other day or so, and you know a fair trade when you see one. No cheating the Sioux or leaving me short either. What's maybe more important, I could trust you with a wagonful of goods."

"Tom?" I asked, turning to where he sat, rubbing his chin.

"I thought to ride out and join the Crows 'fore winter sets in," he explained. "Maybe do some horse tradin'."

"I'd pay you a fair wage," Borden promised.

"Isn't money'd be at issue," I broke in. "We've got bank notes we'll never spend now. It's hard to explain, I guess. We're wayfarers, Tom and me. We never took a job for wages, 'cept maybe scouting for the wagon train, and that's more adventure than work. I never took to farming, and I'm not sure we'd stomach this brand of work."

"You could try it," Laveda argued.

"Wouldn't be so different from swapping horses," Laurence added. "I've done it some, and I could go out with you the first few times."

"Maybe you should take on the job, Laurence," I said, seeing the eagerness in his eyes.

"He's a good salesman," Borden declared proudly. "Be a fair trader when he gets his growth. But a Sioux trades best with a man he respects."

"Can't send your son to deal with another man," Tom mumbled. "I see it clear enough."

"Besides," Laurence said, "I don't know how to make the right signs, and I don't speak the Sioux language. I aim to learn, but that gets me nowhere now."

"Tom?" I asked again.

"Well, the Crows'll still be there a bit," he told me. "And we've been on the move most o' two years now. Be good settlin' in for a time."

I smiled my approval, although I knew he didn't believe a particle of what he'd said. Tom Shea grew restless if he spread his blankets in the same place more than a week.

Nevertheless we set out for the Sioux camps early that next morning. Jesse Borden spared us a wagon, which Laurence drove, and Tom and I led the way. We met with the Oglalas first, and though Spotted Elk wasn't any too pleased to see his old enemy come to trade, there was, at least, respect between us.

I met with a different response from the younger men.

"Ah, it's a sad day," Two Nations declared when he and a dozen other Oglala boys appeared to trade. "A warrior's turned to trading looking glasses to the women."

The others laughed and taunted me. I made my own jests in reply, and after a time voices began to rise. It wasn't until a tall young man pushed me to the ground that tempers really flared though.

"Ah, it must be done right!" Two Nations shouted when I struck my attacker in the face. "Come, we make a game of it."

Before I knew exactly what was happening, Two Nations had paired me with the tall Oglala, Charges Ahead. He had three inches and forty pounds on me, and his muscular arms bore the scars of other battles.

Well, what of it? I asked myself as I stripped off my shirt and handed it to Laurence. I was tanned and hard, too, and the scars left by a Sioux arrowhead on my elbow and a grizzly's claw on my chest attested to my own talent for surviving brushes with death.

"Watch his feet, Darby," Laurence whispered. "I've seen him before."

"Watch his eyes, trader," Two Nations said, grinning. "They speak of your pain."

I glanced at Charges Ahead and understood Two Nations's taunt. There was pain in that tall young warrior's face. More

73

than pain, in fact. Hatred! But where strong feelings will give you strength for the moment, they can work to your disadvantage over the long haul. When Charges Ahead lunged at me, I clasped his arms and used his weight to throw him over my hip. He rose in a fever, and he leaped at my legs like a wildcat, grabbing and clawing. I dodged him, then drove my knee into his ribs. He rolled away, howling in pain. Then a hand reached out and held me in place. Charges Ahead rushed at me, and we collided with a thud. I rolled over backward, and he jumped on my chest.

I felt the air rush out of my lungs, and I wheezed in agony. My chest was afire, and that Indian seemed to enjoy the fact. He slapped at my head, but I fended off the blow. He grabbed my shoulders, but I slipped my hands under his hold and slammed an elbow against his chin.

We rolled away from each other, and I managed to catch my breath. This time when a hand reached out at me from behind, I grabbed it and threw the offender against a lunging Charges Ahead. The Oglalas collided this time, and I gave each of them a solid thump across the chest. It sent the surprised second Oglala to the ground, but Charges Ahead leaped upon me and drove my head into the sandy ground. We rolled along, one on top and then the other. It was a wild fight, with dust and hair flying, man clawing man, or biting, or kicking. Finally the two of us rolled into a wallow, and the muck brought us sputtering to our feet.

The Oglala boys gathered close, and one held out a knife. I felt my insides grow cold as Charges Ahead gripped its bone handle.

"Don't do it!" Laurence yelled. "Fight fair."

"As did our brother, Younger Elk?" Two Nations answered. The words hit me like a fist, and my eyes fell to my feet.

"Enough!" I shouted. "I know of him. I'll not hurt a man who's suffered so. I, too, buried a brother once."

Two Nations translated my words with a new, slightly hushed tone, and Charges Ahead paused. He stared at the knife, then flung it aside, crying out fierce words.

"He says there's been enough dying," Two Nations ex-

74

plained. "You fight well for a *wasicun,* for a white man. Come, we wash."

I turned and followed Charges Ahead and his companions toward the river. We cast aside our clothes and waded into the muddy stream. For several minutes no one spoke. Then Charges Ahead gripped my hands and quietly spoke.

"He says he doesn't speak your words, but he knows your heart," Two Nations translated. "You were the one who carried his brother's body from the *wasicun* camp. We know the pain that rested in your eyes. Yes, you know death. It is well known in the Oglala camps."

"I would've had it different," I said, signing the same meaning to Charges Ahead. "Was foolishness, your brother dying. Men should see more sunrises before the darkness falls."

We swam a bit longer, and afterward I conducted them to the wagon and helped start the trading. Mostly the Oglalas needed flour and powder, and they brought good buffalo robes to swap. I smiled my approval as Tom and Laurence kept the exchanges fair and congenial.

Later, as we headed back to the fort, Laurence recounted my battle with Charges Ahead.

"Strange how much you share with a man you're wrestling," I observed. "There's pain and power you exchange with each other, and a kind of understanding grows. I feel I know those Oglalas a bit. And though they'd surely kill me if we were at war, I got a feeling they wouldn't much enjoy it now."

We went out to the Indian camps three times that first week out, swapping what food we could to weary Brules and Miniconjous as well as with the Oglalas. One wagon train at least visited the fort each day, and by night I entertained the ladies on the post piano and entertained the youngsters with tales.

Lt. Fleming visited with me a couple of times, and it turned out he had a few books. Mostly they were military history and geography, but he had a fiction book or two as well, and I read them each and every one.

"You look like you're taking to settled life," Laveda observed as we walked beside the river following one of the welcome dances.

"Don't know what's settled," I retorted. "Got a roof over my head, so maybe I am partly tamed. Not much settled about trading with the Sioux though."

"Papa's been very pleased with your work," she told me. "In fact, he's spoken of setting up a new trading post at the Sweetwater crossing, maybe going there himself. He thinks Laurence and I could run the store here . . . if we had some help."

"Meaning?"

"I never planned to tend my papa's counter forever, Darby. I've got a home of my own to make one day, and babies to hatch and raise."

"My babies?" I asked. She nodded. "Laveda, who am I to take a wife? I hardly stay in one place long enough to know it. Marry you? Shoot, I'm just bone and trail dust. I hardly have enough whiskers on my chin to make 'em worth shaving."

"Isn't whiskers make a man," she argued.

"Nor tall dreams and big talk," I added. "I don't know that I can be what you want, what you need."

"You'll do," she assured me. "Could be I know you better than you know yourself, Darby Prescott."

"Maybe," I said, clutching her hands. "Can't say it's a notion that doesn't have some appeal to it. Still, we're awful young."

"People die young in this country," she complained. "We've both of us buried mothers who were still young. I want to see my children grown, Darby."

"I guess everyone does. But you're rushing me considerably, Laveda. Be patient."

"That's what they tell the Sioux," she grumbled.

"Sometimes it's the only thing you can say. Or do, Laveda. The only thing."

"Yes," she admitted as we turned back toward her father's store. "But that doesn't make it easier to swallow."

Chapter Eight

Summer was one long pageant of wagon trains. As soon as one company left, another appeared. I worried over the late ones, knowing the hardships of crossing the high passes once snow began to fall. But there was nothing to do about it.

"We had fever on the Platte," one group said.

"Were a long time findin' a good scout," another explained.

Laveda and I often joined in a bit of the singing and dancing that always marked a train's arrival at the fort. It was a brief interlude between long days spent riding among the Sioux camps. Most of the warrior's were off hunting now, intent upon putting in a supply of winter meat, giveaway or not! There was a fair amount of business to be done with the women and old men though.

Laurence thrived on that trade. The younger boys and girls taught him Sioux words to go with the signs I'd passed on, and the old people often shared stories. If it was up to old men and young kids to make treaties, I guess there'd be a lot less trouble about 'em. They made swaps and shared tales and got to know each other. Would've been a good example for others to follow.

I was thinking that very thing the day the Langer company arrived at Ft. Laramie. It was a ragged train, with stragglers spread out all over the place. Worse, they kept no guard on their stock, and the children strayed more than they kept to their wagons.

I guess I wasn't much surprised when the next morning a band of emigrants approached Lt. Fleming with word that three boys had strayed.

"They've gone and wandered off before," a distraught mother explained, "but they never stayed overnight. Been back at supper's call each time. Now, oh dear, I fear they may have met with mischance."

"We're late crossin' west as is," Langer, the captain of the company, said. "Don't see how we can linger long searching for 'em."

"You can't just leave them behind!" the woman cried. "Not my little Joshua! And what of his cousins, Tim and Toby?"

"How old are they?" Fleming asked.

"Tim's fourteen. Toby's twelve. And little Joshie's only ten."

She went on to describe the trio, telling how she did her best with them, what with her husband and brother resting beside the Platte in the shadow of Chimney Rock. The lieutenant was shaken by her words, as was the post's other lieutenant, the hot-headed John Grattan.

"You see any Indians around your train?" Grattan asked.

"Why, yes," Langer said, nodding. "Lots of 'em. They came out to beg flour or trade."

"I warned you there'd be trouble from those Sioux," Grattan told Fleming. "Now they've gone and stolen these children, good Christian boys snatched from their mama's lap."

"You don't know that," I objected, making my way to the lieutenant's side. "This is Sioux country. It's only natural they should be here. You heard these folks. The boys've wandered before."

"Never overnight," the fretful mother said, dabbing a handkerchief against her tear-streaked cheeks. "Were kidnapped, pure and simple. I've heard what Indians do to white boys. Lord, help them. They'll be burned alive!"

A crowd had begun to gather, and I tried to argue my point again. The old-timers echoed my words, but others shouted them down.

"Rouse the command!" Lt. Grattan urged. "Let's show those Indians the keen edge of a cavalry saber!"

"And what if they really did wander?" I called. "You'll start a war!"

"They started that when they took my son!" the woman insisted.

"Hold up there now!" a commanding voice shouted, silencing all others. Tom Shea, still a bit sleepy from a long night drinking with the wagon folks, parted the crowd like ole Moses halved the Red Sea. Even Grattan grew mum.

"Listen to Tom Shea," I said, joining Tom across from the lieutenants. "He knows the tribes and the country."

"I do," Tom declared. "Sioux might make a raid for your horses, but they'd hardly snatch a bunch o' pilgrim boys so close to this fort. If they did, it'd be men did it, and they've mostly gone to hunt buffs. Most likely the three of 'em's gone off and got lost. Thing to do's have a look 'round. Talk to the Indians. Could be somebody's seen the boys. Go respectable to 'em, and they'll help. Ride armed and ready for trouble, they'll oblige you."

"I don't suppose it would hurt to ask the Indians," Langer confessed. "I'll organize some of the men, get them looking around. Lieutenant, you'll speak with the Sioux?"

"Mr. Grattan, take three men and ride to the Brule camp," Fleming ordered. "I'll speak to the Oglalas. If we have no luck there, we'll visit the other bands."

"Yes, sir," Grattan agreed. "I'll need an interpreter. Lucien August would do."

"I planned on taking him myself," Fleming answered. "Shea?"

"Take young Darby," Tom suggested. "He's on fair terms with the Oglalas."

"Son?" Fleming asked, turning to me.

"I'll get my horse," I told the lieutenants.

So it was that I became an army interpreter. By the time I had my horse saddled and picked up a provision bag from Laveda, Lt. Grattan and his three men were waiting. Together we rode to the Oglala encampment. The morning cook fires were still smoking, and women were down at the river, scrubbing clothes. The few young boys not gone to the hunt watched over the pony herd. I greeted a couple I recognized and was sorry I hadn't picked up the Sioux language as Laurence had.

As it happened, that didn't much matter. Two Nations was there. The half-white youngster did the interpreting, and all I did was watch and listen. I saw and heard enough to sour me toward Grattan right off.

"Three white boys are missing from a wagon train," the officer said. "Where have you hidden them?"

Two Nations and I both tried to temper the lieutenant's words, but the bluecoat chief's eyes betrayed his feelings, and the Oglalas responded angrily.

"Why would I take white boys?" one white-haired old warrior asked. "Don't I have enough children to feed with no promised presents?"

Others were less kind. A crowd started to gather, and Grattan wisely ordered a withdrawal. When we got back to the fort, the lieutenant argued for a thorough search of the camps.

"Never find 'em that way," I objected. "Tom and I'll track 'em down for you."

"But we've had no sign of them," a tall emigrant cried. "Miz Heath's beside herself with worry."

"You don't know the country," I explained. "I do."

By late afternoon I had a fresh horse under me, Tom at my side, and was riding out past the wagons.

"Look at 'em," Tom grumbled, pointing to the children wandering hither and thither. "Be lucky if another dozen aren't gone 'fore dusk."

"Worse luck," I added, staring at the muddied ground beyond the camp. A hundred feet had obscured any sign of a trail. It would be blind good fortune if we detected a trail.

I led the way eastward along the river, figuring it likely the strays had set off in that direction. After riding a mile or so, I spotted a corner of cloth in a nest of briars.

"Could be them," I said, reaching down and snatching it.

"Hasn't been here long anyway."

"Not long," Tom agreed when I handed it to him. "Been since the last rain."

We headed up a low hill and began winding through a series of low ravines. After a quarter mile, I spied something off to my right. Tom saw it, too, and we froze. From out of a cluster of cottonwoods emerged a pair of bare-chested riders. One was Two Nations. The other was a bronze-skinned Oglala called Sparrow Hawk.

"Ah, we, too, saw the cloth," Two Nations said, pointing to the scrap. "There are tracks here."

I nodded. Likely the boys had been there, got turned around in the tangle of brush and gully, and were even now awaiting rescue. I thought of how surprised the soldiers would be when Two Nations and I brought the missing boys back to the train. Then, as I glanced toward a small, muddy-bottomed ditch, I saw something move.

"Hello!" I called. "We're friends."

A small, dirt-smudged face peered out from the underbrush. His clothes were in tatters, and briars had scratched his chest and face unmercifully.

"Indians!" the boy screamed, pointing toward the Sioux.

"Friends," I repeated as I swung my arm down and lifted him up onto my saddle. "What's your name?"

"Joshua," he whispered. "Joshua Heath."

"And the others?" I asked, touching his shoulder in the kindly way I'd watched Laveda comfort her brother.

"Down there," Joshua muttered, pointing up the ravine.

Tom and Sparrow Hawk turned that way. Two Nations stayed behind, his face strangely troubled. I helped Joshua back down, then offered him some dried beef from my near-empty provision bag. Joshua gobbled the scraps hungrily, then moved off a ways and sat down, rocking back and forth as he hummed softly to himself.

"Something bad has happened," Two Nations declared. "When our mother died of fever, my brother acted much the same."

I grew tense, then trotted off down the ravine. It took only

81

a couple of minutes to discover the truth in Two Nations's words. Tom knelt on the ground, placing a canteen to the lips of a second tattered boy. A third, larger one lay a short distance away. His head was turned awkwardly to one side. When I got closer, I could see that he was dead, likely fallen from the lip of the ravine into the rocks that held his body like giant oblong fingers.

"Be hard, this homecomin'," Tom remarked.

"Real hard," I agreed. "Hard as it ever gets. Why was it I expected a better end to it, Tom?"

"Guess we wanted it, so that's what we figured," he said as he helped the sorrowful brother to his feet. I led the boy back to where his cousin waited while Tom took charge of the corpse. Half an hour later we appeared at the wagon camp, Joshua hugging my waist, young Toby White riding likewise behind Sparrow Hawk, Tom and Two Nations on the third horse, and the body of Tim White tied atop Tom's mare.

We didn't visit much with the Langer company, and Mrs. Heath had no words of thanks for us, either. Death had struck them hard, and there wasn't any gratitude in them.

Lt. Fleming thanked our Sioux companions and presented them with shiny new knives. I could tell Two Nations would rather the good words have come from Grattan.

Back at Laveda's place, I passed a somber evening, picking at my food and recalling how stark and alone Tim White had appeared. I couldn't erase the image of that shattered body—the pale, ivory-white flesh and the surprised look in his eyes.

As I lay in my blankets that night, fighting off a chill that didn't come from the sultry breeze, Tom sat beside me.

"Can't take 'em to heart, Darby," he said for perhaps the hundredth time. "It's like that on the trail. Death comes sudden and early."

"Don't I know?" I asked. "Doesn't make it a bit easier to understand."

"No," he agreed. "It doesn't. But you bury your feelin's with the dead and get on along."

"Along to where?" I asked. "We got a destination? Seems like we just stagger over one hill to find another waiting. We survive one storm to see another on the horizon."

"Sure, we do," he confessed. "But we do survive. That's the thing to bear in mind, son. Folks do survive even the worst of it. That's all there is to do."

Chapter Nine

As the long, sweltering days of summer continued, I spent more and more time among the tribes. It was strange how easy it was to forget old animosities while hunting and swimming. These same Sioux, or Lakotas as they called themselves, would have gladly lanced my hide last year when Tom and I were among the Crows. Now, having shared the grim discovery of Tim White's corpse, Two Nations and Sparrow Hawk took me as a sort of kin, a far-off cousin perhaps, whose white skin and strange manners were the result of misfortune.

My ignorance of their language was a vexation. As I rode along with Two Nations, Sparrow Hawk, and a Brule boy called Bobtail, the others chattered away. If I attempted a word or two, they took to laughing. Once the Hawk almost fell off his saddle.

"Don't see what's so funny!" I said, scowling at Two Nations in particular. "If I went around close to naked, with a nose big enough to hang a hat on, I wouldn't be laughing at anybody else!"

"Ah," Two Nations responded, "You are so pretty, are you? No white man dares go naked for long. A hawk would mistake him for a hare and snatch him with its talons. Ah, such a sad end for you, Darby."

Two Nations translated his remarks, and the others laughed even louder than before. I bit my lip, frowned heavily, and rode on ahead of them. But those Sioux must've been born to sit a horse. In the wink of an eye they were beside me again, cackling like a bunch of old widows. If my Sharps had been handier, I might've counted a coup or two.

We spent most of the morning at a stream a mile or so north of the Brules' big encampment. First we did our best to empty the stream of trout. I pulled out my line and gazed around for a grasshopper to put on the hook, but my companions went to laughing again. We wound up fishing Sioux-style.

Now it was my turn to laugh. Those boys kicked off their moccasins and eased their way into the shallows. Then they ducked their head under the surface and scouted around for a fish. When they spotted one, they'd kind of reach around behind and below 'em with their hands, almost tickling ole trout's belly. Then they made a grab.

Two Nations was the first to get his hands on a fish, but a bunch of slippery scales isn't the easiest thing to get hold of. That trout bucked like a range pony, and all Two Nations got for his trouble was a soaking!

"Funny?" he asked with wild eyes as I fell to the ground laughing. "You do it."

Sparrow Hawk and Bobtail glanced my way, so I swallowed my amusement and slipped out of my clothes. Tom had showed me how to snatch trout, and I'd done it a few times when we'd lived with the Shoshonis farther west. Was patience a man needed, and a fair bit of luck didn't hurt him any. I dipped my face in the stream twice without spotting a likely fish. The third time I saw a grandaddy of a trout. It wiggled its way past my knee, and I got both hands on its tail.

Mr. Trout didn't much cooperate. He fought with all his might to slip away, but my hands were sandpaper tough from months on the trail, and my fingers never lost their grip. I hauled the fish out of the water and tossed it onto the bank.

"Ayyy!" Bobtail screamed as I climbed out of the stream.

"*Hau!*" Sparrow Hawk cried, smiling with approval as he examined my fish.

"Not so bad for a *wasicun*," Two Nations added.

"You're half-white yourself," I reminded him.

"I know," he admitted. "The stupid half," he added with a grin.

I captured three trout in all, and young Bobtail got two more. As for the others, they had to depend on our generosity for their supper. I built up a fire, and we cooked the trout over the coals. Sparrow Hawk spoke some as we ate, and once he even gave me a friendly slap on the back, Tom Shea-style.

"He's surprised," Two Nations explained. "Never saw a white man cook. Thought you were like the weak ones who need to bring their women with them. Maybe you'll come with us tomorrow and hunt the buffalo."

"Any nearby?" I asked.

"Plenty," Two Nations told me. "Half a day's ride from here. Get yourself a big bull. You'll need a good coat to keep your skinny white bones warm this winter."

Again they laughed, but there were traces of friendship mixed in, and Sparrow Hawk even cut me a reed and notched it to make a flute.

"Now you can court the trader's daughter," Two Nations taunted me. "She's very bossy, this white woman?"

"Not so bossy," I answered.

"I thought all white women were so. They say, 'Do this! Do that.' It's what makes the white men crazy. My father says it's better to marry a Sioux. She doesn't tire so easy, and she will warm you in the winter."

The Sioux jabbered among themselves, and Two Nations grinned.

"Bobtail, my cousin, says he has a sister," Two Nations explained. "Three horses, and she's yours. She's not very pretty, but she works hard. You can teach her what you need done. She's young."

"How young?" I asked, reading a bemused expression on Sparrow Hawk's face.

"One winter younger than Bobtail," Two Nations answered.

"A year younger?" I said, staring at the slight-shouldered Brule. "He's what, twelve?"

"Fourteen," Two Nations said, fighting a smile off his face. "He's got a younger one, too. She's only seen seven snows."

They hooted considerably at my expense, and I made a show of dickering with Bobtail.

"Maybe he'd take a dog or two for the little one," I suggested. "Could have her hold the horses. Or else show you how to fish."

Bobtail understood very little English, and I wasn't altogether certain Two Nations was translating my words exactly like I said 'em. The Brule alternately fumed and laughed. Then as he turned to fetch his moccasins from the stream, I caught sight of something moving through the tall buffalo grass.

Well, I'd been in the mountains long enough to know trouble. And when a hollow popping sound filled my ears, I drew out my Colt pistol, aiming and firing in the same instant.

The concussion drew an instant reaction from Two Nations and Sparrow Hawk. The two of them raced for their weapons and prepared to return my fire. Bobtail flew through the air like a dancing arrow and landed beside the stream. Four feet away an unlucky rattlesnake twitched eerily as it searched for its dismembered head.

"Was a rattler!" I called, pointing at the dying snake. "Was sure to strike Bobtail."

The boy turned and stared at the deadly reptile. Then he gazed up at me. Two Nations let loose a howl, and Sparrow Hawk raced over to embrace me.

"You," Bobtail stammered, concentrating hard on his words. "You . . . save . . . me!"

He walked over, placed his right hand on my chest, then touched his own chest. I nodded, and he gripped my hands.

"This was a brave heart thing," Two Nations announced. "You have saved my cousin's life."

"He wouldn't've died from snakebite," I argued. "We'd've got it tended in time."

But it didn't matter what I said. The Indians had made up their mind that I was a brave heart. Sparrow Hawk located the tail feather of a hawk and tied it in my hair. Bobtail, meanwhile, jabbered away like a bothersome ole jay, and Two Nations had a time of it translating.

"Maybe he will take you as a brother," Two Nations explained. "He asks if you will come to his lodge. His father will give you good food. Tomorrow we'll hunt together."

"All I did was kill a snake," I answered with a frown. "I had my gun handy, and you fellows didn't. Was only that."

Bobtail remained unconvinced, and Sparrow Hawk was certain the snake came to test my fidelity. Now I was proven a friend to the Lakotas. I had to come along to hunt the buffalo or dishonor my newfound friends.

I returned to the trading post a little after noon. I told Tom what had happened, and he chuckled to himself.

"So, you counted your first Sioux coup," he remarked. "Lord, I'd love to see you ride into the Crow camps with this feather in your hair."

"They wouldn't know it was Sioux," I told him. "Could be I just found it myself."

"No such a thing," Tom explained, plucking it from my hair and showing the notches Sparrow Hawk had cut to mark the kind of coup and the subtler markings that denoted tribe.

"Does that make any difference where the buff hunt's concerned?" I asked. "We could use the fresh meat, you know."

"I know," Tom answered. "Makes me nervous you takin' off with a bunch o' Sioux though, ridin' heaven knows where! You could get your throat cut, Darby."

"I've got my Sharps and my Colt," I assured him. "I'll be fine."

"Use caution," he warned. "There's hard feelings around, especially among the younger folks. Treatment by the army's not been good."

"They still haven't held the giveaway."

"No, and trouble's sure to come of that. Sure as I'm standin' here, some young buck's bound to rile the others, and a white skin's none too healthy at such a time."

"Don't worry about me," I said self-confidently. "I'll be with friends, and I know how to protect myself."

When we set out that next day, Two Nations, Sparrow Hawk, an eager Bobtail, and myself, I began to have my doubts. Soon we were among the other warriors. Never had my white skin so marked me as a stranger. I'd begun to pick up a little of the Lakota language, but when it was spoken quickly, the meaning continued to elude me. Not so the scowls and stares cast my way.

"You saved my cousin from harm," Two Nations told me. "You are one of us."

I knew better. Oh, my Sharps was welcome enough on the buffalo hunt, but the streaks of yellow the sun brought to my walnut-colored hair were too often a reminder of how the plains were changing. I didn't complain much when the band split into scouting parties. I rode behind Bobtail's elder brother, a young Brule of twenty-five or so named Finds the Enemy. He didn't talk much, just grunted and pointed, and I didn't make much effort to get to know him. After all, he'd found me already, and the notched feathers tied in his hair spoke of kills made—likely in autumn raids against the Crows.

Two Nations hung back at my side, jabbering away as was his habit. Only now he spoke English, and I laughed along at his jokes, even when they were directed my way.

"You're not so like the other *wasicun* traders," he told me when we rested our ponies at midday. "They speak of changing the land, going here and there. You listen."

"Didn't always," I confessed. "But I've been out here close to a third of my life now, mostly trailing Tom Shea through the high country. He's a fair teacher, you know."

"He fought with the Crows."

"He married one," I explained. "Had a son by her."

"Then he is Crow even now," Two Nations declared nervously.

"They're dead. Long time now. Guess he's kind of taken me in to ease the sorrow."

"Your family is dead?"

"Got a sister, some brothers, a niece and nephew. Faraway, though. In a different world."

"Yes, I know this world. Once my father took me to St. Louis. I wasn't welcome in his brother's house. A man can cut his hair short and put on *wasicun* clothes, but he can't do anything about the color of his skin. You know, they call me Two Nations. I got myself a white man's name, though."

"What is it?"

"Henry Brown."

"I knew a Henry once. He got by all right."

"Not with the face of a Lakota in a *wasicun* world. Two Nations! Better to call me No Nation. I am not so welcome in either world as a full-blood would be."

"I guess not," I said, frowning. "Sometimes I think it'd be a whole lot easier if God erased everything and started over. Too much anger and suspicion among us. But I guess we've got to live in this world, like it or not. Make do."

"Yes," he agreed.

Soon we had other concerns, and our troubles rolled off our backs like yesterday's rain. Finds the Enemy and Sparrow Hawk had located the buffalo, and they urged us forward, motioning and gesturing in a kind of frenzied excitement I shared in my heart. Buffalo were ahead, and I would prove myself to my new friends once and for all.

We rode steadily, silently onward for what I judged to be two or three miles. Then, crossing over a low slope, we spotted dark clumps spread out across the otherwise empty plain.

"*Tatanka,*" Finds the Enemy proclaimed.

"Our uncle, Bull Buffalo," Two Nations translated.

Bobtail was dispatched to locate the others, and we contented ourselves with watering our horses at a nearby spring. It was the worst kind of waiting. The buffs were close enough to smell, and Sparrow Hawk's hands were twitching in readiness. I wasn't any calmer myself.

A band of Brules joined us first. An old medicine man gathered us together and made the required prayers. Then the older men organized the hunt. I found myself thrown in with the boys, left to chase the herd and finish off the cripples. My fiery eyes betrayed my feelings, and Two Nations drew me aside.

90

"They don't know you," he explained. "Sparrow Hawk and I will ride with you."

"Your place is on the flanks, with the other men," I grumbled.

"Our place is with our brother," Two Nations argued. "Come, make yourself ready. No man can tell how a herd may turn. We may have our chance yet."

I warmed a bit to know Two Nations and Sparrow Hawk would sacrifice their honored place and ride with me among the younger Brules. Only Bobtail was missing, it seemed, and with all the other boys clustered around, it seemed he was there as well. We watched enviously the warriors split off as they began encircling the grazing animals. Then, howling furiously, the Sioux attacked.

I wasn't much for sitting back and watching, but there wasn't any choice. Pepper, too, sensed the action up ahead, and I had to press my knees into his ribs to keep him from taking flight. The boys cheered and cried and whooped as their fathers and elder brothers struck down buffs right and left. Then, as the animals turned south and west, Sparrow Hawk waved in that direction. Bands of boys had already broken away, eager to chase after cripples and bloody their lances. I relaxed my knees, and Pepper broke away from the others and galloped at breakneck speed toward the stampeding buffalo. I could hear others on my heels, but they didn't matter. Just then Pepper and I were the only ones on earth save the churning creatures thundering across the landscape just ahead.

I did my best to approach the buffs from the flank, for only a fool rushes head-on at an ocean of horns and hooves. Pepper snorted and whined as the dust assaulted his nostrils and stung his eyes. Then I saw a big bull lumbering along beside me. I wrapped the reins around my wrist and drew my Sharps from its scabbard. Then, ramming back the hammer, I aimed and fired. The rifle exploded, and its projectile tore through the bull's meaty shoulder and pierced both lungs. The bull slowed as blood flowed over its mouth. Then it dropped its chin and fell into the swirling dust.

91

I drew Pepper off and watched the remaining buffs thunder past. Then, as dust began to settle, I approached the fallen bull.

"You did well," Two Nations called from a dozen yards away. He, too, had dropped a buffalo. Sparrow Hawk scowled. Lacking a rifle, he stood a poor chance of striking a buffalo once the herd took to its heels.

"Now comes the work," I remarked, gazing around at the boys already busy with the skinning.

"Ah, it's worth it. You'll have a good coat," Two Nations declared. "Won with skill, not traded for *wasicun* blankets."

I nodded. Then I took my knife and began butchering my kill.

I'd never been overly fond of the work, and when Bobtail and another young Brule appeared, I welcomed their help. By that time I'd taken the hide, and they went to work cutting strips of meat. There were hundreds of pounds of it, more than Laveda's whole family, Tom Shea, and me, too, could gobble in a month. I was glad that bull would fill some empty bellies in the Brule camp.

We were most of the afternoon skinning and butchering. By then the women had caught up to us, and they took over the carcasses. An Indian could make use out of most every inch of a buff, from swatting tail to horn tip. It was a wonder to behold!

I wrapped the hump meat and a shoulder, plus a section of ribs in my buffalo hide and tied the bundle to the back of Pepper's saddle. Then I turned toward the fort.

"You won't ride alone?" Two Nations called as I climbed atop my saddle.

"Done so before," I told him. "Don't worry. I know this country well."

"I'll go with you," the young half-breed offered. "Maybe you'll find me some tobacco at the trader's store."

"Maybe," I answered with a grin.

We headed off south, toward Platte River, and splashed across to the south bank three or four miles downstream of the fort. A small wagon train was creeping along the trail there, and a couple of men stepped out, rifles in hand, to challenge our passage.

"Name's Darby Prescott," I called. "Been hunting buffs out of Fort Laramie. Here's my friend, Henry Brown, out to keep me from trouble."

"Dees fort, is far?" the first pilgrim asked.

"No," I told him, gazing at the pale, weary faces of the company. Children stumbled along with dead eyes, their fair skin sunburned and filthy from hard times. More saints, I thought, recalling the handcart Swedes Tom and I'd met earlier. At least this batch had horses and wagons. Their stock was left to wander, though, and when I spoke of the buffalo meat tied behind my saddle, their eyes gazed up hungrily.

"Maybe we could shoot a couple of buffs for you," I offered. "Get you some fresh meat."

"You and . . . thees Indian?" the second wagon man asked. His wary gaze spoke better than any words might have done.

"You saints?" I asked. They nodded, and I sighed. They were prideful folk and never prone to taking help from outsiders. "Fort's up ahead," I told them. "You want some of the meat? I'd leave you a shoulder for the little ones."

"We tend our own," the first man shouted defiantly. I looked at the nigh-starved children and scowled. Two Nations turned up the trail, and I joined him. Wasn't any point to pressing your help where it wasn't wanted.

Chapter Ten

I was standing outside Jesse Borden's storehouse early that next morning, stripping dried flakes of flesh from my buffalo hide, when a delegation from the wagon train appeared at Fort Laramie. I took no notice at first, for after all I'd seen enough folks come and go that summer to last me three lifetimes. But there was something different. Even for saints, these people appeared stern. They gestured wildly with their hands, and a soldier raced off to fetch Lt. Fleming.

Tom Shea happened along the scene, and I watched as he joined in the conversation. He spoke slowly and calmly, and for a moment or two the more agitated of the Mormons began to cool down. Then the argument resumed, grew heated, and Tom stalked off shaking his head.

"What's all the excitement over?" I asked as he stopped to look over my efforts.

"Missed a bit there," he said, pointing to the bottom of the hide.

"Got it," I assured him as I took my knife and stripped the dried flake of meat from the otherwise flat surface. "Didn't answer me, Tom."

"Seems they've had a cow wander," Tom explained. "Claim the Sioux took it."

"I passed by there yesterday, you know. Lucky they've got any of their stock. Left it to wander. More likely than not, that old cow keeled over dead."

"Could be," Tom muttered under his breath. I could read

concern in his eyes though. This matter of the cow was serious.

"Maybe I ought to say something to Lt. Fleming," I said, hoping he'd offer his opinion. "Or we could ride out and have a look around."

"Better to stay clear, Darby. Soldiers are in a hot mood, especially that young lieutenant they got, and nobody seems to want a peaceful solution."

"Oh?" I asked, putting my knife away.

Lt. Fleming now arrived, and the discussion picked up force. Lt. Grattan and the Mormons clearly wanted something done then and there, but Fleming, I judged, spoke for moderation and patience.

"Trouble is these fool wagon folk don't know enough to be sensible," Tom said, pacing back and forth in front of the storehouse door. "They babble on about savage, murderin', thievin' Indians without knowin' the right side of a buffalo chip from the business end of a musket. Fools and pilgrims! Put 'em together with a few thousand angry Sioux, and we could all wind up scalped 'fore winter!"

It was about as much of a speech as I'd ever heard him mutter, and I stared at him with surprise.

"Can't much happen over a missing cow," I told him. "How 'bout riding out and having a look? I'll bet we find it."

Another time Tom would have rushed to saddle his horse, but he continued pacing. He mumbled to himself and kicked small rocks against the wooden sides of the storehouse. He was worried, pure and simple, and so was I.

The Mormons left, angrily calling on the soldiers to do their duty. I made little more of their talk, as it was a muddle of foreign German-sounding words. But there was no mistaking their feelings.

The soldiers, meanwhile, scurried around getting ready to ride out to the Sioux camps to meet with the headmen. I dreaded the notion of that hothead Grattan squaring away with Spotted Elk. A man who'd just buried a son shot down by whites wasn't apt to take kindly to a soldier's bullying.

As it turned out, the ride wasn't necessary. Word traveled

fast on the plains, and soon a band of Brules approached the post. Conquering Bear led them, his towering bulk and great thick neck silencing the challenge forming on Lt. Grattan's tongue.

When I saw Two Nations, I hurried over to listen in, but Tom pulled me back.

"Only a fool jumps into a bubblin' kettle," he warned.

I knew he was right, but I couldn't help sensing trouble was brewing, and I hated the thought of my new friends winding up in the middle of it. As it turned out, the talk was brief. The Brules spoke calmly, and the soldiers answered out of hand. Even from my vantage point, and without hearing a word, I could tell it was all coming to nothing. Conquering Bear rode off to his camp, and the other Brules followed, all save Two Nations who came over to view my work on the buffalo hide.

"You know hides," he complimented me. I could tell his mind was preoccupied though, and I motioned to the storehouse steps.

"Guess you know those wagon folks think a Sioux stole one of their cows," I told him. "More likely wandered off."

"Yes," Two Nations agreed. "It's happened before. Sometimes we take these animals back. This time a Miniconjou, High Forehead, found the cow. Its leg was broken, and his people were hungry. They ate the cow."

"That what Conquering Bear told the soldiers?"

"He offered to pay for this cow. Five dollars gold. The soldiers said twenty. This is no fair price, but the Bear agreed. Even that was not enough though. The soldiers said to bring High Forehead to them so he could be punished. This isn't what the treaty says. We are to punish our own people. Who tended the killer of Younger Elk? We went to the soldiers, and they said the Sioux must be at fault. What did Younger Elk do to earn so young a death?"

"Isn't fair," I muttered. "I know. Just like putting off the giveaway. But I guess you get used to such things."

"Not everyone," Two Nations said with dark, brooding eyes. "No good will grow from this, I tell you. There are voices in our camps that speak of war. 'Kill the bluecoats!

96

Burn the fort!' Many listen."

"And there are soldiers who'd welcome a fight," I said, thinking of the rash young Grattan. "A day ago I wouldn't've thought it possible. Now . . ."

"Yes, I fear it, too."

Two Nations headed into the store then, and Laveda exchanged lead and powder for a bag of gold coins.

"Needed for the buffalo hunt," Two Nations explained. The look we exchanged said otherwise.

Two Nations wasted no time riding off with his precious supplies. Afterward I stood alone across from the post headquarters and observed the two lieutenants discussing their plans. I couldn't hear, of course, but I knew they'd waste little time mounting a force. Already a sergeant had a detail limbering a howitzer.

"Fools," Tom said, resting a hand on my shoulder. "Plan to ride out there with thirty men and a field piece when the whole of the Sioux people's at hand. Look quick, Darby. Won't a one of 'em return."

"How can you be so sure?" I asked.

"I've fought Sioux," he said, sighing. "So've you. They won't line up and wait for you to shoot 'em. Oh, I figure that Grattan fellow'll get in a pop or two with his gun. Then the Sioux'll swarm like angry bees over 'em, and there'll be some stingin'."

"You forget," I told him. "Most of the men are off hunting. Awful easy to kill the little ones."

He nodded, and his sad eyes drifted off, remembering. I sighed and shifted my eyes back to the lieutenants. They'd come to a decision, and Lt. Fleming dispatched an orderly to assemble the command. Before I knew what was happening, Lt. Grattan was barking orders, and men were scurrying around readying horses or fetching muskets.

I wasn't the only one watching. Soldiers' wives and traders voiced concern.

"Has there been an attack?" a young woman shouted.

"A massacre?" another cried. "Lord help us! We'll all be scalped."

"Nothing to worry over, folks," Lt. Grattan assured the gathering crowd. "We've got an Indian to bring in. We don't expect trouble."

"That why you're taking the cannon?" Jesse Borden asked.

The lieutenant didn't bother answering. He collected the soldiers instead, twenty-five or so of them, and made ready to ride out to the Sioux encampments.

Some bystanders shouted encouragement. Others stalked off sullenly.

I turned and walked to the Borden place. Laveda was standing in the doorway, frowning.

"Fine time the soldiers pick to stir up the Indians," she grumbled. "I've got a dozen pairs of moccasins waiting for me out there."

"Oh?" I asked. "They paid for?"

"Laurence took a load of flour and blankets out this morning."

"Won't he bring the moccasins back?"

"He will if he can," she explained. "He's not full-grown yet, and if trouble comes, he'll be in the middle of it."

"The Sioux know him," I pointed out. "He speaks some of their language. And besides, he's probably halfway home by now."

"More likely swimming in the river," she said, sighing. "Darby, I only have one brother. Do you think maybe you and Tom could ride out and have a look?"

"Can't speak for Tom," I told her. "I'll go though."

"Not alone!" she objected.

"Alone? With a company of soldiers and the whole Sioux nation out there, I'll hardly be alone. Don't worry over me. I know how to duck trouble."

"That's why there are bear claw scratches on your chest, huh? You find Laurence and get back, hear?"

"Yes, ma'am," I said, grinning at her pretense of command. I then stepped outside and hunted for Tom. He'd disappeared. I looked in the stable, and his horse was gone. Like as not Jesse had already sent him out to find young Laurence. Well, I'd have little trouble finding either one of them.

I don't know exactly what notion was in Lt. Grattan's head that sent him riding out to the Brule camp. There's a kind of madness, Tom used to say, that sends a man hurrying to his death. I heard none of the dickering that went on between Grattan and old Conquering Bear, and I don't suppose it much mattered once the dust settled. I was approaching the rear of the encampment when the soldiers arrived, and I was immediately surrounded by some of the older boys. The women and children were making their way from the camp, and they surely thought I was part of the soldier group.

A pair of the bigger boys quickly had me off Pepper's back and pinned to the earth. One had a knife out, and I confess I wasn't feeling any too hopeful of passing another winter on this earth. Suddenly Bobtail appeared, spouting a torrent of Sioux phrases and chasing the knife-wielding young warrior away.

"*Kola,*" Bobtail said, gripping my wrist. "Friend."

"Yes," I agreed immediately. "Seen Shea? Laurence? My trader friends, *wasicun kolas?*"

Bobtail pondered it a moment, then grinned. Quick as lightning he escorted me to the wagon where Laurence and Tom were sitting. They weren't captives exactly, but three warriors stood nearby with loaded rifles. I don't suspect they were there to have a tea party.

"Darby, you young fool!" Tom barked. "How come you to come out here and step in this pile o' quicksand, too?"

"What's happening?" I asked, climbing into the wagon with them. I observed the bartered moccasins were neatly stacked in the wagon bed, and Tom's tall horse was tied to one wheel. Laurence shifted his weight nervously and pointed to the soldiers formed up in a triangle near where the wagon road passed by the Brule encampment. Close to a thousand warriors huddled in the rock-strewn marshes, determined to protect the camp from the soldiers.

"Doesn't look any too good," Tom observed. "If it comes to shootin', you two get that wagon movin' toward the river. Nobody's apt to bother you. I'll see to it."

I nodded grimly, and Laurence hugged the splintery side of

the old wagon and clawed the plank seat.

For a bit cool heads seemed to prevail. Man Afraid of his Horses, a leader among the warriors, seemed eager to start a parley. Grattan, Conquering Bear, Man Afraid, and the interpreter Lucien August all went into the village and talked things over. It looked like some sort of agreement was made. Then somebody shouted. Grattan made a motion to the soldiers, and a pair of muskets discharged. A whole volley followed, and ole Conquering Bear dropped to his knees and clutched his bleeding side.

Madness followed. The soldiers shot off their cannon, but their aim was off, and it flew past the warriors and knocked down a *tipi*. The nervous bluecoats then fought to reload their guns, while out of the marshes hundreds of angry Sioux charged. Others unleashed a wicked shower of arrows. A sergeant shouted, jumped into the wagon in which the soldiers had ridden from the fort, and a mad chase was on. The soldiers not in the wagon were run down and lanced. August, the interpreter, stood stupidly watching until he was cut down.

"Best head to Bordeaux's place," Tom suggested, indicating the small trading post operated by Jim Bordeaux. He carried on a fair business with the Sioux and emigrants, too, though he didn't have the advantage of Jesse Borden's military license. Laurence had the wagon under control, so I clambered out and mounted Pepper. By then the camp was in no danger, and the Brules seemed disinterested in their unwelcome guests.

The soldiers never made it to Bordeaux's place. I saw the wagon stopped halfway, and warriors were crawling over it like ants on a dead rabbit. I thought for a moment some of the soldiers might have survived, but it was just Brule youngsters wearing blue shirts stripped off the bodies. A terrible sense of foreboding came over me, and I turned as if to circle around and return to the fort.

"Best go to Bordeaux's," Tom told me. He seemed to read my thoughts at times like those, and I followed his advice as usual. We found a dozen other whites at the post, including a

100

few of the Mormon emigrants who'd started the whole mess by letting their cow stray. Sioux warriors, women, and even children were busy rifling the store, taking whatever attracted their eye with nary a word from Bordeaux.

"Be the ruin of me, this day," he mumbled. "But at least I'll keep my hair."

After the Sioux finished with Bordeaux, it grew rather quiet. Tom and I slipped outside to have a look around. We located a family of emigrants huddling in the cottonwoods. We also spotted what was left of the soldiers. Most were dead, but one young private still breathed in spite of a severe wound. A pair of stout-hearted women took charge of the young soldier, bandaging his torn body and offering what comfort a gentle voice and a soft hand could provide in the hours of approaching death.

There wasn't anything else to be done, so we gathered what we could salvage of Bordeaux's belongings and packed them in the back of the wagon. Then, with Bordeaux, Tom, and myself leading the way on horseback, and everybody else piled in the wagon, we headed for the fort. There wouldn't be any soldiers there to protect us, but the old adobe trapper's post once known as Fort John still occupied the south corner of the parade ground, and Bordeaux declared it a solid refuge from which we could make a final stand, if worse came to worse.

As we made our way along the rutted trail, we passed a pair of abandoned wagons the Indians had ransacked. A bit farther along, we came to the American Company's warehouse. The Sioux had paid a visit on Doyle Marcus, too. Those treaty goods locked up for months were being handed out right and left by the wild-eyed Indians.

"Let's hold up a bit," Tom suggested, pointing to where Marcus stood complaining that no one had signed his vouchers. He wasn't making much effort to hold back the mob, though.

Up to that point the Sioux hadn't taken much interest in us. Our luck didn't hold. A couple of warriors galloped toward us, then pulled up short so that a shower of dust descended on us. I coughed to clear my lungs and rubbed the sting out of my eyes. Tom slipped back to shield the huddling emigrants. Their bright blue eyes and sunburned foreheads betrayed terror and fear.

"Give!" the first Brule shouted as he reached down and tore a hat from a thin man's head. The second snatched a silver ring from the hand of a young woman.

"Have the Sioux become thieves?" Laurence asked, speaking first in English and then sputtering a group of Lakota phrases. The Indians gazed at us sourly, then departed.

"Got any sense to you, son?" the thin man asked. "They could've scalped all of us!"

"Nothin' an Indian respects more than courage," Tom argued. "Likely stung their pride, those words, even though an Indian don't consider it stealin' to take a trinket or two off an enemy."

"We are not enemy," one of the emigrant women insisted. "We come here only for first time now."

"From Denmark," her husband added.

"Then you wouldn't know," Laurence said. "Once all this country belonged to them. Bit by bit we've stolen it. Can't be any surprise they're angry about it."

Tom waved us along, and we resumed our journey. There were Sioux everywhere, warriors riding by, shouting angrily. Women and children darted here and there. Some of the younger boys shot bird arrows at the wagon, and the wagon children began crying.

"Won't harm you, those arrows," Tom said, reaching down and picking one of the small arrows from the ground. "Child's toy," he added, tossing the arrow to a red-faced little boy.

I wished all our fears could have been salved as easily. The closer we got to the fort, the more we saw of the Sioux. Some rode by to show off the fine presents they'd taken from the warehouse. Others angrily taunted us. A few helped themselves to this and that. Laurence lost his skinning knife, his shirt, and the moccasins stacked in the wagon bed. I gave up my shirt and my boots.

By the time we rolled to a stop at Jesse Borden's door, we resembled a bunch of plucked chickens. Tom was the only one who still had all his clothes. I don't think anybody really wanted to tangle with him, especially after reading his fiery gaze.

"Lord, son, I'm more than a little relieved to see you," Borden said, rushing out and embracing Laurence. "Leave the wagon and go get you a shirt."

"Sure, Papa," Laurence said, scrambling down from the wagon.

"Looks like you're short a pair of boots, Darby," Borden said, turning toward me. "I got some hidden back of the counter. The rest of you folks go in and grab what you need. I already sent Laveda on to Fort John. Get along when you can."

"We have no money," the thin man objected.

"Don't remember asking for any," Borden barked. "Might as well grab something. Sioux're sure to take what you leave."

"We could stay and guard the place," I offered.

"Against that?" Borden asked, pointing to the prowling warriors swarming across the parade ground. "Better to hole up and pray hard. We've friends among the tribe, and I'm hoping they'll remember."

"Me, too," I added, passing him on my way inside the store.

Chapter Eleven

The rampaging Sioux made only a half-hearted effort to pillage the fort. I was able to grab my new Sharps, roll my belongings up in an elk robe, and join Tom at the old trappers' fort unmolested. We entered together, then stared in disbelief at the dazed occupants of the old adobe building. Lt. Fleming and a pair of soldiers bent over a wounded private, trying to find out what had happened. If the poor soldier knew, he wasn't talking.

"Ought to leave the boy to die in peace," an old woman complained. "Ain't you soldiers done enough harm for one day?"

The crowd muttered their agreement. Traders like Jesse Borden and Doyle Marcus, whose rifled shelves and plundered storerooms spelled disaster, sat in the shadows, stunned. Small children huddled with their parents, each trying to bolster the courage of the other. Those with guns stood guard at the windows, awaiting a bloodthirsty charge from the assembled Indians.

I located an unguarded window in one of the back rooms and stood there, cradling my rifle. Behind me I heard folks singing a hymn. There was a sense that we were all sharing a last, terribly final moment. Grim faces glanced up occasionally, but otherwise everyone simply waited for the end.

Laveda stepped into the back room, followed by young Laurence. They appeared calm enough, that is until you took a close look. Laveda had nearly chewed through the fabric on her cuffs, and although Laurence had found a shirt to clothe his bare chest, he'd only got half the buttons fastened.

"When will they come, Darby?" Laveda asked as she sat at my side.

"Papa says before nightfall," Laurence said, swallowing hard as he huddled beside his sister. "I don't think they fight at night, do they?"

"Don't know the Sioux too well," I confessed. "They do a fair bit of raiding after sundown. I'd guess it'd be soon or not at all."

"Why?" Laveda asked. "They must know we've got little food and almost no water in here. Why not come along and finish us?"

"Might do it if it was soldiers," I said. "But these Sioux know some of us. Can't warm their hearts much to think of killing ole Laurence here. Won't have any white boys to outswim down at the river. And if they kill off the traders, who'd bring 'em powder and shot?"

"You didn't see their eyes," Laveda whispered. "I've never seen people so angry."

"At Grattan and the bluecoats," I told her. "Not us. At least not once the sting wears off. Conquering Bear got himself shot good, and I wouldn't be surprised if others were killed. For a fool five-dollar cow, too!"

"Sure hope that Grattan fellow's happy," Laurence mumbled. "Set the whole Sioux people onto us. Won't be anything moving on the trail west now, either. Went and started a war."

"Well, it's the last one he'll start," I said, frowning as I recalled the soldiers' mad race for their wagon, the frenzied flight from the Brule village. "He's dead, sure."

"And so are we," Laurence said, staring with moist eyes out the window. "When'd you say they'll come, Darby?"

"Likely soon," I answered.

It was the worst kind of waiting, sitting in that darkened room, haunted by the hymn-singing or the silence that always followed it. All the time we knew a swarm of arrows might any moment explode through the open window and bring death. Or else maybe some clever Sioux might fire the fodder stored in back and smoke us out into the open.

"You've been in tough spots before, haven't you?" Laveda asked as she rested her head on my shoulder. "How do you, er, get ready?"

"Ready?" I asked. "For a hard fight?"

"No," she said, quivering. "For the dying."

"I never had much chance to think about it," I told her. "When that bear rumbled down at me, I had my rifle, and I was too busy getting ready for the shot. Other time it was cold, and I was near numb. Guess the best way's to think of something else, keep busy."

"Doing what?" she asked.

"I'm not sure. Wish you had some sewing. Wish I had my buff hide to work. Maybe it helps those pilgrims to do a bit of singing."

"You could play your mouth organ," Laurence suggested, pulling it out of the elk hide bundle.

"Darby?" Laveda asked.

I started to say no. After all, I had the window to guard. But just then our frayed nerves needed a bit of calming, and I figured when the Indians finally came, it would be over quick enough. I wet my cracked lips, then put them to the little instrument. It produced a harsh sound, and Laveda laughed.

"Plan to scare the Sioux away, Darby?" Laurence asked.

"If I thought I could, I'd try," I answered, grinning as I took a deep breath and tried again. My hands shook as I ran my mouth along the organ. This time I raised a tune, and I soon transformed it into a fair version of "Sweet Betsy from Pike." Laveda took up the tune and sang along. Laurence joined in the chorus. Soon other heads appeared in the door, and some came inside to join in the music.

That music had a calming magic, and for a while the cloud of doom that hung over old Fort John broke up to let the sun shine through. I wish I'd had the wind to play all afternoon, but my lungs began to ache, and my fingers tired of holding the mouth organ. I finally quit.

"I don't think they're coming," Mrs. Kluger, the widow of one of the slain soldiers, declared. "Look! I can't see even a shadow of them!"

I stared out the window with the others. True enough, the Sioux seemed to have finished with the fort. It didn't mean they weren't huddling close by, preparing an ambush.

"Look there," Laveda called.

I followed her pointing finger to where a thin line of wagons snaked its way toward the fort. It was the Mormon wagon train. I expected 'em to be out there shot full of arrows, but they plodded along unmolested. Children flanked the wagons, driving the stock along. I gazed bitterly at the bony cows and thought what a price had been paid for the one they'd let stray.

The arrival of the wagon train marked the end of our siege. The other Mormons surged out of the old adobe fort, eager to greet their friends. Lt. Fleming regained his senses and began setting the post in order. Meanwhile, Tom came over and drew me aside.

"Told the soldiers I'd go have a look around," he told me. "They've got no scouts, or much of anybody else for that matter. Lieutenant's decided to send a rider east with the news, but he's none too sure what chance a man's got to get through."

"You're not planning to . . ."

"Just promised to have a good glance-over, Darby," Tom assured me. "Sioux made their point. They punished the ones that killed their chief. They got the promised annuity goods. My guess is they've gone to hunt the buffalo and put some miles 'tween their camps and any new batch o' soldiers comes out to settle the score."

"Fair notion," I said, nodding. " 'Cause they will come, won't they?"

"I'd say so, son. Now, we ridin' out there or not?"

"Depends on whether we've got horses," I said, forcing a grin onto my face. "Let's see."

107

Actually, I was more than a little worried that Pepper might now be carrying a young Sioux across the plains, but our horses and the Bordens' stock hadn't been bothered. The storehouse had been visited, true enough, but most everything remained as before.

The wagon folks hadn't been so lucky. They complained to Lt. Fleming in a mixture of English and Danish how the Sioux had surrounded their little train and demanded tobacco, powder, guns, blankets, even tin cups! The other emigrants lamented such misfortune, particularly so since the trading posts had few provisions to offer now.

"Lucky they let you keep your hides!" Jesse Borden told them. His anger reflected the stormy mood of the other post inhabitants, particularly those who'd lost husbands in the ill-conceived attack on the Brule village. I half-expected the two groups to come to blows, but the lieutenant and a few cool heads managed to maintain order.

Tom and I, meanwhile, saddled our horses and rode out toward the Sioux camps. I felt oddly free, riding Pepper, feeling his energetic legs carrying me across the dusty trail. Deep in the pit of my stomach I was afraid—for Tom, for myself, for the Bordens back at the fort. I was a boy of fourteen again, haunted by that mixture of adventure and danger that was life.

As we passed by the looted American Company warehouse, I became ever vigilant. Every rock or gully threatened to conceal the Indians who would bring our death.

"See if you can manage a tune on that mouth organ," Tom suggested. "Music steadies the horses a bit."

I knew it wasn't the horses needed steadying, but I didn't argue. I wasn't able to keep much of a tune going, but the noise did ease my nerves.

We came to the Oglala village first. The Indians had hastily broken down their *tipis* and set off north and west, toward the buffalo hunting grounds. All that remained were tatters of old cloth and buffalo bones, refuse heaps and discarded pottery.

"Gone hours now," Tom observed. He dismounted and examined the ashes of the campfires. He rummaged around a bit, but he found nothing of interest or value.

"On to the Brules?" I asked nervously when he climbed atop his horse again.

"Seems like the thing to do," he answered.

First, though, we came upon the soldiers. I'd seen dead men before, even some the Sioux had taken a particular vengeance upon. Before the victims had been strangers. The ones I looked down on now were familiar.

Pepper shied away from the gory sight, and I wanted to gallop back to the fort. Tom dismounted, though, and I followed him as always. We walked among the arrow-riddled corpses, trying to recognize them. They'd been scalped, and cut up elsewhere, too. Some of the heads had been battered so you couldn't recognize 'em. Boots and shirts had been stripped off, and one or two were naked. Wasn't the Sioux way to waste, after all.

Looking back over my shoulder, I could see the wagon and the other dead soldiers lying between us and Bordeaux's place. Just ahead the cannon stood stark and alone, its cold barrel attesting to the foolhardiness of Grattan's tactics. Beyond, the Brule camp had been uprooted as swiftly and completely as had the Oglala.

"Thought maybe they'd stay to mourn Conquering Bear," I said, steadying myself. My head burned, and my stomach threatened to rebel.

"He's a tough ole bird," Tom said, scratching his chin. "Might be he's not dead after all. That'd be welcome news for all the white men 'round here."

"Yes," I agreed.

We continued walking toward the camp. Lucien August lay butchered where he'd fallen. His tongue was cut from his mouth, and he was cut up considerably. I'd managed till then to hold down my stomach, but now I became sick. I raced off to a gully and retched. I vomited until I thought my heart and lungs were sure to come next. Finally I dropped to my knees and caught my breath.

"Maybe you ought to wait here," Tom suggested as he helped me to my feet. I shook my head and went along with him.

We found Lt. Grattan close to the Brule village. If he hadn't had his watch, we'd never known it was him. I guess thirty arrows were shot through his corpse; some boy's hunting arrows added long after death.

"You're not so much after all," I whispered to the mutilated lieutenant.

"No, not so much at all," Tom added. "Just a fool who's gone and started a war."

After scouting the remains of the Brule camp, we turned back to the fort. If there hadn't been so many, we might have tried to bury the dead. Things being as they were, we didn't have much interest in lingering in that place of death.

Tom turned Grattan's watch over to Lt. Fleming and passed on the grim news.

"Thought as much," Fleming replied, nodding his head grimly. "I'll get a detail to tend the bodies."

I thought it doubtful. The remaining soldiers clearly had no interest in venturing far from the security of old Fort John.

"I could use a steady man to ride east with dispatches," Fleming announced. "I'd pay you full scout's wages, Shea. You know this country, and the Indians wouldn't bother you."

"Oh?" I asked. "Why not?"

"They know you," Fleming said confidently.

"They knew August, too," Tom reminded the young officer. "Lucien wed a Brule gal. Didn't much help him."

"You won't go?" the officer asked in dismay.

"I done my scoutin'," Tom answered, motioning me toward the Borden place. "We got horses to tend and friends to see after."

I took charge of the horses, and Tom went to have a look

at the ransacked trading post. Laurence joined me, but we brushed and watered the animals without saying a word. I knew he hoped for a report on what I'd seen, but I was light-headed, and my stomach remained uneasy. I didn't wish to recall any more of it than was even then flooding my head.

The days that followed were hard ones. Spectral visions tormented my dreams, and I didn't entirely escape them even in my waking hours. Laveda noticed, and she did her best to rouse me from my gloom. But I was a hopeless case, stumbling around, brooding and mumbling and wondering what calamity might befall us next.

Jesse Borden found a tonic for my ill humor though.

"Darby, you helped your papa build himself a house out in Oregon, I hear," the trader declared. "That true?"

"I did," I answered.

"Even make cedar shingles?"

"More'n once. I'm a fair hand with an ax and wedge. Truth is, I thought about working in a lumber camp once."

"I've got myself a problem you can lick," Borden said, resting a hand on my shoulder and leading me aside. "Thing is, next rain hits us, my roof's bound to leak like a barrel been pickled with Sioux arrows."

He might have used better words, as my mind was filled with the arrow-pierced bodies of the soldiers.

"Think you and Laurence might climb up and have a look at that roof?" Borden asked. "I know where there's a fine stand of cedar. I'll bet that Shea and I can fell a couple and drag them back here, if you can cut shingles."

"Who cut the ones up there now?" I asked.

"Did it myself," Borden confessed. "It's why the roof leaks. I'm not much of a carpenter, you see."

I was unconvinced of the fact, but I welcomed the challenge. In no time I located Laurence, and the two of us clambered up onto the roof and inspected the splintered shingles. Someone had fired bullets through the roof, and there were a few places where the shingles never had overlapped right.

"Guess those Indians had themselves a fine time," Laurence grumbled. "Took most of our flour, all the powder, and they'd have us drown from the rain."

"They left you more'n most," I countered. "You've got your stock, and they didn't bust the windows. Flour can be come by easier'n glass."

"And powder?"

"Tom and I've got enough for a winter's hunting. And before that, things'll calm down enough for us to ride to Green River or Scott's Bluff."

"Guess you're right," he admitted. "It's just, well, I thought the Sioux were my friends."

"Some were," I assured him. "Will be again, I'll wager. By and by anger passes."

"But Laveda says the soldiers will come and punish the Indians."

"Might be they will," I told him. "Probably. I fear there'll be trouble, but you can't take it to heart. Nothing you can do about it. Our job's fixing this roof."

That was the wonderful thing about working with your hands. It seemed to cast away fears and doubts and troubles. As I stood outside the trading post, bare-shouldered and sweating as I split the cedar logs and cut the shingles, I felt myself whole again. Laveda brought by mint tea every so often, and we'd sit and talk as if no Lt. Grattan or Conquering Bear or Mormon cow had ever come to the plains.

"One day soon maybe you'll be building a cabin of your own," she whispered. "Up in the mountains maybe."

"Tom and I've done that more'n once," I replied.

"This time, though, it might be a home, a permanent place."

"Not likely."

"Oh, you might need one if you took a wife, raised a family."

"You figure me for my father? I'm no farmer, Laveda. I got no heart for planting things just to see 'em wither and

112

die. My way's to come and go, never stay anyplace for long."

"You've stayed here most of the summer."

"I have," I said, dropping my jaw. "Strange, too. Tom's close to content for a change. Usually he's ready to pull up stakes each time the wind shifts."

"You're needed here," she told me. "For more than shingling a roof, too. You did a good job trading with the Sioux, taking the wagon from camp to camp."

"Well, I wouldn't stake much future in that trade just now."

"I would," she argued. "Papa's talked again of going east, maybe putting together a whole line of stores as towns spring up along the trail. He'd need someone he could trust to stay here and run this place."

"Shoot, Laveda, you could run it yourself. I'm no storekeeper."

"Sure, I could stand behind the counter, keep the shelves in order, maintain the account books. But there's livestock to look after."

"Laurence is good with animals."

"And Indians to treat with."

"He speaks the languages some, too."

"He's sixteen. There'd have to be someone here the chiefs could look in the eye, respect."

"We've talked of this before," I grumbled, getting to my feet. I took the ax, cut a groove, and inserted the wedge. As I split the log, I could tell Laveda was standing there, gazing at me, hoping I'd stop and offer some encouragement. But a man can't be anybody but what he's come to be. And I was Darby Prescott, wayfarer.

As August parted company, Laurence and I placed the last of the new shingles on the roof. We'd not been troubled by Sioux or anybody else in a week or so, and except for attending the burial of Private Cuddy—the poor wounded soldier we'd hauled to the fort in the Bordens' wagon—there was nothing to keep me from stalking deer and put-

113

ting meat by for winter's needs.

Tom and I went often. Sometimes we took Laurence Borden along. Under Tom's watchful eye, that boy was becoming a fair shot. I think even Laveda realized her brother was growing up.

The first cool September nights brought with them a host of visitors. First, a new detachment of soldiers took over garrison duty. They brought a wagon train full of provisions and two full wagons of goods for Jesse Borden. Laveda had barely started the restocking of the shelves when Little Wing arrived with a band of Crows.

"Now we'll have some remembered times!" Tom declared.

Indeed we did, for the Crows had us swimming and wrestling and racing ponies right away. In no time we'd renewed old friendships, and I think we all felt better knowing Little Wing and his men would be scouting the countryside for sign of Sioux.

I think it was the laughter and the pranking of the younger Crows that brought me back to life. They were a hard luck people, struck down by disease and harried by powerful enemies. And yet they fought on, laughing and howling when the chance came to do so. Pepper was constantly challenged by one young man or another, and that spotted pony provided me many a good elk robe and a pair of buffalo hide boots close to as good as the ones liberated by the Sioux.

"You're different," Laveda observed when I returned from a race near the middle of the month.

"Sure, I am," I told her. "I've come back to life."

She stared at me strangely, but I meant those words. My heart and my spirit had died for a time. Now they'd been revived.

114

Chapter Twelve

The new soldiers had been at the fort about a week when I first met Capt. Ernest Powers. He was a tall, pleasant-faced man whose service in the cavalry had caused him to be a bit bow-legged. Even so, he held his backbone stiff and straight, and his hawklike brown eyes lingered wherever they fell, examining carefully each detail before shifting to the next. Streaks of white in his hair and moustache gave him a grandfatherly look. I judged it set some soldiers more at ease than later proved wise.

"I'm Darby Prescott," I told him when he introduced himself just inside the door of the Borden place.

"Shea's boy," he said, nodding. "Understand you're a fair hand at fixing roofs."

"Those that need it," I told him.

"And the Crows tell me you're the very devil on horseback. Don't win all the races, son. I need my Crows ready for winter hunting, not huddling naked in their lodges because a young white scoundrel's won their winter coats from them."

"I'll keep that in mind," I said, matching his grin. "As for hunting, if you'd care to accompany Tom and me, we'll be riding out looking for elk in another week or so. Usually find some good ones up in the Medicine Bow country."

"It's other game I'll be looking for," he told me. "The

115

two-legged kind."

"Sioux?"

"We've a score to settle for Johnny Grattan and his boys. I could use a couple of civilian scouts, especially ones that speak the Crow language. Got a taste for hunting Sioux, son?"

"Got plenty to keep me busy," I grumbled.

"No stomach for fighting Indians?" he asked with raised eyebrows. "Understood it was you and Shea found the bodies."

"It was," I said, biting my lip. "Kind of soured on seeing corpses shot full of arrows."

"Ought to raise your dander, Darby," he told me. "Fill you with an urge to avenge your white brothers."

"My brothers farm in Illinois," I told him. "I've fought the Sioux, and I've hunted with 'em. They're good enough people, and what happened out there on Platte River wasn't their doing."

"Maybe not," the captain confessed. "But it's the army's policy to see them punished. A child disobeys, he gets spanked."

"They're not children," I warned. "You'll find out for yourself, if it comes to a fight."

"It's their turn to learn this time. Come spring there'll be an end put to all this nonsense. The Sioux will learn just like the other tribes that they live by our forbearance, not the other way around."

I just shook my head and set off to find Tom.

He, too, had spent some time with the captain.

"Been thinkin' a lot 'bout headin' east," Tom explained after I described my conversation with the officer. "You never wintered in St. Louis, have you? Fine town that. Been a considerable number o' days since I set foot there. Likely some bartender's gone and buried Tom Shea."

"Be hard on the two of us, crossing that open country with the Sioux riled up."

"They'll be headin' into the Black Hills soon. Make their

116

autumn camps up north."

"I thought maybe the Bordens might use our help this winter, too."

"I aim to catch me a westbound train come spring," he told me. "Fifty-five would be the year for trailin' pilgrims again. Be a need for a man knows his way 'round trouble."

"We could pass the snows here, then head out early for Independence."

"Your heart set on it, Darby? You've gotten to be kind of a regular part of this place. Got a gal takes to you like fresh honey. Maybe you ought to make things permanent, find yourself a preacher."

"Be a storekeeper?" I asked. "Not settled enough for that, Tom. Not by half."

"Then you'd best do some hard thinkin' and some serious visitin' with Laveda," he urged. " 'Cause if we're winterin' elsewhere, it'd be wise to get shed o' this fort 'fore that hollow-headed captain stirs up another hornet's nest."

It might have been a father's advice, and I took it to heart. But before I could draw Laveda aside, her father called me over.

"Darby, are you planning to stay on a while?" he asked.

"I don't altogether know," I answered. "Tom's spoken of going east."

"But not for a week or so, eh?"

"Don't know," I said, glancing around, half-expecting Laveda to appear. "Why do you ask?"

"Well, I've come into some good fortune. A pair of half-bloods, the Le Tour brothers, say they've found themselves a small buffalo herd. They can shoot enough meat to keep us in good stead through winter, but they need some help getting it to the fort. Laurence and I were thinking of taking the wagon and maybe joining in the hunting as well."

"I could take you after buffalo," I argued.

"Know that, son. But we'll be gone close to a week, and with all this trouble about, I wouldn't feel right leaving Laveda so long by herself."

117

"Laurence could stay," I suggested.

"Oh, you wouldn't keep him from a buffalo hunt, would you? It's your fault he's got a shooter's eye."

"You could stay," I countered.

"Well, even an old man's entitled to a bit of a run now and then. Don't you think so?" he asked, giving me a slap on the back. "Well?"

"You know these Le Tours well?"

"I helped birth Pierre," he explained. "Louis hunted fresh meat for us last winter, just as his father did the first year I came west. For all their Sioux mama's blood, they're good men."

"You know the Sioux might not welcome whites to the buffalo range just now."

"Louis says there isn't an Oglala for a hundred miles. Now, can I count on you staying to keep an eye over things?"

"Yes, sir," I reluctantly agreed. "But Le Tours or no, you keep a weather eye out for trouble."

"Sound like an old granny," Borden said, grinning. "Don't you worry over me. This ancient carcass's got some life left in it."

They left the next morning, Jesse and Laurence Borden and the two Le Tours.

"Be three days there, two hunting, and three getting back," Borden explained to Laveda. "We stay gone any longer, rouse that captain and tell him my hair's hanging from a Sioux lodgepole."

"Papa!" Laveda shouted.

"Don't you worry, Sis," Laurence said, brandishing his rifle. "I'll keep an eye on things."

I don't think that was any too reassuring.

Tom and I passed that next week hanging around the fort, giving Laveda a hand when it was needed, swapping tales with the Crows, or working hides into suitable winter coats. Already the wind howled fiercely some nights, and the prairie grasses had put on an amber cloak.

Whenever the wind relented, Laveda and I walked out to the river and talked. Mostly she spoke dreams, while I observed the changing leaves on the cottonwoods and willows. She talked of a future, and I sadly attested to a fading past.

When her brother and father didn't return on schedule, she grew fretful. She spoke to Captain Powers, and Tom asked the Crows to keep an eye out for Jesse, Laurence, and the Le Tours. Still another day, and two more besides passed with nary a word of explanation.

"I'm worried," Laveda confided to me as we bolted the front door of the store that night. "Something's happened to them. I should have spoken up. I was afraid they'd come to harm."

"Your papa has a strong will," I reminded her. "He'd have gone anyway. They're strong, he and Laurence both. They'll get back."

"What if the Sioux found and killed them?"

"Laurence speaks the language, and the Le Tours are related. The Sioux hold no grudge against them. If they hated your father enough to hurt him, they would surely have burned the trading post. They didn't even take your horses."

"You'll go out and have a look yourself, won't you?"

"I'll see if Tom's willing," I told her. "We'll go together."

"First thing tomorrow?"

"First thing," I promised.

So it was that Tom Shea and I left that next morning for the buffalo range. A pair of Crows started with us, but at the first sign of Oglalas, the Crows turned back to the fort.

"Look," I said, pointing to the bare-chested riders.

"Natural for 'em to be here," Tom declared. "Their country, after all."

I thought it likely the Le Tours had also turned away from those Oglalas, but Tom discovered fresh wagon ruts that told a different story.

"Wagon and two riders," he explained. "Bound north

and east. It's them. Got to be, Darby."

"How old are the tracks?" I asked.

"Maybe a week," he said, shrugging his shoulders. "Hard to say with the ground hard and the rains fallin' almost daily now."

I was discouraged all over again. We could be a week behind them. Soon, though, we came on fresher sign. One of the black mules that had pulled the wagon lay dead in a narrow ravine. Nearby were signs of a struggle.

"Sioux?" I asked, exploring the ravine for clues.

"Bear," Tom answered. "Like as not surprised 'em. Kilt a mule and battered the wagon some."

"What about the people?" I asked.

"Well, one at least shed himself some blood."

Tom held up a bloodstained white strip of cloth. The notion of Laurence or his father sliced up by a bear overpowered my faint spirits, and I hung my head.

"No graves hereabouts," Tom pointed out. "Let's get along and find 'em, Darby."

Whether it was the blood or the Oglalas that spurred me on, I'll never know. I urged Pepper into first an easy trot and then a rapid gallop. We cut across the rocky countryside, climbing hill and traversing gully, until I located a thin plume of smoke just ahead. I slowed Pepper and waited for Tom to catch up. Then we approached cautiously.

Up ahead was a small Oglala camp. I thought to turn away and hope we hadn't been spotted, but Tom shook his head and pointed to the Borden wagon. Beside it was a lodge with oddly familiar markings. Tom tried to hold me back, but I rode on unafraid. To my surprise a pair of young Sioux stepped out of the brush and blocked my path.

"Look, here's my knife," I said, casting it aside. "I'll leave my rifle on my horse. I've come to look for two white men, one young and one older."

"For us?" Laurence called out.

I froze. He emerged from the lodge in tatters. One trou-

120

ser leg was torn off completely, and his shirt was open to the belly.

"You all right, Laurence?" I asked. "Your father?"

"Pa took a tumble," Laurence explained, dropping his chin onto his chest. "Bear came along and hit the team. Papa tried to hold the reins, but the horses broke away, dragging him through the rocks. Broke his left leg good, and stove in his insides, too."

"Couldn't somebody go for help?" I asked. "There's bound to be someone who can help."

"Is," Laurence explained. "Medicine man. Two Nations is in there with him now. If I'd thought any of the Oglalas would have been welcome at Laramie, I'd had him ride there. But as things are, soldiers might shoot him."

"What of the Le Tours?" Tom asked.

"Took the money Papa promised and lit out," Laurence answered. "Sure am glad to see you."

"Maybe you ought to go back now," Tom suggested. "I could stay, see Jesse's tended."

"I won't leave him, Darby. I haven't always made him very proud, I know, but just now he's got some new respect for me."

"Had that before," I counseled.

"I never saw it," Laurence said, rubbing his eyes.

"Is it bad?" I asked, suddenly sensing that Laurence hadn't said everything.

"Bad enough," the young man admitted. "Lord, Darby, I'm afraid he'll die. He's weak, like Mama was."

"Let's have a look," Tom said, motioning us inside the *tipi*.

An old white-haired man and two women watched over Jesse Borden. The trader was terribly pale, and he grunted and groaned. His left leg was anchored between two wagon planks tied securely with strips of a shirt.

"Leg's been splinted right," Tom observed. "What else ails him?"

I turned toward Two Nations, who was sitting behind the

medicine man, and the young mixed-blood translated the question. The old Oglala chanted a bit and shook some powder over Borden's chest. Drawing back a blanket, one of the women revealed a chest bound tightly. The ribs appeared broken, and Borden was bleeding inside.

"Nothin' else can be done," Tom explained, even before Two Nations could translate the medicine man's words. "Pure folly to try and move him."

"Then what can we do?" Laurence asked.

"Wait it out and hope for the best. I seen men heal were busted up worse'n this," Tom explained.

Maybe so, I thought as I looked at the faraway gaze in Jesse Borden's eyes. Already he was dancing across some cloud with Laveda's mother.

It was Tom rode back to Fort Laramie with the sad tidings. Laurence and I stayed to do what we could, which wasn't much. Two Nations remained as well, but the medicine man returned to his camp.

"He said the spirits will decide," Two Nations explained.

I knew they already had. Sometime during the night Jesse Borden passed on.

"This is a sad day," Two Nations declared when he helped Laurence and me wrap the body in a blanket and carry it to the wagon. "I will mourn this good man."

"We all will," I said, gripping Laurence's hands firmly. Two Nations then bid us farewell, and we started homeward.

I'd buried a mama and papa myself, and I didn't think I'd ever know that kind of pain and longing again. Now I discovered that it's close to as bad when you've got to pass on news to somebody you care about that will bring them that same kind of pain.

All the way back to the fort, Laurence insisted he would tell Laveda. It was a grim task for somebody so young, grimmer even than driving the wagon that bore his father's body back to the trading post that had been their life those past few years. When we actually got there, Laurence dropped his head between his knees and began sobbing.

"I can't," he muttered.

"Want me to tell her?" I asked.

He nodded soberly, and I helped him down from the wagon. Then I walked to the door of the trading post.

Laveda was watching all the while from the window. Her eyes were already reddening.

"Is Papa gone?" she asked.

"I'm afraid he is," I answered, pulling her close.

"I've got things to do," she said, fighting my hands off.

"There's time to cry first."

"I don't have time for tears," she grumbled. "There's work to be done. I have to get a supply list made so somebody can ride east and replenish our stock. I've got to get supper started, too. Afterward, I have to . . ."

"First you stop and remember your papa," I urged. "Cry for him. He was a good man and earned it. Then we'll see to digging a grave and finding someone to read words over him. All that other can wait."

"Darby?"

"I mean what I say," I barked. "Come on."

I led her to the wagon, and she had a look at her father's frozen face.

"Doesn't even look like him," she muttered. "He was always smiling, telling his little jokes, urging us to work harder."

"Sure," I agreed, noticing the first tear trickle out of the corner of her eye and roll down her cheek. "He's gone on ahead. Be hard getting along on your own without him, but I'd judge he'll be watching."

"Just to keep us at our work, if nothing else," she said, collapsing against me.

"That's better," I told her. "Cry. It s the best kind of healing."

"It doesn't feel any better," she said, sobbing. "Oh, Darby, what will we do?"

"Get by," I told her. "It's all any of us ever does."

We buried Jesse Borden in the little post cemetery that same evening. Most everyone for miles around turned out to pay their respects. A traveling preacher read scripture. Laurence and Laveda recounted some of the better days they'd passed together. The funeral ended with some hymnsinging. Laurence and I covered up the hole and placed a small cross made of picket rails over the spot.

I left Laveda and Laurence to themselves that night and most of the morrow. There were people dropping by, offering help or bringing food. Capt. Powers had the cannon fired off in Jesse Borden's memory. The day after, Tom and I kept ourselves busy tending to a list of chores Laveda had drawn up. We finished late in the afternoon, and she offered us each five dollars wages.

"Didn't do it for money," I said when I refused the money. "Friends do for each other at times like these."

"Times like these," she mumbled. "Pitiful hard times. Laurence won't even talk to me. Blames himself, you know. And me? How am I to run a house and this trading post by myself?"

"You'll manage," I said, mustering a smile.

"Not alone," she told me. "I need help, Darby. Good help. The kind that's there when you need it."

"Laurence will be."

"He's not shaving regular yet. I need a husband."

"And?"

"I was hoping you might have a question to turn my way."

"I don't know that I can be the one you're looking for," I said for what seemed the hundredth time. "Tom's talking about heading east soon. Maybe we ought to take you and Laurence along to St. Louis. You got family there, you told me once."

"An old scarecrow of an aunt," she grumbled. "I'm staying here. This is my home, Darby."

"And mine's a saddle," I responded. "You wouldn't like me all hog-tied and hobbled, Laveda. I'll be around when I

124

can. But I've got some wandering yet to do."

"I hope you're not sorry one day that you didn't put down some roots," she said, swallowing a sob.

"Me, too," I replied.

Chapter Thirteen

It was Doyle Marcus first approached us about bringing in supplies from the East.

"My shelves were near emptied by the Sioux," he explained, "and what remained won't last much longer. I've sent word to the company buyers in St. Louis, and they've started goods west."

"What do you need us for then?" Tom asked. "The trail's well marked, after all. Ten years o' ruts won't blow away."

"Our freight man, Clyde Parkinson, won't move past Fort Kearny without an escort," Marcus explained.

"Well, two men don't make much of an escort," I said, laughing to myself.

"Be enough," he argued. "Word is there'll be cavalry reinforcements sent out in a few weeks. You wait at Kearny for them, then come out together."

"If you've got soldiers comin'," Tom said, "why pay us to go along?"

"Parkinson may need some persuading," Marcus said, shifting his weight from one foot to the other. "It's something you're good at, Shea. If you need other encouragement, I've got two wagons coming with goods Jesse Borden ordered. I'm sure Jesse . . . the Bordens could use those supplies."

"They could," I admitted. "So I guess we ought to go, Tom."

"You talk it over with Laveda?" Tom asked. "I don't know that she'll be too happy to be left by herself, so soon after her papa's passin'."

"Can't wait much longer," I pointed out. "Once the first snow comes, there'll be no getting wagons up the trail."

"He's right," Marcus added.

"We'll think on it," Tom said. "Let you know."

He turned toward the Borden place, pausing only long enough to motion for me to follow. We walked slowly, silently to the front door. He nudged me inside, and I told Laveda about Marcus's offer.

"You were gone most all summer moving goods for the American Company," she reminded me. "Now you're leaving when I need you most. By the time you return, winter's sure to be on the wind."

"Likely," I admitted. "Tell me, Laveda, can you stay in business with what stock you have now?"

"We'll make do," she declared.

"There's enough to keep us fed," Laurence said, joining the conversation. "We won't have a cracker to spare for anybody passing through, and the late trains are always low on supplies. It isn't just us to think of, Sis. What about the wagon folks?"

"They've got fathers!" she yelled. "Let them tend themselves."

"I'll be here," Laurence said, stepping closer and wrapping an arm around Laveda's shoulders. I knew she'd rather it been my arm, but it did calm her down.

"The two of you won't be able to haul the hides and pelts we've collected," Laveda pointed out.

"Nor Marcus's, either," I answered. "He says this fellow Parkinson will take everything back in his wagons."

"I don't like trusting a stranger with our living," Laveda argued.

"Papa did," Laurence said, gazing over at Tom and me. "I knew he planned to do it himself. Was one of the last things he talked about before . . . the bear. Sis, it won't be so long. We'll have the whole winter together."

"Will we, Darby?" she asked.

"I'm not one to read the future in the clouds," I told her. "It'd be late to make it to St. Louis though. We'd still have a chance to go east first thaw, then get us a train in Independence."

"Be a late one," Tom grumbled. "But I suppose it'd do."

Laveda nodded somewhat reluctantly, and I trotted off to tell Marcus he'd hired himself a pair of wagon escorts.

We left two days hence. I wanted the chance to lay in a good supply of wood for the Bordens, and Tom wanted to trade the Crows out of a good horse. I had an easier time felling three willows and cutting them into lengths for the fireplace. Laurence split some cottonwood logs into stove wood, and it seemed our axes sang out from dawn to dusk.

"You remember what I told you about aiming at a running target?" I asked the sixteen-year-old as we stacked the wood outside the back door that led to the living quarters.

"I remember," he said, swallowing hard. "I'll look after her, Darby. She's my sister, you know."

"Truth is, she'll need less of it than either of us," I remarked. He smiled his agreement. But when Tom and I saddled our horses the next morning, I noticed Laurence had placed his father's rifle over the front door.

"Sure you wouldn't rather stay?" Tom asked as I climbed atop Pepper.

"That's all been settled," I told him. "Besides, who'd keep you from falling off Scott's Bluff or drinking too much bad whiskey?"

"There'll come a time for us to part company," he warned. "Be soon, I figure."

"I don't," I barked. And I didn't want to talk about it, either.

We rode eastward, me atop my spotted pony and Tom on a big, broad-shouldered buckskin stallion coaxed from the Crows. Normally we'd have brought along a spare horse each, especially for such a long ride, but Tom thought it a poor notion, us having four animals to keep track of. We were likely to have some hard riding, and extra horses would have to be left behind.

"Better to have a good one under you, and trust you're fast enough to outrun trouble," he philosophized.

"Or hide from it," I added with a grin.

The two of us then galloped east in the shadow of the North Platte, our eyes watching for trouble while our hearts raced with the wind.

We managed almost thirty miles that first day, for the trail was clear, and there were only low hills to cross. Another day would find us at Jonas Redding's trading post at Scott's Bluff.

"Best find ourselves a place to camp," I suggested as Pepper began to show fatigue.

"Marcus said there's a new place just ahead called Midway Wells," Tom said. "Halfway 'tween the bluff and Laramie."

"Somebody had himself a good notion," I observed. "Fresh water's always welcome along this stretch, and there are those like us known to make frequent rides to Redding's place and back."

"Pretty soon the whole Platte'll be dotted with grog houses and trading posts," Tom grumbled. "Not like the old days, when a man had to load his wagon at Independence and rely on those goods to get him to trail's end."

"Progress," I told him.

"Worse curse ever visited mankind!" he exclaimed. "Roads and soldiers! Pretty soon won't be a place left where a man can curse nature or race his pony."

"Some call that civilization, Tom," I said, laughing.

We appeared at Midway Wells half an hour later. No one would have mistaken that place for civilization. There was a hut built of rough planks pried from broken-down wagons, and the shallow wells provided water so muddy I wouldn't let my horse drink it. Around back a few Oglala and Brule *tipis* rose near the river.

"Not much to recommend itself, eh?" Tom asked as he pulled up short. "I'll bet they can cook us up some dinner though. Likely got a jug or two. What do you think?"

"I think it'd be safer eating rattlesnake skin," I said, hesitating to join him.

"Come on, Darby," he urged. "Take the horses down to the river and leave them to get a drink. Then come along inside the place. I'll get us some food and a jug."

I frowned, but he laughed and told how it was just to chase off the melancholies.

I was sour on Midway Wells from the first moment. Even when a Pawnee girl brought over two platters full of elk steaks buried in an ocean of baked beans and turnips, I failed to smile.

"Eat up," Tom encouraged. "It's nigh good as Laveda ever cooked."

I tried my steak, and I admit it was tasty. The turnips were a little soggy, but the beans tasted of ginger and honey. All in all, it was a better trail meal than any man had a right to expect.

Tom bragged on the food, but it was the whiskey brought out his smile. The single swallow I tried nearly burned the lining from my throat and set my lungs on fire.

"Shouldn't give a boy a man's drink," a familiar voice called.

I turned and stared at No Nose, our old Oglala acquaintance. The Sioux reached for the jug, but Tom pulled it away.

"Buy your own," he barked. "And watch your tongue, horse stealer."

"Yes, I knew you would come here," No Nose replied angrily. "I see your horse. Maybe we see who's thief. I take horse. You steal land."

"Land's everyone's, ain't it?" the owner of the place asked. "Here, No Nose. I've got a jug set by for you.

Bring in some skins, did you?"

"No," No Nose said, folding his arms across his chest. "Trade you scalps."

"Scalps?" the owner said as No Nose grabbed the proffered jug. "I don't buy scalps."

"Your scalps," No Nose said, pointing to the owner, his wife and son, the Pawnee girl, and the white men playing cards behind Tom. "Deal?"

"Sure, No Nose," the owner said, nervously motioning his wife toward the door. She dragged along a rebellious boy of eight or so. The Pawnee girl also retreated. When she opened the door, three other Oglalas entered the dimly lit hut. They showed no hint of friendship. Each held a flintlock rifle.

"I take horses now, eh, Three Fingers?" No Nose asked Tom. "I maybe cut you, too."

"You could try," I said, cursing myself for leaving the Sharps outside. I had my Colt, though, and Tom had his.

"You wouldn't want to do that," Tom said, resting one hand on the table in front of him and showing off the pistol he held in the other. "I got no talent for shootin' Indians. Have a bad habit o' clippin' ears, takin' off chins and elbows, makin' a mess of 'em."

"Please, gentlemen, there's a better way to settle this," the owner pleaded. "Let's use some sense here. Bring in your friends, No Nose. I'll send my boy out to fetch a fresh jug from the storehouse."

"Nobody goes!" No Nose shouted, motioning for his companions to block the door. "Now, maybe we have some fun. Maybe we take your gun, Three Fingers. Maybe we cut some hair from these *wasicuns!*"

No Nose spit a torrent of Lakota words at the other Indians, and they howled their approval.

"Maybe you want to start with me," I said, swallowing the cold sensation in my gut as I stood. I'd already drawn my pistol, but No Nose hadn't noticed. Now he stood staring at two drawn revolvers aimed at his belly.

"You will all die," No Nose promised bitterly.

"Everybody does it sometime," Tom said, grinning as he cocked the hammer of his pistol. "Your move, horse thief. Show these brave hearts what a big chief you are. See if you can't find your knife 'fore I cut you in two!"

"Pa?" the boy cried, edging his way closer to his terrified mother. "Pa, do somethin'."

In the end it was one of the cardplayers acted. He jumped up and made a grab for his rifle. One of the Sioux leaped on him instantly, and the both of them rolled across the sawdust floor, grappling and clawing like a couple of mountain cats.

No Nose drew his knife and stepped toward Tom. I cocked my pistol and fired a second later, and No Nose fell back against the bar, dazed by the bullet I'd fired at his head. If my hand had been steadier, I'd killed the villain, but things being what they were, my shot had merely taken a slice out of his earlobe and clipped one of his braid's.

"Ayyy!" a young Sioux howled as he flung himself across the room. Tom dropped a second one, and the others retreated out the door. I intended to fire, too, but the Pawnee girl stepped in the way, and that Indian needed but a second to bypass Tom and slash out with his knife.

"Lord, help me!" I cried as the blade sank into the tender inside of my thigh and slashed downward toward the knee. Pain surged through me, and I screamed to high heaven. The young Sioux raised his knife again, but there was no Pawnee girl in the way now. I fired, fired again, and again and again until my revolver emptied all its chambers. The bullets simply tore that Indian's chest to pieces, and he fell in a bloody lump at my feet.

"Darby?" Tom called as I collapsed on the floor.

"Tom?" I gasped.

No Nose had stood clutching his face, watching it all, but the wild look in Tom's eyes set him in motion. The door was blocked, and the single window was behind Tom. No Nose screamed and bulled his way right through the side of the hut, tearing planks apart as Tom rushed after him. I don't know what happened thereafter, for I was too busy trying to stem the blood oozing out of my leg.

"Lord, he's opened me like a tin of beans," I said, sobbing at the sight of the gash.

"It'll be all right," the barman's wife said, gripping my hand as she tore open my trousers. "Looks worse than it is. Joe, go fetch Ma's sewing box."

The boy hurried to a nearby chest and began rummaging inside it. I managed to glance around the smoke-choked room and see that both the cardplayer and his Sioux antagonist lay lifeless near the far wall. Two others, the man I'd shot and the one dropped by Tom, also littered the floor. The Pawnee girl huddled beside the door, tending another of the cardplayers.

"He gashed you proper," the woman said, forcing my eyes away from the corpses by the wall. "I'll sew it up, but you're sure to take fever. Are you far from home?"

"Home?" I asked, blinking a mist from my eyes. "Far? Yes, very far," I told her. "Where's Tom?"

"Here," he answered, making his way through the splintered side of the hut. "Got the horses ready. Saw to it everything was there, too."

"Good," I said, gritting my teeth as I felt the woman's needle pierce my hide. "Tom, you there?"

"Right here," he said, sitting beside me. "Never did know a boy so good at gettin' himself sliced by bears and such. Almost did yourself proper this time, I tell you. Good thing you grew some this year. Elsewise that blade'd sliced you open from belly to toe."

"Would take some time explaining it to Laveda," I said, trying to smile in spite of the pain eating at my insides.

"I'd guess so," he said, brushing the hair back from my eyes. "Lord, I should've listened to you, son. You knew

133

this place was trouble. I read it in your eyes."

"You couldn't know," I told him.

"You did," he muttered. "Ought to trust you to know, Darby Prescott. We've trailed together too long not to."

I didn't talk much the rest of the time the woman did her stitching. It hurt, and I was growing weak besides. The boy stood beside me, staring at the bloody mess that had been my leg, and I tried to manage a grin for him. Whatever my mouth produced sent him racing to his father's side.

Once the wound was closed and bandaged, the barman knelt beside me and somberly turned to Tom.

"You can't stay here," the man whispered.

"You don't mean to send this boy out like he is, sliced up and near bled white?" Tom cried.

"That No Nose has friends," the barman explained. "The other gentlemen have already left. The two of you killed a buck apiece, and that won't be overlooked. Not a chance of it. I'd get clear 'fore the devils come back."

"What about you?" Tom asked.

"I got a place up in the rocks to hide. We'll be all right. No Nose has had run-ins with folks before, but he favors whiskey, and there's no other place he can get it."

"Darby?" Tom whispered, and I lifted my head. "Got to get you clear o' here. I'm goin' to tear one o' those *tipis* down, use the poles for a travois. Figure you can stand bein' drug a ways?"

"Lot better'n being carved up some more," I answered.

"Watch you go slow," the woman warned. "Wouldn't want to open that leg up again."

"No, ma'am. Thanks for your help," Tom said, fumbling in his pocket for a gold piece.

"Don't want your money," the barman insisted. "Just get clear."

"Do our best," Tom promised. He then hurried outside to make the travois.

As the sun sank low into the hills west of us, I bobbed

along in my bed of blankets and buffalo hides. Pepper whined a bit at having to drag the extra weight of the long pine poles, and I silently promised him it wouldn't be too long I'd be on my back. Tom, meanwhile, got us four or five miles to the east before stopping. He made camp beside a small spring, and we passed the night there. I lay there mumbling feverishly, calling for Mama, and fleeing from one nightmare to the next.

I didn't find much rest, and when morning arrived, I discovered Tom bathing me in cool water and cursing ill luck and fevers.

"Doesn't hurt so much now," I said, glancing down at the blood-soaked bandages.

"Can't see how it could," he told me. "You've bled more'n any man I ever saw."

"Tom," I said, staring at an ugly black scar on the near horizon. "Tom, they're coming for us. Look. Dust!"

"Not dust," he assured me. "Smoke. The Sioux went down and burned the grog house. So you won't need to argue me out o' stoppin' there on the way back through."

"Are the people all right? That woman was kind."

"Married a fool though," he muttered. "I expect they holed up."

"You could have a look."

"I got a job o' work to do just now," he said, scowling. "Now quit yappin' and leave me to get it done. Hear?"

I nodded and closed my eyes. I wasn't much able to do otherwise.

Chapter Fourteen

My leg swelled up like a melon, and I spent one whole day feverishly thrashing about, mostly out of my head. I wasn't much better the next day either. Bad off as I was, I had occasions when I fought my way out of the shadows. It was then that I realized how worried Tom was.

"Rest easy," he always told me. "You'll heal up by and by."

He might have deceived me with words, but his eyes couldn't lie. My leg throbbed and festered, and I realized it.

The third day Tom examined my leg and satisfied himself the gash had scabbed over enough to move me. He tried to help me rise, but I'd eaten almost nothing, and I was as weak as a newborn fawn. I struggled to pull myself onto Pepper's back, but my vision blurred, and I collapsed into Tom's trembling arms.

How he got me mounted, I'll never know. He did though, and we got back down to the main trail. I blinked my eyes into focus a bit later. Up ahead strange white phantoms swayed back and forth beside the Platte, and I moaned. I couldn't feel anything except the ropes that kept me slumped across my horse.

"Help's come," Tom called then, drawing us to a halt.

"Help?" I asked. "Laveda?"

"Wagon folks," Tom explained. "Be gettin' you better 'fore long, son. Be good as new, once I get a proper poultice on that leg."

I only heard the words. They had no meaning. I did feel hands reaching up, untying my ropes, and easing me onto the ground.

"He's little more'n a boy, Pete," a woman called. "What could he have done?"

I blinked my eyes to clear my vision. There were shapes bending over me, but I couldn't make out the faces. One held a long, polelike object. A rifle! And as other figures gathered, I knew I was far from a welcome guest.

"Tom?" I called.

"It's goin' to be all right, Darby," he whispered. "This woman's goin' to have a look after you."

"You're not going?" I asked.

"Just a bit. Got work to tend, and there's the herbs you'll need for that poultice."

I sank into a feverish stupor, and everything grew dark.

When I awoke again, I found myself lying in the shade of a willow down near the river. A damp cloth kept my head cool, and somebody had made a bed of hides so that I rested in cloudlike comfort.

"Well, it's time you woke," a pleasant-faced woman said, bending over me so that she could touch my forehead. "Still got fever, but I'd expect that. It'll pass."

"Who are you?" I asked.

"Mabel Harper," she said. "Who're you?"

"Darby Prescott," I told her.

"Well, Darby Prescott, you've been a fair-sized amount of trouble to me this day, and if you weren't already sliced up proper, I'd probably do it myself. How'd you come to be in such a fix?"

"Was a Sioux did it," I said, frowning as the memory

137

swept over me. "Down at Midway Wells."

"You don't say," a masculine voice broke in. I turned my eyes to the other side and saw a somber-eyed man of forty or so holding a shotgun.

"We were by there this morning," Mabel explained. "Somebody burned the place to the ground."

"I saw the smoke," I said, closing my eyes a moment as the energy seemed to leave me.

"Might've been Sioux," the man said. "Might've been you."

"Why would I do such a thing?" I cried, trying to rise. A sharp pain raced up my leg, and I fell back moaning.

"Leave the boy alone, Rufus!" Mabel warned. "He's weak."

"I'll leave him alone when he gives me some answers," the man countered. "I was riding ahead of the train early this morning. Saw a man down there who looked a lot like that old goat you travel with. Was digging graves!"

"Graves?" I asked nervously.

"Three of them," he answered. "Had to be sure of it, so me and a couple of the boys did some digging. Was a man, a woman, and an Indian girl."

"You needn't've disturbed 'em," I said, recalling the kind attentions of the woman and the terrified eyes of the Pawnee girl. "Tom would've told you."

"They were cut up some," Rufus added. "Were a time dying, I'd guess."

"They had a boy," I mumbled.

"Found him later on, down the trail a bit. Must've given 'em a run 'fore they caught him."

"It's hard news you've given me," I said, shaking my head sadly. "The woman sewed up my leg, maybe saved me from bleeding to death. The barman, well, he knew the odds of selling whiskey to renegades, but the woman and that little boy . . ."

"See, Rufus Didier," Mabel declared. "He's shook to

138

his core. Told you he didn't have a hand in that business."

"He was there! Admits it!" Didier argued. "I tell you the two of them are renegades themselves. Or road agents. Who else travels east on this trail all alone, with September passing and winter coming early?"

"You're scout for this company?" I asked the fiery-eyed Didier. "Then maybe you've heard of Tom Shea. He's my partner. We were bound for Fort Kearny to escort some freighters to Laramie. Ran across an Oglala called No Nose, a bad character. Was one of his fellows stuck my leg."

"And you just sat by innocent as a babe?" Didier asked.

"I pulled my Colt and shot one of 'em dead," I said, fighting to keep tears from falling. "Don't you see? That's why those folks died? 'Cause No Nose lost half his ear, and had men killed, too. He's not one to let a thing lie."

"Then you're being here puts us in danger," the scout declared.

"I'd judge it so," I confessed, turning to Mabel. "When Tom gets back, he can get me off to the hills. I'll mend in time."

"You wouldn't mend at all in his hands," she grumbled. "That woman stitched you did you no favors, Darby. Wounds need to bleed so the bad humors get out. That Shea fellow brought you to me white as death, with your leg swollen double."

"Did he lance it?" I asked, looking down toward my leg. I couldn't see past the linen covering my belly. I wiggled the toes on my right foot, but when I tried to move my left, I couldn't. "God, you didn't cut it off?" I cried.

"You got to us any later, even that wouldn't've much helped," she said. "No, I sent him off to find his Indian herbs and opened it up myself. Pure mess, that leg.

139

Black blood and puss drained all afternoon. Got that poultice on now, and the fever's down. Swelling's bound to linger awhile, but you ought to be better soon."

"Well enough to ride?" I asked.

"I wouldn't," she advised. "Not for a week. But I know men, and boys are even worse. You should rest it seven days, but you'll be testing it in two."

She grinned a bit, and I forced a smile. The recollection of the family at the springs troubled me, and I wished Tom was back. Even so, it felt more than a little good to be alive.

Tom returned an hour or so later, dragging an elk carcass behind his big horse. After paying me a brief visit, he set to skinning the beast and offering hunks of fresh meat to the wagon folks.

"Papa, should we take it?" a boy asked when Tom cut a shoulder roast.

"Why would you share your kill?" the boy's father asked.

"Payment for your kindnesses toward Darby," he explained to the hesitant pilgrims. "It's fresh meat, can't you see? I haven't poisoned it!"

That night Mabel stewed her portion of the elk and fed me a bit of it with some mashed tubers. My stomach fought it for a time, but I managed to keep most of it in me.

"It'll take solid food to get you on your feet," she told me. "We'll be moving along westward in the morning, and you'll only have that Shea fellow to nurse you."

"He's a good hand at it," I told her. "I've given him practice."

"Well, you see that leg's given time to heal," she scolded. "You'll have a devil of a scar, though the worst of it's too high up for modest folk to get a peek at. Unless you wear those trousers I cut off you. Made a ruin of 'em, I fear."

I shared her laughter, then glanced over at Tom.

"Figure you can get me some buckskins put together?" I asked him. "Can't much ride to Redding's place wrapped in a sheet of bed linen."

"Traded some wool pants off one o' the wagon folk," he assured me. "But I figured maybe we'd turn back to Laramie, give you a chance to mend proper."

"I'll be all right," I argued. "It's late enough."

"I plan to see you on to Laramie myself," Rufus Didier said, walking over with his shotgun. "I'm none too satisfied you didn't have a hand in killing those people at Midway Wells."

"I told you we didn't," Tom said, staring angrily at the scout.

"But what proof have you of it?"

"I told you," Tom stormed. "That's enough for any mule-headed pilgrim!"

"People hereabouts know Tom Shea's word," I interrupted. "Ask the soldier captain at Fort Laramie. Talk to Doyle Marcus at the American Fur Company post, or old Bordeaux, or Laveda Borden. They'll say as much."

"I'll do just that," Didier promised. "When we all get to the fort."

"I'm not headin' that way," Tom said, eyeing the scout coldly.

"You are now," Didier said.

Tom started to reach for his knife, but half a dozen rifle barrels rose to challenge the move.

"This boy's not fit to travel," Mabel argued.

"He'll be all right in the back of the supply wagon," Didier replied. "George, get some rope and bind Mr. Shea here's hands and feet. Same for the boy."

"He's not walking anywhere," the man answered. "I'll tie his hands though."

"I'll be a long time rememberin' this," Tom vowed.

"No," Mabel said, chasing the men away from me.

"He's got enough troubles without being hog-tied. I'll watch him. You men go tend the stock."

"Worried over a one-legged youngster!" Tom growled. "Ought to concern yourselves with gettin' through the Sierras 'fore winter freezes the passes."

"We'll get through," Didier said confidently.

"Will you now?" Tom asked. "More likely spend the winter starvin' up there."

A couple of the children muttered questions, and I frowned.

"Is he right, Ma?" a little girl cried. "We goin' to starve?"

"We'll be fine, dear," her mother responded. "We've got powerful courage, Mr. Shea. You'll see."

"Hope so," Tom told them. "You'll have need."

I knew it was so, but I also knew there were times when it did no use to argue. It was like the folks who'd warned Lt. Grattan to step lightly when dealing with the Sioux. Now there was a man with no ears for reason, boasting how he'd ride through the whole of the Plains tribes with thirty men! Rufus Didier was a man to keep his own counsel, too, and Tom's jabbering only got him a rag stuffed in his mouth.

I didn't want to think how he must feel, tied and gagged like a thief. Me, I was near as helpless, what with one of the wagon men standing guard over Mabel and me all night.

"Figure me to run away?" I asked.

"Just avoidin' troubles," a red-haired farmer explained. "We've had our share of trials on this trail, and we've grown cautious."

I thought of a hundred replies. "Some grow cautious and others grow stupid" would have made the point. But I wanted no rag in *my* mouth, so I bit my lip and let a terrible weariness whisk me away.

For a time I floated on a cloud, an eagle able to soar

142

over the mountains. I felt whole again, strong and free of pain. I touched the earth and became a buffalo, thundering across the plain. Then a terrible silence descended, and I was once again a man.

"Watch well," a voice whispered. "Use your eagle eyes. Listen with bull buffalo's ears. Danger is near."

I awoke with a start. Once I hadn't put much stock in dreams, but I'd gotten sensations before, heard voices, and seen figures in my sleep. I glanced to my side. Mabel lay sleeping in her blankets. Across the way a strawhaired boy of fifteen or so rested his head on the stock of his rifle.

My first instinct was to rouse him, but the hammer was at half cock, and I worried that boy might set his piece off in panic. Better to give Mabel a nudge, I decided. I took a deep breath and reached toward her. The sound of muffled feet stepping lightly through the buffalo grass froze me stiff.

There were other noises, too. Over by the supply wagon Tom struggled to loosen his bonds. The two night guards spoke of a wagon with a bad wheel. Then there was a rush, and the guards were dragged off out of sight.

"Lord, don't let it be No Nose," I whispered as I searched for my pistol. Naturally the wagon folks hadn't left it nearby. I tried to raise myself by the hands, but pain exploded through my leg. I might as well have had a cannonball chained to my ankle!

"Mabel," I said, rousing her.

"You all right, boy?" she asked, sitting up sleepily.

"Get me a gun," I pleaded quietly. "We've got visitors."

"Lord Almighty!" she shouted. "Indians!"

Her yell set the camp in motion. My guard took his feet and managed to kick his rifle against a water barrel, setting the gun off. A chorus of curses followed as people rushed to see what was happening. It was a sight,

143

and I might've laughed had there not been serious trouble about.

"Get your britches on, Henry!" a woman called as her husband fumbled with his musket.

In a daze caused by darkness and weariness, people ran around half-clothed, calling to Didier or yelling at their children. Then a woman screamed.

"They've taken my Lucinda!" she cried. "Wilfred? They've snatched him, too!"

Pain or no pain, I wrapped the sheet around my waist and grabbed the adjacent wagon wheel. I managed to pull myself onto my good right leg, but I was too lightheaded to go anywhere.

"Hold it there!" the young guard called, frantically reloading his rifle.

"You want to help, get over there and untie Tom Shea!" I yelled. "And give me that rifle. You'll still be loading it tomorrow."

"Do it, Chance," Mabel urged. "Must be plain to everyone it wasn't them set these Indian's on us."

The boy passed his rifle over, and Mabel found a buckskin bag with shot, powder, and wadding.

"They're most likely already a mile away," I muttered as I rammed down the ball. "Lord! They were in here slick as bear grease."

"Give me that," Mabel said when I finished loading the rifle. "Could be I can get off a shot at the last of 'em."

She rushed out toward where the horses had been grazing, but the Indians had planned it well. They, the horses, and eight children had vanished into the night.

"Lord help them," Mabel cried.

"Lord help us all," I echoed as I collapsed to the ground.

I drifted in and out of a light slumber the rest of that night. Figures stirred all around me. Parents searched the nearby gullies, softly whispering the names of vanished children in the vain hope that they might merely have wandered off. Others, beset by nightmares, cried out in their sleep.

I was sitting up long before the sun first cracked the eastern horizon. Men chopped wood or mended harness to cast their minds from the terrible fix facing us all.

"I don't understand a bit of it," Rufus Didier said when the company assembled to discuss what to do. "I see taking the horses, but why the children?"

"Sell 'em off as slaves, I'll bet," one woman suggested.

"Not Wilf," a grieving lady sobbed. "Not Lucy!"

"Could be they mean 'em as hostages," Tom said, eyeing me solemnly. "If so, they'll come along by daylight and offer you a swap."

"And if not?" Didier asked.

"Adopt 'em into the band," I explained. "I heard of it. Sometimes when sickness has hit and there are lots dead, they'll stage a raid, take some young ones in as replacements for those that died."

"And leave our hearts empty instead?" Mabel asked.

"Most of the time the parents have arrows in their hides," Tom said grimly. "Best figure out who's missin', then send word to the fort."

"How?" Didier asked. "They've taken our horses. It's thirty miles!"

"Tom's right," I said, nodding sadly. "Pick someone with good legs and get 'em started."

A dozen volunteers stepped forward, and Didier dispatched a pair of them. Provision bags were packed for them, and prayers were made. Then they set off westward.

"If I'd had two good legs, I might've stopped 'em," I grumbled as Mabel brought me a malted broth for breakfast. "Or if Tom was handy."

"Still figure me for a raider?" Tom asked Didier.

145

The scout stumbled past us, dazed. His was the worst of plights, the watchdog who'd slept while his master's treasures were taken. Now Didier faced seventy mourning companions stranded on the North Platte on foot, with no prayer of reaching golden California before the snows blocked the Sierra passes.

"Don't feel too sorry for him, Darby," Tom told me. "We're afoot ourselves."

Chapter Fifteen

The thing about being at the bottom of the deepest gully in creation, Tom once told me, is that you've nowhere to go but up. I've noticed how it is that when you've been hit square on the jaw and tossed face first into a buffalo wallow, the Lord kind of takes pity on you and lets the sun break through the clouds. There I was, surrounded by moans and sobs, wondering what I could do to help, when I look out to the Platte and see a slight-shouldered Sioux leading Pepper and Tom's big buckskin toward the wagon train.

"Pa, Indians!" a boy called, and the wagon people rushed to get their guns.

"Hold up!" I shouted. "Look to his face. He's got no paint on, and his horse's tail's hanging loose, not tied up for war."

"Hold your fire," Didier ordered. "May be an invite to a parley."

As the young Sioux appeared, I saw he was followed by others. They were too faraway to see, but the horses were familiar. I'd seen three of them at least when I'd gone buff hunting with the Brules.

"Tom, I think I might know some of 'em," I called.

"How's that?" Didier asked. "You bring those savages down on us, did you?"

"Hush!" Tom growled.

There was a stir among the wagon people then, and I gazed around us. A hundred or more warriors emerged from the ravines and surrounded us. I swallowed hard and looked to Tom for direction. He shrugged his shoulders and stared at the ground. The others, too, saw what a hopeless fix we were in. Despair painted their faces pale, and families huddled in prayer.

"Look," Didier shouted, and I turned back around. The young Brule rode toward the camp, driving Pepper and the buckskin to us. Then he climbed off his own horse and walked toward the camp, making signs that he wanted to talk.

"Who'd send a boy to meet with us?" Didier asked.

"Didn't anybody send him," I said, recognizing the face at last. "He came on his own. To talk to me."

"What!" the people cried. "You're a renegade after all."

"No," I said, grabbing the wagon wheel again and painfully pulling myself onto my good right leg. "Just a friend. Was once, anyway."

"Darby, don't be a fool," Tom said, rushing over and taking hold as my good leg began to buckle. "You've been on your back close to a week now."

"Can't be helped," I argued. "Can't you see he's recognized my pony. He knows I'm here."

Tom nodded, then turned me over to a pair of stout-armed men. He managed to bring my new trousers over, and between the three of them, they got them pulled up over my swollen leg and fastened so that I didn't step out half-bare to open the parley.

"Be careful of that leg," Mabel warned. "You've already got it bleeding."

I looked at the red droplets staining my bare toes and frowned. There was nothing else to do though. They'd have brought other horses if it was someone else they wanted to see.

Tom got me onto Pepper's bare back, and I hugged my eager pony's strong neck and got him moving out toward the young rider. Once I arrived, another figure emerged from the encircling Brules.

"*Hau,* Brother," I called to Two Nations. "*Hau,* Bob-

148

tail."

The boy grinned his answer.

"You're white even for a *wasicun*," Two Nations observed when he arrived. "Leg?"

"Guess it's hard to hide even with trousers," I said. "Took a knife in the thigh."

"These whites?" Two Nations asked.

"Oglala," I mumbled. "Was riding with No Nose."

"And now we come to steal your horse. It's a hard day for you."

"Been lots of hard days lately," I said, frowning. "But it's good brothers don't take from each other."

"There's that," he agreed.

"Wasn't just horses taken, Two Nations. There's children missin'."

"Not missing," he objected. "They've found new homes."

"Now you know these folks won't forget that."

"They only live if Finds the Enemy chooses to let them."

"He's chief now, is he?"

"He leads the young men," Two Nations explained. "Those making the surround."

"Then I guess we ought to get him together with the wagon people so they can work things out. They haven't got much to trade, Two Nations, but they—"

"Trade?" he asked. "Anything they have is ours if we choose. Look around you! What do you see?"

"Death," I told him. "For the wagon people, sure, but for others, too."

"But not for you," Two Nations said, motioning to young Bobtail. The boy grinned again, then babbled away at me.

"I don't understand," I said, catching only one or two recognizable words. "What's he saying?"

"He says he owes you a life," Two Nations explained. "His brother is generous. You and Three Fingers can go."

I nodded. Now things got clearer. Part of me wanted to bid Tom join me so that the two of us could ride off and never look back. But I knew Mabel was back there, poor simple woman, and she'd saved my life even as I'd saved Bobtail.

"I can't," I told them. "I went to those folks feverish and close to dead. There's a woman lanced my wound, drained and cleaned it, saved my leg and likely my life. What manner of man would I be to leave her when she's in trouble, her and the others?"

Two Nations became grim.

"You won't go?" he asked.

"We've got a lot of differences, your people and mine," I said, speaking more to Bobtail than to Two Nations, for he was caught in between worse than I was. "One thing's the same though. The best of all of us is the man who keeps his promises and stands by his friends."

Two Nations translated the words, and more, I guessed, for the two Brules spoke back and forth for several minutes. Then Bobtail turned and rode away.

"He goes to see his brother," Two Nations said. "It may be we won't meet again on this side of the shadows. I'm proud to have ridden with you some."

"As I am," I said, gripping his wrists. Two Nations then returned to his people, and I rode back to the wagons.

"Well?" Didier asked. "What'd he say?"

I managed to slide off Pepper's back, but my first step sent me to the ground in a heap.

"Leave him some air!" Mabel complained, pushing people out of the way. "Let's look at that leg."

"No, I've got to tell them first," I said, raising myself into a sitting position. "It's a young batch have us surrounded. Their leader's never had much use for whites, and I figure he's hot to do some killing to get back at those who killed his chief last month."

"You were out there a long time," Didier pointed out. "They told you more than that."

"The small one who brought my horse is called Bobtail. I was out hunting with him and his cousin, and I killed a rattler that was sure to strike the boy. To his thinking," I explained, "he owes me. Brought my horse so I could ride away. That would satisfy the debt."

"And the rest of us?" Mabel asked.

"Tom could go, too. The rest of you, well, you couldn't."

"Dear Lord," Mabel said, sinking to her knees. "They mean to massacre us all."

"It's why they took the little ones first," Didier surmised. "Didn't want them killed by stray shots."

"When do you go?" the red-headed farmer asked.

"Sir?"

"When do you leave? You said they offered you free passage. I want to send a letter to my brother, explain what happened. You'll take it, won't you?"

"I'll write my sister," a woman said. "You can take her what money we've got left."

"I told them no," I said, steadying my trembling arms.

"What?" Didier asked.

"Tom?" I said, wincing as pain surged through my leg. "Tell it to 'em."

"Tell us what?" Mabel asked as she tore the trouser leg away and began cutting through my bloodstained bandages.

"Debts work both ways," Tom said, folding his jacket and resting it under my head. He owes Mabel here for her tendin' him, so he can't leave."

"You should save yourself," Mabel argued. "I'm an old woman who's seen her best days. Buried two husbands and may a third," she added, winking at me.

"Then you're all dead for certain," I muttered. "Me staying gives you a chance."

"What?" they asked.

"That boy's not goin' to rest easy if he can't pay off his marker," Tom said, grinning at me.

"And his brother's their leader," I added. "I figure we'll

151

have us a parley after all."

The others cheered some. Only Mabel scowled. She set about cleaning up the mess I'd made of my leg by reopening the wound.

"Pure determined to bleed to death." she grumbled. "Men are born fools. But some have their moments, don't they, Darby?"

"Yes, ma'am," I agreed.

It happened I figured right for once. Two Nations reappeared with Finds the Enemy, and the other Brules dismounted and sat beside their horses. Tom and Didier went out to treat, but it wasn't long before they returned to fetch me.

"That Brule's about as lock-jawed and quick to fight as any I've seen," Tom said, "but he's got a soft spot for that brother. Says he wants to see you're all right first. Then we'll bargain."

"We're only safe as long as the boy stays among us!" one of the wagon folks objected.

"We don't do as he says, we're all of us crowbait 'fore mornin'," Tom barked. "Sit yourself down and leave it to those who know what to do. With a smile or two and some pretty compliments, I just might wrangle those kids back from him. Maybe even some of the horses."

In the beginning Rufus Didier was determined to speak. He told how unprovoked was the raid.

"There'll be serious trouble, too!" he warned. "I sent men to the fort for help. Any minute soldiers could appear."

"Ah, you sent two men," Two Nations said, grinning. He spoke to Finds the Enemy, and the warrior gestured to his men. They quickly produced the messengers, the both of them stripped to their drawers and bound head to toe.

"Now, threaten us more," Two Nations said, scowling at the wagon scout.

"Didn't come to make threats," Tom said, satisfied Didier would leave the parley to him. "Came to talk of friendship and brothers. Came to speak of now and to-morrow, not of fools like Grattan who only want to shine their sword and strike the defenseless. You know me and Darby. You know we speak from the heart. Listen to our words for the truth that's in 'em."

I'd seen Tom at work before, but even I was amazed at the craft he displayed in bringing Finds the Enemy around to our point of view. When Two Nations described how measles had plagued the band and taken the lives of seven children, I spoke of the death of my own little brother Matthew.

"It tears at me to think of those people and the empti-ness they feel," I said, wiping my eyes.

"Dry your eyes, Two Nations counseled after he and Finds the Enemy spoke a bit. "I'll go get the children myself. We'll bring some horses, too, the big slow ones to pull the wagons. We keep the saddle ponies."

"I'm grateful," I said, turning to Didier. He, likewise, offered thanks, and handed over a box of pipe tobacco. We smoked to seal the bargain, and an hour later Two Nations and some of the younger Brules brought back the captives, as well as twenty mules and such oxen as hadn't been slaughtered for meat.

"Get the teams hitched," Didier commanded as fami-lies welcomed back their hollow-faced youngsters. Clearly the three boys had suffered little save in the ex-change of their clothes for a narrow strip of buffalo hide. The girls, unused to the harsh world of a Sioux woman, had gotten a switch or two applied to their backs. Their bare feet bled from abuse, and they'd had their hair cut and braided.

"I hope the soldiers ride every one of those red devils into the dust!" one mother screamed as she comforted her daughter.

"Not me," the red-headed farmer argued. "I've got my Hollis back, and I say, Praise the Lord."

"Praise the Lord!" others shouted.

Tom helped me to a small rise overlooking the trail,

and we looked on as families consolidated their stock and possessions so that they could continue their journey. Wagons were abandoned, and fine possessions were spread out along the trail.

"You watch that leg now, Darby," Mabel scolded as she prepared to follow the train west. "Won't have this old woman around to tend you anymore."

"Guess I'll have to be careful," I told her. "Godspeed."

"I'll be a time remembering you, son," she called.

The wagons snaked their way along the trail, leaving me behind like so much trail dust.

"Up to ridin'?" Tom asked.

"I was born to sit a horse," I answered.

"Then it's on to Scott's Bluff and Redding's store. Bet he'll have a jug set aside for us. How'll that be?"

"Won't be near as welcome as a new pair of britches," I said, grinning. "These are torn to tatters."

"And that pilgrim robbed me dear for 'em," Tom lamented. "Better to shoot a buck and use its hide. Or turn you Sioux and cut a breechclout. Fool boy. You always were hard on clothes."

"That's what Mama used to say."

"Always did think she was far too level-headed a woman to get herself hitched to a mess o' Prescott's. Now let's get along. We've two days ridin' 'fore I get that jug. Maybe three if that leg o' yours starts to fester again."

"You leave me to tend my leg," I grumbled. "You keep a watch for No Nose. I've had enough trouble out of him!"

"Ain't it the truth?" Tom said, nudging his buckskin into a trot. "That too hard a pace, Darby?"

In truth the jarring had my leg convulsing with pain, but I shook my head. Just then it felt good, that pain. It meant I was still alive!

Chapter Sixteen

We moved slowly eastward, holding our time in the saddle to what my leg could endure. At night Tom would inspect the awful-looking black scar and drain it as needed.

"Goin' to run out o' bandages if it doesn't get itself well soon," he told me as I lay staring at the towering monolith of Scott's Bluff a few hours away.

"Maybe you ought to leave me to the buzzards," I said, grinning.

"Got too much respect for buzzards to do 'em such a wrong," he replied. "Prescott meat's too salty, I figure, and stringy to boot. Could leave you with Redding while I head along to Fort Kearny."

"Then who'd keep you out of trouble?" I asked. "It's getting better, Tom."

"Is it?" he asked. "Well, the rest of you's thinner'n a fence rail, and nigh on wasted away."

"Elk steak would take care of that," I told him. "Or some venison. I'll bet there's game to be found somewhere nearby."

"Not close," he grumbled. "Wagon folks've scared every sensible creature south to Kansas or up into the Black Hills."

"Bet there are fish in the river."

"Could be," he said, passing over a coil of fishing line and some hooks. "Make yourself useful."

I managed to hook three trout and a fat old catfish.

Tom fried them up over a small fire for our supper. After days of struggling to keep food in my belly, I devoured the fish like a starved man. Tom rummaged around in his packs and located some dried buffalo strips, and I ate those, too.

"Sure sign you're better," he announced as he rolled out our blankets alongside the embers of the fire. "Out to eat us poor. Won't be long now 'fore you're good as new."

I wasn't quite so sure. But when we rode past Scott's Bluff to Jonas Redding's trading post down on the river, I dismounted on my own for the first time since the set-to at Midway Wells. True, I'd fallen off once or twice, but this time I even took a rickety step or two.

"Time we made you a crutch," Tom announced as he led the horses back to the river. "See if ole Redding's about."

I took a deep breath and hopped toward the front door of the trading post. The place appeared deserted, and I had to bang loudly on the door three times before a window cracked open.

"Darby Prescott, what in blazes are you doing here?" Redding asked, sighing with relief. "Thought certain it was Sioux come back to talk me out of more powder."

"Had some trouble?" I asked.

"Nothing but," he said, opening the door. As I hopped over to a keg and sat down, he frowned and nodded knowingly. "Looks like you found a bit yourself. Shea with you?"

"Took the horses to the river," I explained. "He'll be along."

"Well, I won't claim company's not welcome. I had a girl and some Pawnees here till that fool Grattan stirred up the Sioux. The lot of 'em hightailed it east. Can't blame 'em much. I'd go myself, if my livelihood wasn't tied up on these shelves."

"I figured most of the Sioux were up north in the Black Hills."

"Not all," he said, frowning. "Bunch of Oglalas bothering the wagon road, running off stock or demanding presents. I have to keep powder and shot—not to mention my extra rifles—in a hole under the floorboards. Elsewise those Oglalas'd have every bit of it by now. Trade's pure gone to perdition!"

That night as we sat around Redding's table, eating trout and taking sips from a jug of corn liquor, the trader lamented the hard times.

"Seems the world's grown sour," he grumbled. "Wagon folks come through here expecting to pay St. Louis prices. They ask you for favors like that's the real business you're in. 'Can't I just have a stick of candy for little Caleb? He ain't had any for months!' They think me hard-hearted for turning a profit. Ought to say a prayer I haven't vamoosed east like everybody else!"

"They've got their own troubles," I said, recalling the many hardships of trail life. "And the ones that come through now are late for getting across the Rockies."

"Too late," Tom added.

"It's a late year," Redding observed. "Never remember so many companies staggering in this late in September. Horses are thin as death, and the kids aren't much better."

"Be a lot of graves dug come winter," Tom observed.

Yes, I thought. Winter was always a season of death. I took out my mouth organ and blew a sad tune I'd picked up from ole Sgt. Hicks at Fort Laramie. Hicks lay on the plain now, his big booming voice silenced by a dozen flint arrowheads, and his friendly face covered by a few inches of trail dirt.

"Find somethin' livelier," Tom said, and I blew a bawdy melody the new soldiers had brought west with them.

"That's better," Redding said, clapping along. Soon the gloomy spell lifted long enough for a chorus or two of "Farmer John's Hogs" and "Sweet Betsy from Pike." Tom had washed away his melancholy with a liberal swallow or two of the corn liquor, and he sang his own version of the tunes, "Farmer John's Gals" and "Collette from St. Loo." I almost fell down laughing.

157

We left Redding's place early the next morn. Watching the trader bid us farewell, I actually believed he'd miss us. Living out there on that lonely stretch of river was a torment, and I hoped the Pawnees might come back after a time. The longer I was away from Laramie, the more I appreciated Laveda and missed my sister Mary and her family out in the Willamette Valley.

My leg continued to improve as we followed the North Platte southeastward past the familiar landmarks of the old Oregon Trail. I waved to Chimney Rock, and I struggled up Windlass Hill from Ash Hollow. As always, I was put in mind of that first time west, when as a weedy fourteen-year-old I'd first met the grizzled old frontier scout Tom Shea. I'd done a fair measure of growing since then, and I wasn't a tenderfoot anymore.

"Rememberin'?" he'd ask me whenever I broke out in a grin or sadly dabbed my face with a kerchief.

"Jamie McNamara's buried along here somewhere," I remarked when we swam in the Platte a day or so shy of Fort Kearny. "If there was a marker, I could visit him."

"You don't need a marker to do that," Shea said, growing thoughtful. "You talk to a friend's spirit anytime you want. They're never faraway."

"That what you do with your son?" I asked.

"Most ever night," he said glumly.

"I guess some pain never entirely passes."

"Not altogether," he admitted. Then he took to splashing me, and I counterattacked.

When we finally reached Fort Kearny, I felt like celebrating. Tom had cut me a cottonwood crutch, and I was getting to where I could hobble around on it pretty well. I put some weight on the leg now and then, but the knife had cut deep, and there was mending yet to do. Best way to heal, I thought as I climbed down from Pepper's back, is to be heading home. Or at least to what feels like home.

Fort Kearny wasn't much to look at. It was a world away from St. Louis and Washington, and the soldiers acted accordingly. One batch sat around the edge of the parade ground, puffing on their pipes and swapping tales. Only one of them wore a regulation tunic, and it was open to the waist. They put out a powerful odor, too. The few women and children I spotted kept upwind.

We had no trouble locating Clyde Parkinson. He was prowling around a line of parked wagons, complaining there wasn't enough grease on the wheels and that the canvas covers hung loosely.

"Mr. Parkinson, to keep 'em tight you got to retie the blamed thing twice every day," one of the drivers argued.

"You got nothing better to do," Parkinson barked.

"I just think—"

"Company doesn't pay for you to think!" Parkinson shouted. "I gave you a job, and I expect you to do it. Unless, that is, you'd care to be discharged out here in the middle of this godforsaken wilderness."

"No, sir," the nervous driver replied. "I'll get to it directly."

"I'd consider it wise," the freighter said, storming off. He nearly ran me down. "Watch where you're walking!" he yelled.

"I'm not walking anywhere," I told him. "Hobbling around some. I figure other folks'd look where they stepped."

"Oh?" he asked, his forehead wrinkling up like a piece of dried venison. "Around here boys learn to stay out of my way."

"That right?" I asked. "Well, I don't see it posted anywhere. And I haven't been a boy since I buried my mama in the Bear Mountains back in '48."

His gaze grew in ferocity. But when I wouldn't back off, he regained his composure.

"You got business here, do you?" he finally asked.

"With you if your name's Parkinson," I explained. "Doyle Marcus sent Tom Shea and I out here to escort you to Fort Laramie."

"Two of you?" he asked. "And one a cripple to boot?"

"Wasn't when I started out," I said, biting my lip to

159

keep from laying my crutch alongside his nose. "We ran across some renegade Sioux a day out of the fort. Got cut up some, but I'm better."

"Is that why you're a week and a half late?"

"We were slowed some, I'll admit. But we're here now, and we'll start for the fort in the morning."

"The devil we will!" he shouted. "I've got ten company wagons, and two more loaded for a fellow named Borden. I didn't get them all the way out here to see Indians carry them off like the supplies at Fort Laramie. I demanded an escort, and two men won't do."

"Well, we're what's here," Tom said, ambling over and joining the conversation. "All you'll find, either."

"Marcus said something about reinforcement for the post coming," I said. "We didn't pass any, so they must be here, too."

"Refugees from Missouri jails," Parkinson complained. "Who will guard us from them?"

"We'll do the guarding," Tom said, putting his battered nose in the freighter's face. "You just get 'em loaded and hitched."

Parkinson stood there babbling about this danger and that, but Tom only laughed and motioned for me to follow him to the post headquarters.

I first wrote off Parkinson's reluctance to a sharp case of Sioux fever. Nobody who'd read the exaggerated reports of what Easterners were calling the Grattan Massacre would willingly head west along the Platte. But when Tom and I walked out to greet the horse soldiers assigned to accompany us to Laramie, I began to suspect Parkinson had reason to fret. I found the whole bunch of them, twenty-one by my count, splashing around in the river stark naked. They were pale white and skinnier'n the blades on a yucca plant. You'd have to look real hard to find ten minute's work for a razor, too. Half-starved and one-legged as I was, I made those soldiers seem like children wandered off from a schoolhouse.

"Hello there!" Tom called as we reached the riverbank.

"Anybody in command here?"

"I am," the thinnest of the batch declared. He trotted to the bank, splashing a companion or two on the way. He shook himself like a dog to chase off the water, then placed a pair of wire spectacles down over his nose and looked us over.

"You'd be Shea," he said, taking Tom's hand. "Heard a world about you, sir. And you'd be Prescott. Well, I'm delighted to meet you at long last. Tomorrow we set out for Fort Laramie, I take it."

"That's the plan," Tom said, sadly shaking his head at the boyish figure who was climbing into the uniform of an infantry lieutenant.

"I'm Lt. Nathan Bailey," he explained. "Folks generally call me Nate. We're detailed to accompany you, but I might as well tell you, if we come across threatening hostiles, my orders are to engage them and punish their misdeeds. That hasn't set too well with your freighter, Mr. Parkinson."

"Don't suppose it would," Tom muttered. "Got the impression he's used to doin' things his way."

"Or not at all," the lieutenant agreed. "My command will be drawn up and ready at dawn."

"Then we leave after breakfast," Tom declared. "Now all we have to do is tell Parkinson."

As it turned out, we had to do a good deal more than tell Clyde Parkinson.

"I'm not going anywhere!" the freighter hollered when Tom and I roused him shortly before daybreak. "These wagons are my responsibility, and I'll see them safely up the Platte or stay right here. No twenty snotnoses and a pair of renegade whites will stand up to the Sioux. We'll wait a bit."

"You'll find yourself snowbound and less use than horseshoes on a snake," Tom barked. "Now, listen real good, 'cause this is the last time I'll say this. I been hired to move those wagons. Don't matter whether you go or not. You start up with me, and I'll take a knife to your hide and skin you so your own mama wouldn't know you."

"You wouldn't dare," Parkinson said, looking around for help.

"Wouldn't wager *my* hide on that, fellow," Tom said, drawing out his skinning knife. "Now, we got an agreement?"

Parkinson gazed at the razor-sharp steel and nodded his head.

"Watch him, Darby," Tom told me. "He says anything contrary to the drivers, you let me know. I've had all the trouble I can swallow for a while, and I'll have no more!"

The words had a profound effect on Parkinson. I could tell the freighter was steaming underneath, but he bit his lip and kept quiet. The drivers got their teams hitched and secured the goods loaded in the wagons. Then, with the sun still rising in the lower quadrant of the eastern sky, we headed off up the Platte.

The first day of our journey was uneventful. We made good progress along the muddy river, and we made camp on a rise overlooking the rutted trail. Early the next morning we resumed our journey, pushing man and beast hard. Tom wanted to move twenty-five miles a day, but the soldiers were afoot and of limited endurance. Tom had half of them riding on the wagons at a time. Every five miles they'd swap off with the marching group. Even so, ten miles seemed to stretch them to their limit.

"What'd I tell you?" Parkinson blubbered. "Soldiers! We'd be better off on our own."

"If you really believe that," I suggested, "we could go ahead on our own."

"With bloodthirsty Indians ready to cut our throats?" Parkinson exclaimed. I felt another tirade coming on, but Tom drew out his knife, and Parkinson grew quiet.

We were rolling along in good shape that next day, when a musket shot brought Tom and me galloping to the rear of the train.

"I got one!" a skinny private hollered, pointing to a

162

lump of brown flesh slumped beneath a willow alongside the river.

"Indians!" the driver beside him screamed. "Indians!"

Tom and I rode over and had a look. What I saw chilled my insides. A young Pawnee, maybe twelve years old, lay beside a fishing pole. A single round red hole pierced his right side just below the ribs. I managed to dismount and limp to his side. Turning him over, I saw the ghastly mess the big musket ball had made of his belly.

"Ought to come see your handiwork!" Tom called, and the soldier hurried over. When he saw the boy's solemn, lifeless face, the private dropped his gun and fell to his knees.

"Lord, he wasn't but a child," the soldier muttered.

"He was just fishing," I said, spitting the bitter taste out of my mouth. "Fishing! This is his country, after all."

"Oh, yes, feel for the little Sioux butcher!" Parkinson said. "You forgotten Grattan so quickly?"

I turned and drove my right fist into Parkinson's midsection, doubling him over.

"First of all," I said, my eyes ablaze, "he's Pawnee. Not Sioux. Second of all, it wasn't the Sioux fired off their cannon into a peaceful Brule village!"

"Darby?" Tom called from his horse.

"A minute more, Tom," I replied. "Parkinson, I'm half-lame and forty pounds smaller, but you want to continue this, just speak up. I'll keep myself handy."

The soldiers had gathered around the young corpse. They examined the Indian as if they were in some sideshow, and the dead boy was a freak on exhibit. Then they stepped back. An older Pawnee rode over with two other boys, likely brothers.

"Why?" the man asked, staring at the lifeless figure. "We make no war with Americans. Pawnee's good Indians. We fight Lakotas, help white man."

"Was a mistake," the lieutenant said, stepping forward. He took some bank notes from his pocket and offered them to the Pawnees.

163

"Can you buy life?" the Indian asked. "Keep your money! Give me back my son!"

The three Indians began a woeful chanting, and Lt. Bailey motioned his men back to the wagons.

"A sad mistake," the lieutenant told Tom. "I'll watch the men more closely. You don't think these Indians will strike the wagons?"

"No," Tom said sadly. "They're Pawnees. They already know it's the white man set the sun in the heavens."

"Well, that's fortunate."

"Is it?" Tom asked, grinding his teeth. "Don't know as I agree. But it's the way of things, and a man needn't make himself sick frettin' over it."

It was much later that we first encountered the Sioux. Tom and I were up ahead, scouting the long descent down Windlass Hill, when four or five young Oglalas galloped by whooping and howling like dogs who stepped on a hot coal. Tom watched them a moment, then shouted right back. I did the same, and soon the hollow echoed with our voices.

It was a battle of yells, the kind of thing old-timer's spoke of around a winter fireplace. Anger and suspicion passed as we laughingly taunted each other.

"Wasicun," a young man called, "where have you hidden your women? They're all so fat and ugly. Maybe we shot them for buffalo."

"An educated Sioux?" I asked Tom.

"Some've been to mission school," he explained.

I thought about Two Nations, and about No Nose. Those who wanted to learn seemed to pick up English fast enough, and there'd been a lot of intermarriage among the traders and tribes.

"Hey, *wasicun,* come down and let us put an arrow in your chest!" the Oglala continued. "We have many arrows. We make you a present maybe."

"No, thanks," I hollered in reply. "I'd have to shoot you with my Sharps in return, and I've only got fifty or sixty bullets. I understand Oglalas take a lot of killing."

"Yes!" he said, howling his delight. "We let you live, *wasicun*. Another time maybe we hunt you."

"Another time!" I shouted.

He gave a final yell, then turned and led his companions off into the nearby cottonwoods.

"Sioux are comin' south to make winter camp," Tom said, examining the hill. "Best we make a quick job o' this. Wouldn't want to be here when their daddies come 'round."

"Figure they will?" I asked.

"Oh, you can bank on that, son. Bet your life on it."

Chapter Seventeen

From Ash Hollow to Scott's Bluff, we were rarely on the trail alone. Often parties of Sioux or Cheyenne warriors approached, making brave talk and hurling insults. Other days impoverished bands of Pawnees would appear, offering to watch our flanks in return for a bit of flour or some gunpowder.

"What use would they be?" Parkinson asked. "Why, my old gray-haired grandma would be more use in a fight."

"They fight well enough," I replied. "And you already know how well they die."

The words stung, and Parkinson responded almost generously to the Pawnees' request.

We arrived at Scott's Bluff late in the afternoon, and I couldn't help howling with relief. Now we were but a hard two days from Fort Laramie. In no time I'd be shed of those wagons, Parkinson, and the responsibility that kept me from sleeping soundly at night.

"Got to admit you fellows know your trade," Parkinson said grudgingly as we approached Redding's place upstream. "I thought you both crazed and sure to get us killed, but you were right all along."

"Disappointed?" Tom asked.

"Enormously pleased," Parkinson said, "and considerably relieved. I didn't think it could be done. All the way from Nebraska with not a shot fired in anger."

I thought to remind me of the Pawnee boy, but I didn't.

It was as close to a thank you as Parkinson was apt to manage, and I was weary of our verbal melees.

Often it seems just when you think the struggle's over, and you're settling into a snug bed for the night, something comes to jolt you awake. That's what it felt like when we turned a bend and saw dust clouds rising from the direction of Redding's place.

"Trouble!" Tom shouted, and the soldiers formed a line in front of the lead wagon. Lt. Bailey took charge and ordered us to move forward with caution.

"He thinks he's fightin' Napoleon," Tom remarked as the soldiers shouldered arms and marched onward. "Best you and me watch our tail, Darby. Sioux won't run up and stand still for you to shoot 'em. They'll buzz around like bees and sting you hard!"

I knew it well. Memories of Grattan's riddled body plagued me, and I fought the shadows that were threatening to choke me.

"Look there," I said as a pair of young archers appeared out of nowhere. They were as startled as we were. One fired an arrow over Lt. Bailey's head and grabbed his companion's arm. The two of them retired in haste.

The soldiers' line had dissolved momentarily, but the lieutenant managed to regain control. He then waved his pistol over his head and led a brief charge toward the trading post. Jonas Redding threw open the door and greeted his saviors warmly.

"Lord thank you, boys," the trader said over and over. "I'll pop a cork and pass the jug."

When we rode up, he grinned.

"Gave up on ever seeing you boys again," Redding declared. "Haven't had a moment's peace since you left. Sioux and more Sioux. I've got a dozen people holed up in my store, most of 'em set afoot by raiders, and three of 'em arrow-shot."

I frowned. I'd felt like we had reached a refuge. Instead we'd ridden into a fight.

Worse, we weren't given much of a welcome by Redding's guests. You'd think thirty-five men, most of 'em soldiers, would have raised spirits a bit, even brought on a smile or two. Instead we heard mostly complaints.

"If you soldier boys hadn't gone and shot ole Conquerin' Bear, I'd still be up in my cabin sippin' Missouri corn," one old trapper said. "Now you got the whole Lakota people runnin' 'round tryin' to shoot arrows into anyone with a white face. My little Betsy lost a piece of one ear, and the missus had thirty pounds scared off her."

"Had 'em to spare," one of the soldiers remarked.

"Maybe I ought to shave a few off you, sonny!" the trapper barked. "How 'bout it?" he added, pulling a knife.

"Save it for the Sioux," Tom suggested. "They'll be along, I'm guessin'."

"Sure, they will be," a sorrowful-faced woman declared. "Wouldn't you, if you'd seen your huntin' range torn by wagon trains, game scattered to the corners of the earth? Wouldn't you, if you'd buried sons and daughters struck down by pox and measles and Lord knows what other white man's diseases?"

"Sure, I would," a young man whose dark complexion and long, straight nose hinted of mixed parentage. "Every young Sioux's out to count coup, earn himself a warrior name."

"And here you've brought in wagons stuffed with trade goods," the woman added. "It's like a second giveaway. They'd be blind to've missed 'em, and they're sure to take a crack at 'em."

"That's why we've got the army along," Parkinson explained.

"Them?" the trapper cried. "They couldn't fight their way out of a bawdy house. Ain't a one of 'em's fullgrown. Bet they'll run at the first shot."

"No, they'll stand and fight," Lt. Bailey promised. "I know my men. There's not a coward among them."

"All the worse for them," Redding said. "If they ran, some would live. I counted four, five hundred warriors out there this morning. More happening along every hour.

Poor odds, friend's. Poor indeed."

"Hopeless," the trapper muttered.

I myself didn't deem it so, and as for there being half a thousand warriors on Platte River, I thought it unlikely. Tom and I helped the drivers form their wagons into a defensive circle, then drove the horses within.

"So what else can be done, Tom?" I asked.

"Get some rest and leave things to happen as they may."

"You think they'll come?"

"No," he said. "They've been riled up some, but they don't have a quarrel with us. Winter's comin' soon. There's meat to dry and helpless ones to look after. What's the use of comin' up here and gettin' kilt? They know we've got rifles, and some of us can shoot. No chief wants himself remembered as the one who led the young men to their deaths."

"I guess not," I admitted.

That night I sat alone on my blankets, working the stiff muscles of my leg and flexing the knee. It wouldn't be long until I discarded my crutch and was whole again. Off in the distance, the campfires of the Sioux flickered like tiny yellow stars lost in an ebony sky.

I felt confused. A year ago I'd considered the Sioux enemies, heartless murderers who had struck down many among my friends, the Crows. Now I thought only of Two Nations, little Bobtail, Sparrow Hawk, and all the others I'd hunted with and swum with and raced horses against. They were just people, no better nor worse than the rest of us. There were good and bad men among each band. I could muster no hatred for the invisible faces who sat beside those fires. I understood them.

Morning found us preparing to leave. Again Parkinson argued to the contrary.

"It's lunacy!" he said, quivering with rage as the drivers hitched their teams. "We'll be killed, wiped out to the last man. We've got supplies. We're safe here, in this good position."

"No one's safe holed up," Tom argued. "We move fast,

169

and we'll be seein' patrols out o' the fort soon."

"We're not far," I added. "But if you'd rather stay here, do it."

We weren't the only ones intent on leaving. Most of the refugees pleaded to go along, and we shifted supplies around so they could crowd together in the rear wagon. Two others were emptied so that soldiers could ride in them. Men afoot were too tempting a target for a Sioux horseman, and the wagons provided a stable platform for marksmen.

"Well, you comin' or stayin', Parkinson?" Tom finally asked as he prepared to lead the way west along the river.

"Coming," the freighter muttered. "Better to take my chances with the army."

"Sure," I grumbled, knowing it'd be Tom Shea'd get us through, if we escaped at all.

I think we were all a little nervous in the beginning, especially the soldiers. They'd grown accustomed to drilling and marching. Riding in a wagon with a loaded rifle, awaiting a Sioux charge, made them witless and jittery. They'd fire at anything approaching the train, and Tom and I had to shout out a warning when we rode alongside.

Gradually we rolled along, and Scott's Bluff grew smaller and smaller on the horizon. The soldiers began to breathe easier, and I thought perhaps the Sioux might have left the Platte entirely. They hadn't. A bit after noon the first column of them appeared on the opposite bank of the river.

They laughed and chatted and occasionally taunted us. But they kept clear of rifle range. It wasn't death, after all, that they sought.

Those Sioux riders were masters at mock combat. From time to time a group of them would charge into the Platte, howling and screaming and driving icy darts of terror into my heart. Often another band would emerge from a gully on our other flank and mount a second charge. There we'd be, fighting to catch our breath and decide when and where to fire. Then the Sioux would turn away, laughing

170

and thumping their shields with their knees, as if it was the finest joke ever played.

"Wish they'd stop," I grumbled. "They've got me frazzled. Maybe I ought to fire at 'em this time. My Sharps's got the range."

"You kill one, and the rest'll come on us like locusts," Tom warned. "Leave 'em to have their fun. Every hour we're closer to the fort."

Yes, I thought. But what if the Sioux are there ahead of us. What if they've killed all the soldiers, burned the place to the ground? What if Laveda . . .

I couldn't stand the notion. I wanted to kick Pepper into a gallop and race ahead. We could make those last thirty miles. I was certain of it.

I might have done just that if Finds the Enemy hadn't popped up. There he was, coup feathers tied in his hair, naked save for a breechclout, and accompanied by a dozen other young Brules. I spotted Two Nations and Sparrow Hawk a bit farther back. Likely they'd been allowed to come along and hold the horses. Or join in if the danger wasn't too great.

"*Hau,* Prescott!" the warrior called out. "*Hau,* Three Fingers."

It might have been as close to a greeting in English as the broad-shouldered buck could manage. He was all smiles, though, and he held his eager companions in check while Two Nations rode forward.

"Hold your fire!" I shouted to the soldiers. "I know this one."

That didn't have much effect on most of the bluecoats, but Lt. Bailey ordered the muskets lowered, and the soldiers complied.

"Bobtail paid his debt," Two Nation's explained when he joined me along the flank of the wagons. "How many lives do you want us to give you?"

"As many as are needed," I answered. "You wouldn't want to fight us, Two Nations. We've got too many rifles. Lots of people would die, and for what? To prove you're

171

good warriors. We know it already."

"You have many good guns and powder barrels," he pointed out. "You give us some."

"Can't do that," I told him. "They're not mine."

"You'll have to give up something," he demanded. "Finds the Enemy has said it."

I thought to give them Parkinson, or at least part of him, but I figured the Sioux had troubles enough. Instead I rode over to the fourth supply wagon and pulled a box of fresh tobacco from the piled goods.

"Take this," I said. "Save it for the day we'll sit down around a fire and smoke together. The day we know peace again."

"Be a long time," Two Nations said, dropping his chin onto his chest. "Even my own father is not welcome among us now."

"Some wounds are deep," I told him, thinking of my thigh. "But most heal in time."

"Yes," he agreed. He held up the box and howled loudly. Then he raced back to present Finds the Enemy with the gift. In moments the Brules had vanished across the river.

We camped that night near the charred remains of Midway Wells. Just ahead a wagon train formed their camp circle beside the Platte. I could hear music and laughter carried on the wind, and once things were secured, Tom and I rode out to visit.

We were met with suspicious eyes.

"You're late headin' west," Tom observed. "Be snow in the passes soon."

"Sometimes," the gaunt leader of the group replied. "But the almanac says winter'll be late this year."

"Late?" I asked. "What almanac is that?"

"Davy Crockett's Almanac," the captain of the train explained, holding the book in his hand. A sketch of the hero wrestling a bear appeared on the cover, but what I noticed was the year. It read 1852.

"Lord, that's two years past," I complained. "And it

172

wasn't right that year, at least not for this part of the country. Was there ever a frostbiting freeze-your-tail winter to match '52?"

"Not as I recall," Tom agreed. "You got women and kids with you, and your horses are near starved. No oxen for the hard climbs! You'll all of you be dead if you try it."

"Who are you to say so?" the captain asked. "I've read all the guidebooks. I know the way by heart, and although we've had all the misfortunes known to man plaguing us so far, I'm confident we'll get to California before the first snow falls."

"Remind me what he said, Darby," Tom grumbled. "We'll write confident on his grave board."

"He's right about the passes," I said, nodding to Tom. "We've both of us been up the trail and back before."

"Oh?" the captain asked. "And your names?"

"Tom Shea," I said, pointing to Tom. "Me, I'm Darby Prescott."

"We've heard of you, Mr. Shea," the emigrant leader said, grabbing Tom's hand and shaking it heartily. "Lord, what good fortune. I'm Jeremiah Conover, late of Indiana. We could sure use an experienced scout."

"Even I couldn't get you across this year," Tom warned. "Not alive. Maybe you can hole up at Fort Laramie till spring."

"We mean to be rich by then," Conover complained. "Come with us. Bring the boy, too."

"He's no boy," Shea objected. "And he's not fool enough to freeze in the high country. Really just stopped over to see who you were and tell you we've got a band of soldiers with us. You might care to follow us tomorrow, seein' how you're in Sioux country."

"But I thought they were friendly?" Conover asked.

"Not lately," Tom said, shaking his head. "Don't you follow what happened up the trail? There was a lieutenant got himself and thirty men kilt attackin' the Sioux. The big chief of the Brules, Conquerin' Bear, went down, too.

173

Now all the Sioux've put on their dark eyes and are huntin' white men."

"Didn't know," Conover confessed. "Well, we're certainly glad of your offer. We'll do our best to keep pace. Think over my offer, too. We'd pay you well."

"Buy me a handsome grave marker, I'll bet. Good luck with, you tomorrow," Tom concluded. "And afterward. You're sure to need it."

"We aim to get on, friend," Conover said as we turned away. "God willing, we shall."

"Fools," Tom muttered. "Pure gold-plated fools."

I nodded my agreement.

That night as I lay between my blankets, I was visited by a strange dream. Shadowy figures walked a frozen world. One called out my name. Another cried a warning.

"Darby, don't go," Laveda's voice whispered. "I need you."

"You'll all of you wind up frozen!" a different voice shouted. "Heed my orders, you men. Stay here. Leave the dead to themselves."

The world grew brighter then, and I saw a parade of brightly dressed children scattering flowers along a velvet path. Bright reds and yellows mingled as the light-footed youngsters danced and sang.

"Here's the gate to heaven," they sang. "Here's a world without pain."

There were other words, too, but I didn't hear them. Instead I watched a line of familiar faces. There was little Jamie McNamara, his red hair bright as ever.

"Comin', Darby?" he asked, peeling off his clothes. "Let's catch a quick swim."

Mama came next. Her gentle hands took my head and pressed it to her bosom.

"I've missed you so, Darby."

Papa rested a weathered hand on my shoulder and nodded silently, sadly.

Up ahead the velvet path dissolved in a cloud. Through a hole I peered down at a world painted white. Tall pines

174

were clothed in shawls of ice and powdered with white mists. Amid this scene a line of tiny wagons lay smothered. Women and children coughed and huddled as their last ounce of life flickered and went out.

"I'm death come to walk the earth," an eerie voice spoke. "I've come for you, Darby Prescott."

I awoke with a start. I was soaking with cold sweat, and I could barely move. I closed my eyes, and the phantom voice called me again.

"No!" I shouted.

There was a stirring among the soldiers, and a pair of them raced over. They gazed down on me, shivering with cold fear, and their eyes drew back in alarm.

"It's nothing," I reassured them. "Just a nightmare."

"Oh," one of the young privates said. "I get 'em sometimes, too. They pass."

"Sure," I agreed.

"Been dreamin' again, eh?" a weary Tom Shea asked. "See anythin'?"

"More'n I cared to," I told him. "Mama, Papa, even Jamie. And a phantom calling my name."

"Ghosts! Put the fool up in front of the whole Sioux nation, and he'd never flinch. But put a shape in his dreams, and he's come apart like a bad pair o' moccasins. Bear-killer Prescott, the Crows call you. Remember that? Well, Bear-killer, catch yourself some rest. Tomorrow's a long day."

"I'll try," I told him. But each time I closed my eyes, the spectre returned, and I finally sat beside the wagon and watched the stars move across the dark sky overhead. That, at least, could bring me no harm. It was familiar.

Chapter Eighteen

We rode up to Doyle Marcus's American Fur Company outpost late the following afternoon. The last two or three miles we were escorted by lines of boisterous Crows. They darted in between the wagons and back out again, waving blankets overhead and shrieking like eagles. It was a sight to remember!

Behind us, scattered across three miles of open plain, the wagon train lumbered along. I'd ridden alongside them four or five times, offering encouragement or trading taunts with the children. I thought to kindle hope or spur defiance, but mostly I witnessed the weariness and dejection that would spell death come first snow.

"Don't take 'em to heart, Darby," Tom advised. "You won't sleep nights if you do. We got our own concerns."

Concerns, yes. Problems, no. The lead wagon arrived at Marcus's storehouse to the sound of a bugle blown by a young sandy-haired corporal. Marcus then stepped out with a tray of mugs and pointed to a beer keg resting against the front door.

"Bless you all, boys!" he shouted. "Soon as those wagons are unloaded, the drinks are on me."

Well, I never saw so many soldiers volunteer to help empty a dozen wagons. In fact, Tom and I had to almost shoot one or two before they left the last two wagons alone.

"These are bound for the Bordens' store, up at the

fort," I explained. "Anything you take off just has to go back in."

The soldiers weren't convinced until Clyde Parkinson affirmed our story. He handed us a pair of vouchers to sign, accepting delivery of the goods.

"I'll turn 'em over to Miss Borden," I told the freighter. "She'll want to look everything over."

"The best thing about the conclusion of this trip is getting free from you two," Parkinson complained. "Never have I seen a pair of men so utterly unfit for civilized company."

"Comin' from you, sir," I said, imitating his Georgia accent and making a mock bow, "I take that as high praise. High praise indeed."

The soldiers laughed heartily, but their lieutenant hushed them. We were no longer on the trail, and a man like Parkinson—one with Washington connections—deserved pampering. I left them all to enjoy the keg, collected the two drivers, and got them started for the fort.

"It won't take too long, will it?" a round-faced teamster named Schmidt asked. "I'll bet those jaspers have that whole keg drunk 'fore I get my first sip!"

"You just concentrate on getting this wagon up the trail," I told him. "One thing Doyle Marcus is never short of is strong spirits."

The drivers laughed, and I rode on ahead. I could glimpse the post outbuildings, and I imagined Laveda waiting anxiously in her doorway, eager to welcome me home. The Crows had gone along ahead, and surely everyone knew we were on our way. Nevertheless we rolled onward with hardly a nod of acknowledgement. Soldiers went on lounging on the barracks' porch. Two men polishing the brass fieldpiece paid us no heed. And finally, when I waved the teamsters to a halt beside the door of the Borden store, I saw no Laveda waiting. As a matter of fact, the trading post appeared utterly and completely deserted.

I was dumbstruck and terribly disappointed. Jonas Redding had offered us a kinder welcome, and he thought us responsible for the likely ruin of his trade. Here Tom and I'd gotten these wagons across the windswept plain despite pain and peril, and our thanks was . . . nothing.

"Laveda?" I called. "Laurence? Your supplies are here."

"Where do they go?" Schmidt asked. "We unload quick, eh? Got to hurry back to get a nip of that beer."

I pointed to the storeroom, and the two drivers hurried to roll barrels and carry baskets inside. They paid no heed to proper placement, and I said nothing. Bitterness was welling up in my chest so that it threatened to choke me.

"Comin' along?" Schmidt called when the last of the supplies had been unloaded. "Mug of beer'll lift your chin, Prescott. Shea?"

"I'm behind you," Tom said, urging them on. "Be along later," he told me, winking. "She can't be far. Have a look around."

I approached the parade ground, taking care to march along the edges like the soldiers did. Sometimes a young lieutenant would take particular offense at a civilian treading upon that privileged sod, and I figured I didn't need a run-in with soldiers just now.

"Have you seen Miss Borden?" I asked a pair of loafing privates.

"Who?" one of them asked.

"Laveda Borden," I said. "Tall young gal with hair blond as yellow morning."

"Nope," the second said, grinning. "I'd remembered one looked like that."

Up by the post headquarters, I ran across Capt. Powers.

"Have you seen Laveda Borden?" I asked.

"Why, yes," he answered. "She and her brother are over at my house with Mrs. Powers. Having tea, I believe."

"Thanks," I said, leaning on my crutch and gazing toward the house. Life was a vexation, and women were the worst part of it. I took a deep breath and resumed my journey.

As I hobbled along, I tried to make sense of the captain's remarks. Having tea? Laveda? And Laurence? Well,

178

who would have thought I'd be hunting buffalo with the Sioux a year ago?

I knocked lightly on the door of the captain's house, and a spry Negro woman in her early thirties quickly appeared.

"I've come in search of Miss Laveda Borden," I told her. "She here?"

The servant gazed at my dust-covered boots, at the split side of my trousers, and the cottonwood crutch.

"Who you say you were?" she asked, blocking the doorway with both arms.

"Darby Prescott," I said, anxiously tapping my crutch. "Is she here or not?"

"I'll have a see," she answered. The door closed, and I heard a bolt slide into place. Like as not Mrs. Powers and Laveda were that moment hearing that a sandy-haired devil was standing at the door with a big stick, no doubt aiming to murder everyone in the house.

After a bit, the door reopened. Laurence stood there, grinning.

"It's all right, Delores," he told the maid. "It's ole Darby, all right. In bad need of a wash and some dinner, too."

"You haven't got much on your bones, either," I told the young man. "Can I see Laveda?"

"She'll be along," he said, joining me on the porch. "Has some business to finish up."

"Over tea," I grumbled.

"Yeah," he said, laughing. "Tea. This Miz Powers is one for fancy living, I tell you. Has servants and silver teapots and fine china. We've got some odds and ends I picked up off the wagon trail or bought off emigrants needing flour, but she puts a palace to shame, Darby."

"Got the supplies in," I told him. "I guess we could go along and start putting them in their proper places."

"Looks to me like you'd be better served with a long rest," he said, eyeing my leg. "Lord, would you look at that scar!"

179

I glanced down. My trouser leg flapped in the light breeze, exposing the jagged black lines cut into the pale flesh of my thigh.

"We had some trouble," I explained. "Ole No Nose happened along."

"He's played a trick or two on the soldiers, too. Killed three men from a wagon train last week. That leg'll mend, won't it?"

"Mostly has," I replied. "Soon I'll put this ole crutch in the fireplace and be free again."

"Laveda won't like that much. To hear her talk, what you need's a ball and chain. That'd keep you around longer."

"Guess it would," I agreed, laughing.

We made our way back to the storehouse. Tom hadn't come back, and Pepper stomped around, complaining I hadn't seen to his needs.

"I'll do it," Laurence said when I reached for the weary pony's reins. "You get yourself in the store and find some decent trousers."

"We've got the supplies to see to first," I reminded him.

"They'll wait. There's nobody standing in line to buy flour just now anyway. I'll get some water heated, and you can scrub up."

"And Laveda?"

"She'll be an hour jabbering away with that Miz Powers. They're planning themselves a harvest party. Harvest? As if we've got anything planted out here!"

"Not a bad notion, though," I observed. "Do some of us good to forget our troubles."

"Figure to do a lot of dancing, do you?" he asked, laughing.

"Tend my horse, Laurence. I'll be waiting for the bath."

A half hour later I lay in a wooden tub beside the cook stove, soaking in soothing hot water. I felt like I'd scrubbed a month's trail dust from my hide. Likely I had. For the first time I'd gotten a really good look at the jagged scar on my leg.

"It's not bear claws," I mumbled. "It's a real battle scar, one that reminds you of the pain."

Laurence popped in and out of the kitchen. Once he brought me a file to grind down my toenails. Later he produced a razor.

"Not used to seeing you with a beard," he said, studying my face a moment. "Makes you look older. Maybe I should try letting my whiskers grow. What do you think?"

"Thought you *were* letting 'em grow," I said, grinning.

"Get shaved," he said, scowling as he pushed the razor into my right hand. "Here's a mirror."

"Don't like me with a beard?" I asked.

"Laveda hates whiskers. It's her you plan to please, isn't it? I'm not much use as a dance partner."

"Nor am I just now," I grumbled, staring at my scarred thigh. "But I won't stay lame forever."

I was still soaking in the tub when Laveda returned to the store. She poked her head into the kitchen, and I hurriedly covered the open top of the tub with a length of cloth.

"See you're home," she said.

"You keep looking, you're apt to see more'n that," I retorted.

"I guess I'm missing a real treat then. Delores, Mrs. Powers's maid, said your trousers were flapping in the breeze so a modest woman had to turn aside."

"Well, a modest woman wouldn't be disturbing a fellow during his bath."

"Maybe not, she said, laughing. "Want me to get my shears and clip your hair? It's gotten wild."

"You'll let me get dressed first, I hope."

"Well, I don't know," she said, grinning. "I might just grab the shears and come on over. You're gone weeks, and nary a whisper to tell me you're all right."

"Who'd I whisper to, Laveda? Trail's hardly full of dispatch riders. I didn't exactly get swamped by your letters! I come back, and nobody greets me save a bunch of loafing soldiers and a few horseflies."

181

"I'll make it up to you tonight," she promised.

"Tonight?"

"That's why I was at the captain's. Mrs. Powers and I are planning a harvest dance. A wagon train pulled in, too, so we'll invite those people, the soldiers, everyone for miles."

"Crows, too?"

"I don't think the captain's lady would favor that idea," she said, scowling. "She's a real lady, attended a women's seminary in Philadelphia and everything. Darby, you should see her gowns! I'm borrowing one for the dance."

"You know I've got a lame leg, Laveda. I don't think I'll be doing much high-stepping."

"You don't have to," she replied. "The piano's still here, and one of the wagon people tuned it. It sounds wondrous. You'll play, won't you?"

"Only if you promise to spend part of the evening on the bench with me. I get melancholy playing music all alone."

"I'll be with you every second."

"Not every one," I argued. "You ought to have a bit of fun, too, and you wouldn't want a revolt among the soldiers."

"Guess not," she said, grinning.

She left the kitchen, and I busied myself rinsing off the soap. I finally climbed out of the tub, rubbed the moisture out of my weary hide, and stepped into the new cotton shirt and woolen overalls Laurence had found. A bit later Laveda clipped my hair, and I felt like a human being again.

The dance was quite an event. Soldiers put on their best blue coats, and the officers' wives arrived in full dresses, wearing ribbons in their hair. Parkinson's teamsters appeared clean-shaven and a bit wobbly from their drinking spell. Tom even showed up, though he was a bit out of place in his elk robe and weatherbeaten leather hat.

The wagon folk put on their Sunday best, too, but that wasn't saying much. Most of the children arrived barefoot, and hard days on the trail made them a little too eager to help themselves to the generous platters of food laid on tables for the whole throng. I gazed at worn knees, at bleeding gums, and legs dotted with flea and mosquito bites. I don't think there was a decent coat among the whole company, and when the wind began to blow, the little ones huddled together in misery.

I did my best to stir them to song. I played and played, until my fingers began to swell and my wrists ached. Finally I could do it no more, and Laveda helped me to a nearby table.

"They're in a bad way," she told me. "I swapped bags of flour for pocket watches and wedding bands today. They won't make it west this year, will they?"

"If they try, the children will surely die," I said, sighing. "Tom told 'em as much, but nobody was listening. You can't help a body who doesn't have ears or sense."

"They asked me if I could recommend a guide," she whispered. "I told them to ask Tom. If anyone alive could get them through, he could."

"You mean the two of us could, don't you?"

"I mean Tom. You've got a place here, Darby. I need your help. There's so much to do before winter hits."

"I thought you understood, Laveda. Tom and I're partners."

"He wouldn't stand in the way of you being happy."

"Wouldn't have to. I wouldn't consider letting him try it himself."

"Even if he asked you?"

"Don't you understand anything?" I asked her. "Only reason he'd leave would be so he could go off and get his fool self killed. He's all alone, just like I was when he took me in. What kind of man would I be to cast him aside now, when my need's less and his is greater?"

"I suppose you're right. Truth is, there's plenty of work for four people."

"At least till spring," I told her. "Then we'll probably head for Independence and pick up a company bound for

Oregon."

"And what of me? I thought maybe we'd be speaking to a preacher soon."

"It's pushing things, Laveda. A lot. I'm still half buffalo tail and trail dust. Give it time."

"Time?" she growled. "Time? Give me time! I've heard that till I'm blue in the face. It's late enough, Darby. I've waited and waited, while you hauled goods to Green River, while you escorted Parkinson to the fort. It's time now. I need you."

"I know," I told her. "Part of me wants to stay with you forever. But the rest of me itches for open country and cloudless skies."

"Yes," she said, resting her head on my shoulder. "My trouble is that I love both halves."

I felt the warmth flow from her into my chest, and I wrapped my arm around her. I felt a wonderful sense of belonging. And at the same time I knew nothing had changed in the least.

We left the others and walked out along the river as we had a thousand times before. Overhead a million stars glittered in the heavens, and the crisp autumn air brought new life to my dust-choked lungs. It was a strange walk, for I don't think a dozen words were shared in two hours. Then, when we finally returned to the trading post, Laveda gripped my hands and whispered, "I love you, Darby."

"Got kind of fond of you, too," I replied. She then wrapped her hands around my chest and squeezed tightly. I drew her to me, and for a time we were two parts of the same whole. Then I stepped away.

"Darby?" she called softly.

"Time we took to our blankets," I said. "We'll talk more tomorrow."

Tom was waiting for me when I limped through the door of the storehouse.

"Did a fair job with the music tonight," he told me. "Was good for an old man's heart to hear so much singin'

184

and carryin' on. Got to missin' the trail lately."

"Those wagon people came to you, didn't they?" I asked.

"Came to offer me a scoutin' job. They've got troubles, what with worn-out stock and the people not much better. Asked me to get 'em through South Pass, maybe up to Jim Bridger's fort."

"What'd you say?"

"Told 'em I'd have to ask my partner. We still partners, son?"

"Till you decide otherwise."

"I been thinkin' on it considerable. Seems to me that little gal needs a good man, Darby. I'm fond o' you, and I like the cut o' Laveda Borden better every day I'm 'round her. You've got the beginnin' of a home here. Might be you should put down some roots and plant yourself here."

"I'm twenty years old," I told him. "If I was Sioux or Crow, I'd have a wife now, maybe even some little ones. But life out here's so uncertain. I might've died from that gash in my leg."

"Death can come anywhere," he told me. "For a lonely man, it's just the passin' of a cloud past the sun. Got no meanin' to it. For a man who's built himself a family, there's a future."

"How come you never married after the Crow woman's death?"

"Don't know for certain. Partly I never figured there would be anybody to touch my heart like she did. Hard to go from a buffalo roast to shoe leather, you see, son. Was easier to cut the feelin' part out of me."

"Didn't do much of a job at it. I see you with the wagon kids. You're as generous with them as you were with me," I told him. "It's why you're talking to me about taking these wagons on when you know they'll wind up in some snow-blocked pass dead of cold and starvation."

"Maybe so," he grumbled.

"Laveda wants me to stay the winter. I told her I would if you did. We're partners, after all."

185

"You've passed the need, Darby. Man looks to a woman for more than sharin' a trail."

"And if we get hitched and have kids, who'll they look to for a grandpa's tales? Not Laurence. I was thinking maybe we could get us a few Indian ponies, start breeding 'em. Then when people come through on worn-out horses, we'd swap, fatten up the spent horses, and trade 'em to the next batch."

"Burkett does that at Green River."

"Makes some fair deals, too. That'd keep us busy, Tom, that and helping with the store."

"Got it all planned, do you?"

"Either that or head east come spring and get us another wagon train."

"Dependin' on how you and Laveda suit each other, eh?"

"That's it exactly," I admitted. "And depending, too, on how well we do in the horse trade."

"Well, I suppose a man could do worse," he said, sighing. "I'll sleep on it."

"Do that," I urged. "And then say yes."

Chapter Nineteen

The first snow came a week later. It seemed only yesterday I'd walked in my shirtsleeves beside the Laramie
River with Laveda. The Crow boys had splashed naked
in the shallows the day before. But that was life on the
plains. One day the sun blazed high in the afternoon sky.
The next the weeping moon gazed somberly upon a
world frozen white.

"Winter's come," Tom grumbled, as he sat rocking
away beside the fireplace at the Bordens' quarters back
of the trading post.

"Early this year," I noted as I put another log on the
fire. My leg was aching, and I sat beside the hearth in
hope that the warmth might ease the suffering.

"It could have waited till November," Laveda said as
she knelt beside me. "Pity those wagon folks. They'll
never get through to California now."

"Nope," Tom agreed, staring in his far-off way. "Knew
it. Told 'em so, in fact, but who listens to them that
know?"

"Nobody," Laveda said bitterly.

"Good thing we got all that wood cut, eh, Darby?"
Laurence asked. "Now you've got your leg cut apart, it's
just me works that ax."

"I'll lend a hand tomorrow," I offered.

"Wasn't looking for help," Laurence said, frowning. "I
was just thinking how sometimes you do a thing, and at

the time it seems like a lot of nonsense. Stacking stove wood under clear skies, with the sun half-melting you as you work. It turned out smarter than I thought."

"Stick around ole Bear-killer," Tom said, laughing to himself. "You'll pick up a thing or two. I taught him most of it myself, you know."

"In a tale-spinning mood, Tom?" I asked. "I could stand a story."

"Not tonight," he said gloomily. "But you might raise a tune on that fool mouth organ o' yours."

I drew the instrument out of my pocket and obliged him. I chose the old, familiar trail songs, and the Bordens sang along. Tom might have joined in once, but he seemed oddly distant that night. He never looked on winter as the best of times, but he was more at odds with the season than ever.

"Was a fool thing to do, ridin' down to Kearny," he said, when I took a breather from the music. "Should've been up in the Medicine Bow country, gettin' a cabin started."

"The old one's still there," I told him. "The Crows told me."

"Too late to get meat in," he muttered. "Too late to fell trees and season a woodpile. Just plain too late!"

"Tom, what's troubling you?" I asked. "Got cabin fever?"

"No," he said, managing a faint smile for Laveda. "Just seem old tonight. Feelin' the years, I suppose."

"Papa used to say that," Laurence remarked. "If we'd got those buffalo when we rode out with the Le Tours, we'd have enough meat to last us till spring. And Papa died in the effort! I should've seen it through."

"You looked after your papa," I said, as Laveda walked over to her brother and took his chin in her hands.

"For some, winter's been here a long time," she whispered. "Won't pass for a long time."

"No, but we can bring in fresh meat," I declared.

"Tom and I've hunted elk lots of times in late October, even on into November."

"Best season for hides," Tom pointed out. "Animals put on their heavy coats for the cold months."

"I'd look good in an elk robe, don't you think, Sis?" Laurence asked. "You'll take me along, won't you, Darby? Tom?"

"Not a thing lightly undertaken," I cautioned.

"Well, it's for blamed certain you're not going, Darby Prescott!" Laveda stormed. "There's plenty here to keep the four of us busy till spring, and you're too thin by half to ride out into a blizzard."

"It's not a blizzard," I objected. "Just some snow."

"You can't even walk right!" she complained.

"I can," I argued, tossing my crutch onto the embers of the fire. Tom laughed, and Laurence gave a whoop.

"When do we leave?" the boy asked.

"Never," Laveda said, planting a hand on each hip. "There are Sioux out there, remember? Thousands of them. They'd like nothing better than to hunt down a few whites, especially those friendly with the Crows."

I frowned. It was true. The Crows camped on the Platte had done a fearful lot of raiding against the Sioux winter camps. There'd always been bad blood between the two tribes, but it was worse than ever just now. The Crows had left to winter in the Big Horns, and a few Sioux bands had returned to the Platte basin.

"Sioux won't bother us," Laurence said confidently. "Darby's on good terms with the Brules, and I speak more than a little of their language. We won't stay gone too long, will we, Tom?"

"Two, three days," Tom said, stoking the fire. "Would taste good, a thick elk steak fried up with some o' Laveda's honey bread and a few ears of corn."

"Darby, that leg needs rest," she asserted. "You know it. It hurts you even now, sitting by a warm fire. It's certain to be worse out there in the open, with the wind howling and the snows burying the earth."

"Might at that," Tom said, sighing.

"The leg doesn't want rest," I argued. "It wants a hard ride or two, steep climbing in the hills, clear air to breathe, and an empty horizon."

"You're a fool if you believe that," Laveda said, shaking her head. "Haven't you bled enough for one year? You warn the wagon people not to tempt fate. Then you turn around and do the very thing yourself!"

"It's different," I told her. "Tom and I've wintered in the mountains. We know when to take cover and when to start a hunt."

"And when the clouds smother the sun, and the sweat between your toes turns to ice, will you say that still?"

"More'n likely," I replied with a grin. "Wagon scout's bound to be half-fool at least, crossing this sunbaked, snow-plagued country more'n once. But hunting's another matter. We'll ride west two days, looking for game. What we find, we'll shoot. If we see nothing, we'll come back. Either way, we'll be home in three days' time."

"Half a week," she complained. "*If* you keep to your word. And what am I to do all this time, sit around darning socks?"

"Lots of wood you can chop, Sis," Laurence suggested.

"You!" Laveda fumed. "Chop, eh? You'll be lucky if I don't start with your toes."

"Good thing I've been running races with the Crows," Laurence told us. "Used to be she could catch me."

"Now I'll have to creep up in the dead of night and hack away while you're sleeping," Laveda said, casting a chilling gaze at her younger brother. "Who knows what else I'll cut? An ear. Your nose maybe. That wagging tongue for sure."

"That's not so funny, Laveda," Laurence said, stepping back. "I tell you, fellows, she's pure devil when she takes the head off a chicken!"

"Or a boy," she said, grinning.

"Well, I wasn't so set on takin' Laurence here," Tom said, "but I'm hanged if I can think of any peril on the

190

trail equal to an ax-totin' sister."

I laughed along with him, and the Bordens exchanged scowls. We then shifted the subject to preparing for the hunt. Tom and I soon set about assembling our thickest hides and heaviest boots. Even so, I figured it would take two days to sew some new buckskin trousers for myself, and outfit Laurence so he wouldn't freeze the first night out.

We set out early on a bright clear morning. The November air was crisp, and in spite of the dull aching of my left leg, I welcomed the adventure. Once I was atop Pepper, the world seemed familiar, and I was at home.

Tom led the way south and west into the mountains. Elk loved the high country, the massive pine and spruce forests of the Medicine Bow country. That was a land I favored myself, and glancing back at Laurence, I read the same excitement in his bright, eager eyes.

"Blow us a tune, Darby," Tom urged, and I put the mouth organ to my lips. The cold steel near froze me, and I had to stick the instrument under my arm for half an hour before I could tolerate its touch.

"Figure we'll each get us one?" Laurence asked as we began the long, gradual climb through the foothills. "I could stand an elk robe myself. Sparrow Hawk showed me a fine one last summer. We buy 'em up, you know, but they fetch too good a price to keep the good ones for ourselves. Figure you can make one out of the hide for me, Darby?"

"Son?" Tom asked, turning to me with a grin.

"You'll never learn to do it that way," I said. "I'll *teach* you, help you work out the stiffness. I'll show you how to scrape the flesh, how to tan it. But you'll do it yourself. An elk hide's to be earned, eh, Tom?"

"Always," he agreed.

"That's how it's done among the Sioux," Laurence said, nodding respectfully.

"They're not particular wrong about such things," Tom said. "Fort soldiers may not say so, but then they wouldn't know a hawk's talon from a pine cone without some sergeant tellin' 'em."

"Men teach the boys, and women teach the girls," Laurence went on to say. "Fathers or uncles pass things along. I got no papa now, you know. Nor uncles, either. Just a sister."

"She'll teach you more than working elk hides," I told him.

"But there's things she doesn't know."

"Then you hunt up the man who does," Tom said somberly. "It's the way an orphan gets along. And if you're lucky, that man'll turn out to be a good one."

"I figure he is already," Laurence said with a grin as he closed the gap between us.

We were weaving our way through snow-draped pines a bit after midday when I spotted the elk. There were a dozen of them, and they dug through the snow to chew the soft grass. A young bull kept watch on the flank nearest us, and I only just managed to wave Tom to cover and pull Pepper behind a large boulder before the cautious animal spotted me.

"Got lots to our favor," Tom whispered, as we dismounted and drew our rifles from their scabbards. "Wind's in our face, and I don't think they've seen us. To get a sure shot, we need to close in. Care to lead, Darby?"

"Stay close to Tom," I cautioned Laurence. "Let him be your guide."

The boy nodded, and the three of us made our way through the trees, slowly but surely closing the range. When we were fifty feet or so away, Tom tapped me on the shoulder. I loaded my Sharps, then fixed the cap in place, and cocked the hammer. My companions did likewise.

Tom examined the animals below. He pointed Laurence toward a doe near the center of the herd. He motioned me toward the far left, where a trio of bull elk grazed. He himself aimed at a giant of a bull with a rack of antlers to match any I'd ever seen.

Tom raised the five fingers of his good right hand, then counted down to one. I waited patiently, confident in my rifle and my aim. When the last finger vanished, Laurence dropped the doe. I blasted the middle buck, and Tom fired at the giant. The first two fell as though dropped from the sky. The old grandfather elk jumped up and back, and I saw bright red blood flow from his chest.

The rest of the elk took instantly to flight. The grandfather watched them go, then turned in an opposite direction, and dragged himself across the snow-covered hillside.

"I got mine clean," Laurence boasted. "You hit yours, too, Darby. Tom, what happened?"

"I kilt him," Tom said, staring at the bloody splotches on the ground. "He's dead. Only trouble is, he don't know it."

I thought I detected a trace of a smile on Tom's face.

"Laurence," I said, "Make the throat cuts and start the skinning. I'll go with Tom."

"You stay here," Tom barked. "This is 'tween me and Granpappy Elk."

I believe just then an invisible bond linked the two old-timers, and nothing would have kept Tom from stalking that bull elk.

"Fine trophy those antlers'd be," Laurence remarked enviously. "Bet we could get a fair offer for 'em at the trading post. Thirty, maybe even fifty dollars."

"Tom won't bring in the antlers," I explained. "Hide and meat, sure, for there's need of 'em."

"Maybe I ought to follow him, take those antlers myself."

"You get to know Tom, you'll come to understand his ways," I said, placing a firm hand on Laurence's shoulder. "It's a good way. It keeps you going when the days are long and the hills are steep. And you take your rest knowing you can rise in the morning and hold your head up high."

Laurence flashed a puzzled look at me, and I grinned back. Words were never meant to convey that sort of truth. It had to be lived to be learned.

We had the animals skinned and butchered, and still Tom didn't return. I finally decided it was time to have a look. Leaving Laurence to watch over our kills, I set out on Tom's trail. There was no trouble following. The elk's path was painted with red splotches.

I found Tom a hundred yards or so ahead. He was standing on a rocky outcropping, looking down at the dying agonies of the great bull elk. I stepped to his side, and he gave me a welcoming smile.

"Fool elk's dead," he muttered. "Anybody can tell it. He's bled himself white, and he's only got to lay down and get the dyin' over. Stubborn ole cuss! Won't give up."

"I know the type," I said, grinning. "Got him for a partner."

"Figure so?" he asked solemnly. "Figure I'm dead and don't know it?"

"No," I replied. "That wasn't my meaning at all. I meant you always go on, even when it seems impossible. Don't give up."

The elk turned then and stared as if to plead for an end.

"It's hurting, Tom," I told him.

"You know, son, pain's sometimes the only thing let's you know you're still livin'. But in the end, you welcome its passin'."

He raised his rifle and fired. The elk dipped its head into the snow and fell, finally and completely dead.

"Let's get him skinned," Tom said, waving me down the hillside. "Be a fine coat from this one. Figure you can teach the boy what he needs to know 'fore he works it soft."

"You mean let him work this hide?" I asked.

"Make a robe to be remembered, don't you think?

194

That's a thing best given to one who's got time left to make memories."

"You're not Methuselah," I complained.

"No?" he asked. "Sure feel like it sometimes."

We made camp atop the mountain that night. Elk steaks simmered in a frying pan, and stars danced through a strange mist overhead. When the meat had cooked, we ate hungrily, mixing in wild onions and some carrots Laveda had sent along. I never felt as hungry, and I don't recall eating half as much before or after.

Once we'd eaten our fill, Tom took a look at the horses, and I dug three trenches into which I laid the glowing embers of our fire.

"Cover 'em with dirt," I told Laurence, "and they'll keep you warm through the night."

"You sure?" he asked, gazing at the shroud even now draping the moon. "Feels a storm coming."

"Could be," I admitted as I rubbed the stiffness out of my leg. "Good thing we didn't ride any farther from the fort. We'd have a devil of a time getting all this meat back."

Tom returned, and he gave Laurence a hand filling in the trenches. I then handed over a blanket roll to each of my companions and spread my own over the warm ground.

"Strange night," I observed as the wind howled eerily through the pines all around us.

"Strange night," Laurence agreed.

Tom said nothing. I could tell his mind was elsewhere, wandering through a hundred memories. I pulled my blankets tight, then managed to scramble out of my heavy clothes. A man got to sweating during the day, and that sweat froze solid on him at night. It wasn't any too pleasant an experience!

I never could tell exactly when the snow began falling. By the time the drifts tickled my nose and woke me from a sound sleep, four or five inches had fallen. Tom was near buried, and Laurence was shivering like the last November leaf on a willow.

"Wake up," I urged, shaking Laurence to life. I then roused Tom. The three of us retreated to a protruding shelf of rock and burrowed ourselves in.

"Came on us sudden, wouldn't you say?" Laurence asked. "Laveda'll be fit to be tied."

"Felt it all day," Tom grumbled. "Should've turned homeward after shootin' them elk. But I wanted a last night under the stars."

"Not many you can see," I pointed out.

It was then the phantom appeared. It was willowy white, with savage eyes and a terrifying whine of a voice. Laurence covered his eyes, and I fell back against the hard rock wall, shuddering as I remembered my strange dream coming back from Fort Kearny.

"Ain't spirit," Tom declared. "Can't be."

But the demon hurried toward us, flaying its hands and screaming like a singed hawk.

"No!" I hollered.

"Darby, what is it?" Tom asked, gripping my shoulders.

"Death," I said, shivering as icy fingers gripped my insides. "Lord, help us! Help us!"

But we were out there alone, and the Lord had his eyes elsewhere.

Chapter Twenty

The shadowy, ice-covered figure stumbled toward us. In the heavy mist he lumbered toward us like a wounded buffalo, his hairy chin dripping frothy icicles. It might have been a monster plunging through Devil's Gate, and I shrank away from it.

"Help . . . me," a faint voice called. "Help!"

Then the frozen specter collapsed in the snow.

It was Tom who hurried toward it. He knelt beside the ivory shape and shook it like he was rousing a dozing boy.

"Darby, give me a hand with him," Tom called.

I blinked my eyes, as if that might clear the mist. It didn't. Tom called again though, and I pulled on my clothes. Then I struggled to reach the two shadowy lumps ahead. My hands trembled as I reached Tom and bent over the frozen shape.

"Help us," a voice mumbled again and again.

"Let's get him to shelter," Tom urged.

I grabbed a stiff arm, and Tom took the other. We then dragged the ice-covered shape to the outcropping, and I scurried around, collecting bits of wood for a fire. Tom was already lighting a bit of dry kindling, and I began peeling the damp bark from the logs with my knife.

Laurence huddled in his blankets and watched with alarm.

"Give me a hand with the fire," I told him, and he

crawled over. He drew out a knife and cut shavings of pine. I nodded as he fed them to the sputtering white smoke that struggled to ignite. My larger slivers finally began to blacken, and a bright yellow flare erupted.

Gradually as I stacked larger and larger sticks on the fire, it cracked into life. Thick gray smoke burgeoned forth, and a warm glow spread across the frozen ground and through the tips of my fingers, up my arms, into my chest. Laurence rubbed his hands over the flame, and Tom dragged our frozen guest over. We pried his saturated woolens from his pale flesh and rubbed life back into his ashen frame.

Bit by bit the fire restored life. At the same time, I recovered my senses and began to slow my heartbeat. Laurence huddled close by, his wide eyes betraying his own fears. Only Tom remained calm. He was like that, of course, for he'd seen it all before.

"Puts me in mind o' that boy you drug into our camp short o' Fort Hall," he told me. "Nigh as frozen."

I stared at the grizzled features of the mysterious stranger. His matted beard had turned white, and his wild, fear-crazed eyes blazed intently.

"Who are you?" Tom asked. "Where've you come from?"

"Mountains," the stranger mumbled. "Help."

"Who are you?" Tom asked again.

"Stewart," the shivering man managed to say. "Help us."

"Help who?" Tom asked. "Who?" Stewart seemed lost, bewildered, and Tom gripped the man's shoulders and shook him hard. "Where've you come from, fool? Who're we to help?"

"Wagons," Stewart said, dropping his eyes to the ground. "The train. God help us. The little ones . . ."

"A wagon train?" I asked. "Up here?"

"Took the cutoff," he explained. "Through the mountains."

"What cutoff?" Tom cried. "Which mountains?"

"Medicine Bow. The Medicine Bow!" Stewart screamed. "Indian scout led us through. Shortcut to California. Snows hit, and they left us."

"There's no shortcut to California through this country!" Tom shouted, angrily shaking the stunned Stewart. "No wagon trails at all."

"It's just rocks -and ridges!" I exclaimed. "And you took a company in here?"

"Yes," he said, sobbing. "Was an Indian. Said he knew the way. Tried to hire a scout at Fort Laramie, but they all said it was too late to go west."

"It was," I said grimly.

"Know that now!" Stewart shouted. "But we're trapped, and the stock's all gone. People are freezing! The Indians ran off with the horses, and we lost two men trying to stop them."

"What Indians?" I asked, feeling a nervous sliver of ice work its way down my spine.

"Friendly sort, with good English. Had a bit of his ear shot away and a misshapen nose."

"No Nose," I said, staring somberly at Tom.

"Then they're all of 'em dead," Tom told me.

"Dead?" Stewart cried. "No! You've got to help 'em!"

"We've run across No Nose before," I explained. "He's put on his bad face toward the whites. Isn't just horses he was after. He wanted blood."

"Can't be," Stewart whined, glancing at Tom, me, even young Laurence, in hopes of hearing some encouragement. None was forthcoming, and he dropped his face into his hands and started sobbing.

"You can't be certain they're all dead," Laurence whispered. "Might be some are out there right now, freezing from the cold."

"And how would we find them?" I asked. "Look out there. You can't see ten feet in front of you, and snow's swallowed any trace of a trail."

"You're not even going to try?" the boy asked, turning to Tom. "You know this country better than I do, Tom.

199

There's only a couple of gaps you could run wagons through. One's just a mile or so from here."

"Is he right?" I asked, scratching my head in hopes the snow-covered world would become familiar. "Could they have gone through there?"

"Seems likely," Tom said, gazing bitterly at Stewart. "He couldn't've come far. We might get lucky."

"Please," Stewart pleaded. "You have to try."

"Tom?" Laurence asked. "Darby?"

I frowned. I looked out and saw only the nightmare reality, remembered my dream. There was death, seemingly grinning at us from beyond the mists. And all I wanted was to get back to Laveda and the fort.

"You've got to try," Stewart argued. "You have to."

"It's just frozen farmers and little children," Laurence added. "You were one yourself, Darby. I remember your stories."

"What're we to do, Tom?" I asked. "We could get back to the fort, get a party of soldiers, and come back."

"Be three days doin' it," he grumbled. "Boy, you up to a hard ride? Think you can get those elk and this pilgrim back to the fort and get help started up here?"

"I've been out here with Papa a dozen times," Laurence said confidently. "But how will I manage with just one horse?"

"You'll have all three," Tom said, pointing at the animals stomping restlessly in the nearby pines. "Where we're goin', horses won't help. You have them soldiers bring some wagons though. They'll be needed."

"I'll get started soon as I get the saddles on," Laurence promised.

"No, wait for dawn," Tom insisted. "Get some rest. We'll need to thaw out this fellow and get a bit more out of him. Darby, drag the saddles and such over, too, and look to the horses."

"We leave at dawn, too, don't we?" I asked.

"Only thing to do," he answered, gazing sadly at Laurence.

"Never could walk away from a fight, eh?" I asked. "Whether with a bear or a Sioux or a mountain."

"Never could," he agreed, managing a smile.

We got a bit more rest before the sun cast an eerie yellow haze across the eastern horizon. It didn't provide much warmth, either to body or spirit. As I wearily shook myself to life, I gazed over at Tom. His stern face replied silently to my grim frown.

"Best help the boy ready the horses," he told me. "I'll build up the fire some, and we'll fry up some o' that elk meat. For what lays ahead, we're apt to need full stomachs."

I nodded, then roused Laurence. Together we shook Stewart to life, and the three of us warmed the saddles and dried the blankets. Afterward we collected the horses and did our best to rub the cold from their icy backs and shoulders. Pepper in particular stirred restlessly, and I knew he sensed my own fear. It was hard to explain how I dreaded setting off with Tom into the heart of those mountains. Up ahead, likely buried by the sudden snowfall, lay wagons and people—perhaps the latter as cold and lifeless as the former. The wind continued to whine, and I was overcome with anxiety. My leg stiffened, and I limped to the fire and tried to loosen the constricted tendons.

"Maybe you ought to go along with Laurence," Tom said as I winced in pain.

"And leave you alone up here?" I asked. "Not likely that. We're partners, remember?"

"Never thought otherwise," he told me, resting a tired hand on my shoulder. "Only I never figured to push you past your limits."

"Let's get the elk frying," I told him. "Won't get easier sloshing through this snow."

"No, that's sure," he agreed. "And Laurence ought to get along to the fort, too."

We huddled beside the fire and tried to warm ourselves as the elk strips crackled in the skillet. We ate the meat greedily, and I felt new strength flowing into my limbs. We cooked up some extra to keep us going on our long ordeal, and I put some in a bag for Laurence and Stewart.

"Keep at it, boy," Tom advised, when we tied the rest of the meat on Pepper's back and helped Stewart onto Tom's big buckskin. "Go slow till you're in open country, then get along to Platte River. Snows'll be lightest along the river. And when you get to the fort, start them soldiers headed out here fast."

"Yes, sir," Laurence answered.

They headed north and east, and we watched them go with somber eyes.

"Now it's our turn," I said, turning southwest.

"Best give me the lead," Tom answered.

I kicked snow over the fire, threw a provision bag over my shoulder and nodded. Tom then started through the snowdrifts, and I followed.

We were all of the morning winding our way slowly across the rocky slopes. It was strange how strong and sure were Tom's steps. He was oddly confident, and he urged me to blow a tune on my mouth organ. I tried, but my numb lips couldn't manage it. In the end, we sang a few old trail songs, adding a bawdy lyric or two in place of the milder words we'd once shared with wagon folks.

"One good thing 'bout all this snow," Tom remarked as we struggled through the drifts.

"What's that?" I asked, as I stumbled over a hidden rock and fell face first into the snow.

"No Sioux likely to worry us on this march."

"No," I agreed, laughing. "None of 'em that stupid. They'll be huddled up in their buffalo robes, with warming fires blazing in their *tipis*. Only fool whites'll trudge around in this weather."

"Sorry you came?" he asked.

"Today?"

"No," he said, pausing a moment to stare westward.

202

"No, I was thinkin' 'bout when you left your sister back in Oregon. And maybe 'bout your leavin' Illinois way back when."

"Never gave it a second thought," I said, grinning. "Had myself some high times since then, and more'n a few adventures. And there never was better company along the way."

"I always found it up to the mark."

I grinned and quickened my pace. For a time we followed a rough trail through the pines, and I thought we might have stumbled across the wagon path.

"More likely a forest fire or a rockslide cleared out the pines," Tom said. And when the clearing ended in a tangle of snow-covered boulders, I saw he'd been right as usual.

"Where now?" I asked.

"On," he muttered, waving his hand toward the southwest. "Hope we see or smell or hear somethin'. Or that you have one o' your dreams."

I'd had my dream, but I kept that to myself. He'd lost none of his confidence, and I sensed a profound belief that he'd find those wagon folks. For my part, I only hoped it would be before they were all frozen.

We crossed a low hill and made our way along a sheet of ice that once might have been a creek or pond. I recalled skating on a pond back home in Illinois with my brothers, laughing as we fell bottom first on the rock-hard surface and skidded along like stones rolling down a hillside. We always collected ourselves along the shore, gingerly regained our balance, and set out all over again.

"Winter's a bitter hard season," Tom suddenly observed. "Full o' cold and ice and death."

"Papa told me once that things had to die so you appreciated harvest. You said yourself it's fitting that the old give way to the young."

"It's a truth," he agreed. And for the first time I heard him cough as he fought to catch his breath. I felt the cold taste of the air myself, and my lungs ached. I coughed, too, and my leg began to ache. We'd gone a long way already, and there was no sign of the wagon folks.

We trudged another mile and a half through that frozen wilderness before I saw a flash of metal in the faint sunlight. I pointed that way, and almost immediately Tom and I both sniffed woodsmoke.

"Easy, son," he warned when I prepared to charge forward. "There's No Nose to keep in mind."

I halted instantly. There wasn't a bit of me wanted to tackle that renegade in such awful country. Worse, my Sharps was riding back to Fort Laramie in its scabbard. Tom and I had our Colts, but whether they would fire was a question. They'd been exposed to cold and damp, and the powder in the cartridges was suspect.

I'd stepped behind the cover of a tree when I heard a baby cry.

"Mama, I'm cold," a child spoke up.

A considerable amount of mumbling and grumbling ensued, and none of it was answered by harsh Lakota words.

"It's them," I said, struggling on.

"Darby, go slow," Tom urged. "Remember that wagon captain you come across at Fort Hall. He'd've kilt you for a biscuit."

I slowed my pace and let him catch up. I recalled that stranded wagon train all too well—the circle of frozen children surrounding a cold fire, while twenty feet away others remained safe and secure. I'd turned over a week's provisions to that captain, and he'd dragged them off and gorged himself while children whined with hunger! In the end the other wagon people had torn their leader to pieces over some dried venison and crumbs of bread.

"You remember it, too?" Tom asked.

"The world turns in circles, it seems," I told him.

"Does indeed. Let's have us a look."

The first people we discovered were huddled beside a small fire, sheltered by a wagon turned on its side. The people glanced up at us with empty, lifeless eyes. No one howled or announced their rescue. They just shivered and ignored everything else.

The next batch were piled under a canvas wagon cover, the bunch of them packed like a tin of sardines. A small boy grabbed my right hand with an iron grip and pulled off my glove.

"Mama, I've got a glove," he called in triumph as he slid it over his own pale, bluish fingers.

"My lord, it's Shea!" a tall, hollow-eyed man proclaimed. "Shea! Come from the fort to rescue us. Praise God! Stewart got through!"

Now some of the people came to life. A few even gripped our hands or slapped our backs.

"How many horses did you bring us?" a sandy-haired fellow asked. "Twenty? Wagons?"

"Ain't you got any stock left at all?" Tom cried.

"We killed a mule for food," a woman explained. "The other one run off. That renegade guide of ours took the others."

"No Nose," I muttered.

"That's the one," she said.

"Well, get hold o' yourselves," Tom pleaded. "Gather close to your fires. Stewart's gone on to the fort, and it won't be long 'fore soldiers come with wagons."

"We got wagons!" the fair-haired man shouted. "And the horses are up with No Nose. I say we go get 'em."

"With our bare hands?" another asked. "Got three knives and Granny Bassett's old musket. You know the Indians took all the guns."

"We could sneak up on 'em," the blond man suggested. "I've got my whole life tied up in those horses o' mine."

"Thank God you're alive," a young woman suggested. "But—"

"You ever try to sneak up on an Indian?" Tom asked. "A Sioux especially? He'd eat you for breakfast and spit out the leavin's."

205

"You could lead us," the blond man said. "Shoot, I'd go. Others, too."

I gazed at Tom with alarm, but he shook his head and ordered the fires built up.

"We'll wait for the bluecoats," Tom declared. "I've fought all the Indians I ever want to tangle with."

We did our best to bring the wagon folks to life. Tom and I got some of the younger men busy chopping wood so the fires could be built up, both for warmth and so that the soldiers could find us. We burned pine branches on the largest fire so that a tall pillar of gray smoke rose skyward. We got the people up and moving, and we saw to it everybody got a sliver of our provisions. The ones really bad off—mainly the smaller children and a few old people—were set close to the fires. Women rubbed their limbs and bodies, working out the numbing cold and breathing new life in to take its place.

The soldiers appeared toward nightfall, if it was possible to tell when dusk started and daylight passed. Mostly it went from gray to grayer. I'd expected Capt. Powers and a column of soldiers escorting three or four wagons. As it happened, Laurence Borden rode in with two privates atop a single open-bed supply wagon.

"All the captain would offer," Laurence said, scowling. "Laveda's at him for more, but . . ."

"Captain figured they'd all be dead," one of the privates explained. "Don't they have their own wagons? Horses?"

"There are too many for us to take," the second soldier said. "We couldn't even take all the children."

"All the children aren't here," the blond man explained. "That renegade Indian took ten or so and some of the women."

"What?" I asked.

"It's why I said we should go after 'em. Now there's no choice, is there, Mr. Shea?"

The others gazed at Tom, and he frowned.

"You boys got rifles?" Tom asked the bluecoats.

"Muskets," the first soldier answered.

"Get 'em and come along. Darby, check your powder. Looks like we've got a war to fight."

"Tom?" I asked. "No!" I wanted to tell him about my dream, about the dreadful sense of impending doom that was growing in my heart. But the people shouted their encouragement, and the sallow-cheeked children whimpered and called out for mothers and brothers and sisters.

"Got to be, Darby," Tom said. "Shouldn't worry a bear-killer, though. We'll live to raise a jug down on the Green River again."

"Will we?" I asked.

"Can't leave ole Burkett to drink it all himself," he said, laughing as he slapped my back. "Now let's get our plans made, folks. Who's got a gun?"

I left Tom and the blond-haired pilgrim to work it all out. Me, I stumbled over to the fire and tried to fend off the cold.

"Thought there might be trouble," Laurence said, joining me. "Brought your Sharps."

"Thanks," I said, taking the rifle.

"Got my own rifle, too."

"Tom'll put it to good use," I said somberly.

"But I —"

"Look after the little ones," I said. "There's a girl over there wheezes like a north wind."

"Darby, I —"

"Stay here," I told him. "Take it for a brother's advice."

"But I can talk to 'em," he argued.

"You can't talk to a man with no ears to hear your words," I answered. "Tell Laveda I'm thinking of her."

Chapter Twenty-one

There were nine of us altogether that set off to find No Nose's camp. Tom and I carried our rifles and pistols while the soldiers had their muskets. The blond-haired man, Thurman Conwell, brought along a burly Alabaman named Green and a Georgian named Maggs. The three of them had old pistols. Rounding out our company were a pair of boys, James Collard and Kurt Bromberg, brought along to take charge of the horses we hoped to capture.

We weren't much of an army, and if there'd been any other way to get that half-frozen company back to the fort, I'd have left No Nose to himself, captives or no. The dream was still much on my mind, and the whining wind seemed to taunt me at every turn.

"I'm waiting," the eerie voice seemed to say. "Death's here waiting for you."

I stared at Tom's shadow ahead of me and noticed his steps grow less certain. He heard it, too, or felt it anyway. I gripped the Sharps firmly and continued. What else was there to do?

We were half an hour searching for No Nose's camp, when a pale flicker of light in the distance drew us there. We plodded close to another hour before coming across two *tipis* and a large council fire. Overlooking them on a rocky ridge stood a solitary sentry. Down below a second guard kept watch on a knot of women and children who huddled beside the fire in their tattered clothing.

"There," Conwell said, pointing them out. "It's them."

Tom clamped a hand over the fool's mouth and waved me to one side of the narrow passage through the tall pines that served as a path. I feared the sentry might shout an alarm, for he certainly heard the words. Instead a tall young Indian cautiously approached us, calling out a challenge as he held his rifle at the ready. Tom nodded, and I jumped out and wrenched the gun away. The Sioux drew a knife, but Tom clubbed him across the head, and the blade dropped harmlessly to the ground.

"Now it turns interestin'," Tom whispered as I dragged the sentry to cover. Conwell drove his knife into the unconscious Indian's chest all the way to the hilt, and air rushed out of the dead man's lungs.

"You needn't've done that," I said as the wagon man withdrew his knife.

"I lost friends to those murderers," Conwell explained. "You've seen Sioux take prisoners. Ever imagine what those ones down there've been through? Save your sympathy."

I started to reply, but Tom hushed me.

"Not time for nonsense," he said, frowning. "They'll take note o' their picket bein' gone quickly. Darby, I'll take these soldiers and make my way to the *tipis*. That way we can cut down anybody there."

"And what do I do?" I asked.

"Take those three men, creep down, and get that other guard," he explained, pointing at a slight young man (wearing a captured woman's cloak) who was watching the captives. "We'll see the others don't trouble you. You get the prisoners and help 'em get clear."

"Yes, sir," I agreed.

"What about us?" young James asked.

"You take charge of the horses," Tom said, pointing toward a dozen or so shapes prowling the far hillside. And once Darby gets those people to you, head for the train. No time to be wasted gettin' everybody back there

209

and along to the fort."

"Yes, sir," the boys said in unison.

He waved me forward then, and I wove my way down the hill, cautiously keeping to the trees so that they hid the deep prints my feet formed in the snow. My leg ached considerably, but I refused to rest. The night was growing colder each second, and the chattering teeth of the scantily clad captives reminded me of the shivering folks back at the wagons.

My three companions followed slowly, trying to mimic my actions. They were loud and clumsy, and I'll never know why the guard didn't hear them coming. He had turned his back toward me in order to scold one of the captives when I made my move. I lunged out of the pines, half stumbled a few feet, and plunged my knife into his back. My hand felt his warm blood as the blade nicked a rib and drove deep into his vitals. He made but a brief gasp before falling forward.

"Emily, it's Papa," Green said, snatching a girl in his big arms and holding her tightly. Maggs embraced a lithe young woman and took the hand of a ten-year-old boy.

"No time for that," I whispered, waving the way toward the horses. My comrades seemed frozen though, and the captives mulled around, ignoring the danger present in the nearby *tipis*. Soon enough it made itself felt.

I don't know which of the Sioux first called out, but it took no time at all for No Nose to emerge from the first *tipi*. He called out angrily and fired his rifle toward the huddle of captives at the fire.

"Get down!" I shouted, grabbing the two closest children and pulling them to the ground with me. Green's boy yelped and fell, holding a shattered wrist, and I held back an urge to scream. The other Sioux now cut through the buffalo hide walls of the *tipis* and fired rifles or arrows. The fire illuminated the captives and made them fair targets, but a volley from Tom and the soldiers distracted the renegades long enough for Conwell to get the wagon people moving along toward the horses. One of No Nose's men, seeing it, made a solitary run toward Maggs, but I fixed the Sioux in my sights, and the Sharps dropped him to the ground.

"More death," I grumbled as my stiff fingers fought to reload the rifle. It was then I first noticed the barrels of powder on my left side. There they were, not five feet from the fire, ready to blow me halfway across the Rockies. I dragged myself toward the trees, but an arrow split the air just behind my ear, and a rifle shot drove me down into the snow.

"Darby, you all right over there?" Tom called.

"Not full of holes yet, if that's what you mean," I answered. "Keep 'em busy a moment, how 'bout?"

There was a brief pause. Then the soldiers opened up on the first *tipi*, and Tom unloaded his Colt at the second. I moved to where the first powder keg rested, bashed in the side, and made myself a fuse from a strip of my shirt. By then the Indians were giving me a fair measure of attention, and I fired two shots at them with my Colt. As they took cover behind the *tipis*, I lit my makeshift bomb and rolled it toward them. The flaming cloth rolled along like a parade of fireflies in the ebony darkness, and I hugged the ground as I waited for an explosion that didn't come. The damp ground extinguished the flame, and No Nose himself made a leap for the keg. Before I could send a bullet through his shadowy form, he dragged the powder inside his *tipi* and out of harm's way.

"Fool thing that was to do," I grumbled, knowing I'd just managed to resupply the enemy. Even so it was a fair notion. I made a half roll over to the second keg and bashed it open. I heard arrows slice the air nearby, but low to the ground as I was, I made a tough target to hit. This time I took my whole shirt and twisted it into a ropelike strand. The wind sent slivers of icy pain through my ribs in the brief moment I abandoned my coat, and I had a hard time getting my numb fingers to work.

211

Finally, I rammed the fuse in place, lit it, and rolled the barrel down toward the waiting Indians.

"Ayyy, yahh!" One of the Sioux howled as he saw the second bomb coming. It rolled straight for the lefthand *tipi,* and I huddled with my Sharps and ducked as the Indians made a frantic try to escape. The soldiers dropped two of the renegades, and the others were blown off their feet by the earth-rending concussion that followed the ignition of the powder keg.

"That'll teach the devils!" Maggs screamed from the top of the hill.

"Isn't a man alive could've survived that blast!" Conwell added.

Young Collard and one of the rescued youngsters stepped out to have a look then, and I shouted a warning.

"Get back, you fools!" I hollered as one of the stunned Sioux rose and started toward the youngsters.

Green crouched and fired his ancient pistol, but the shot missed badly. Tom and the soldiers were creeping toward the singed *tipis* from the far side, but I knew they'd never be able to stop that Sioux.

"Kill 'em all!" No Nose suddenly screamed, and a tremor ran down my back.

"No" I shouted as I watched the disfigured fiend rush toward the crowd of wagon people carrying a torch in one hand and the intact powder keg in the other. I had but a second to think, and my pistol was already following the faint outline of the first Indian. James Collard's frozen face danced in the faint light cast by the council fire, and I winced. My thumb cocked the hammer, and my finger fired the gun. Once, twice, I cocked and squeezed. The charging Indian fell on his face.

I turned to stop No Nose, but he was on me already. He swung the torch like a club, striking my jaw and sending me reeling backward. I lay there dazed as Tom slung young Collard out of the way and drove a knife into No Nose's fleshy side. The Sioux grunted and

212

dropped to his knees, then gazed brightly at Tom. With a final defiant scowl, the renegade rammed the torch into the powder.

There was a brief flash, and a whole section of mountain erupted. My ears rang with the sound. Splinters of pine, slivers of rock, and all manner of dusty debris cascaded about us. I gripped the ground as it shook. Near the crest of the hill children screamed, and men cried out in terror.

I couldn't rise for several moments. My shoulders and back were bruised and battered by the barrage of rocks, and I could feel blood trickling across my left cheek from a gash just below my eye. My legs simply wouldn't function, but I couldn't stay there, not knowing Tom might be up there in trouble.

I clawed my way along what was left of the hill. Pine branches burned like rows of church candles, illuminating the powdery white mist that hung like a shroud over the scene. Where No Nose had touched off the powder, a crater three feet deep spread fissures out across the hillside. I thought for a moment that No Nose might have blown the wagon folk to high heaven, but James Collard tumbled into view, dragging along a terrified child that might have been a younger twin.

"Tom?" I managed to call. "Tom?"

I moved past where a pine had fallen across the council fire. A leg protruded from beneath the trunk, but its bare, bronze-colored ankle identified it as Sioux. Over by the remnants of the *tipis*, the soldiers dragged the bodies of the renegades toward a solitary pile. Conwell was prying a ring off the finger of the second guard. He looked up a moment as I walked by, his face exhibiting traces of guilt.

"He's got no need of it," the wagoneer explained. "Got to pay for the food that'll keep my family alive this winter."

I finally managed to get my legs working, and I painfully stood. Up ahead Collard and the younger boy were

213

sitting beside a pile of boulders. Only when I got closer did I see Tom's shattered form encircled by the rocks.

"He's hurt bad," James said, trying to wash blood and dirt from Tom's face as the younger boy dragged rocks from Tom's legs and chest.

"Tom?" I whispered, collapsing at his side.

"Fool thing to do," he muttered as a spasm of pain racked his chest.

"Rest easy," I pleaded. "We'll get you in a wagon. Laveda and I'll get you healed up just fine."

"Not this time, son," he said, coughing violently. Blood trickled from his lips, and his face grew pale.

"It's my fault," James said, trembling as he touched Tom's shoulder. "We were supposed to stay with the horses, but Mr. Conwell said it was all over, and I . . ."

"Sure," I said, fighting to wipe the wild look from my eyes.

"Boy's got to be curious, don't he, Illinois?" Tom asked.

"You haven't called me that in a long while," I said. "Not since we took to traveling regular."

"Guess you put me in mind o' the trail west," he told me. "Fool boy, out to prove himself a man, and hardly big as a pine saplin'. Had the innards though. Never short o' gumption, that Illinois Prescott. Was as much of a man at fourteen as most ever are."

"Helped to have a good teacher," I whispered.

"Teacher? I ain't even had schoolin'."

"You taught me all the important things," I said, rubbing my eyes.

"No, you had 'em learned yourself that first day we met, in the muddy street in Independence, with the rain drippin' off your hat and splashin' onto your toes. You knew how a man does his best, when and where he can, and he never looks for ease in a life that's got none to offer."

He moaned a little, and I bent over him in an effort to ease his discomfort.

214

"Funny, ain't it?" he asked. "Always figured it'd be a buff's horn or a Sioux arrow laid me low. Here I am kilt by a pile o' mountain."

"Not killed," I said. "Hurt."

"Son, I've got a rib twistin' in my lung, and I can't feel a thing past my belly. I know full well when to end a tale, don't I? This is the last turn, Darby. Trail's at an end."

"No," I argued.

He reached out his hand and gripped mine faintly. I gazed into his sad eyes and fought to hold off my tears.

"Blow me a tune, will you?" he asked.

I reached into my hip pocket and pulled out my mouth organ. It felt like ice, and my lips could hardly move across it. I stifled my heaving chest and managed a few notes.

"Oh don't you remember," he said, coughing. "Remember," he added, coughing again. "Sweet Betsy . . . from Pike."

"Who crossed the great mountains," James took up in a surprisingly sweet voice.

"With . . . Ike," Tom whined, wincing as pain tore through him.

"I'm sorry, Mr. Shea," James said, grasping Tom's other hand. The younger boy sobbed, and Tom fought back the pain long enough to grin.

"You been a good part . . . good a son," he said faintly, "as I could've grown . . . myself. Did my best . . ."

"I know," I said, pressing his hand with my own as if to give him strength. "Tom?"

"Put me high," he said. His eyes rolled back then, and his chest collapsed in a final spasm. Then he was still.

"Lord, no!" I shouted, tearing through the snow and uprooting clumps of grass. "Why?"

But there was only the whining of the wind and the numbing cold to answer. Every part of me ached, and there was no comforting hand eager to provide a balm for my troubles. Once I had thought I'd been grown the day Mary and I buried Papa, but I now knew that hadn't been so. Tom had been around to fend off the worst troubles, to help me steady my feet as I set forth on the hardship-littered trail of manhood.

"Tom?" I called.

And when he didn't answer, I knew I was truly alone now. He'd left the trail to me and asked but a single favor—to rest in the high country he loved.

I bent over his shattered body and picked it up. Once he'd seemed taller than the Rockies, and I'd been so very small. My shoulders had broadened though, and life had worn him down. My legs buckled a bit as I started up the ridge. Melted snow had become ice, and I slipped more often than not.

"Maybe you could use some help?" James Collard said when I fell the fifth time. I gazed over at the solemn-faced fifteen-year-old. I hadn't known he was even there. "My brother Jacob," James added, stepping to one side so that the smaller brother could no longer hide behind his elder. "We could maybe carry his legs, couldn't we?"

"It's for me to do," I told them.

"You were his friend, and I figure it's true," James admitted. "But it was us he saved from the blast. You can't get him up there all alone, you know."

Jacob shook his head and reached for one of Tom's boots. I sighed and nodded. James took the other boot, and the three of us started up the ridge together, carrying the man who had brought us life when death opened its jaws wide.

We put Tom in a small clearing overlooking the North Platte. Even with the world below painted white, I recognized the familiar route of the Oregon Trail. I decided he would feel at home there, looking down on the pilgrims, watching one batch or another making the long crossing. And I thought it would give me comfort riding past, to know he was up there looking down.

The ground was too hard for digging, and we had no

spade anyway. I recalled how he spoke once of the rock cairns the Scots built as grave sites to commemorate the deaths of valiant warriors in Tom's native Highlands, and I only regretted old Duncan Macilvain or one of the other Hudson Bay Company men wasn't around to blow a reel or two on some bagpipes. We placed the body in a grassy spot where we scraped away the snow. Then we dragged rocks over and erected a cairn to cover him.

"Seems a sad place," James observed. "Maybe later, when it's not so cold, we can take him back to the fort."

"No, his place is here, under the open skies, with the hawks and the eagles for company," I told the boys. "His wasn't an easy path, you know, and his heart was torn more than once. He gave what he could, and there aren't many poorer 'cause he came this way."

I drew out my mouth organ and struggled through a sad version of "Shenandoah." I knelt beside the cairn a moment afterward, hoping to come to terms with it all. But I kept seeing his grinning face and hearing his voice. I bit my lip and started down to where the soldiers were organizing the captives on the anxious horses.

Tom's pain had passed. Mine was only beginning.

Chapter Twenty-two

There never was a longer night. I rode at the head of the weary, near frozen army of refugees, toward where their comrades waited for the longer journey on to Fort Laramie, but I was really all alone. Tom wasn't there to keep us from the brush snags and rock slides. He wasn't there to warm my trembling chest by telling of the time ole Buck Jasper got caught in an ice storm and froze his bottom in a saddle so solid a smith had to cut him loose with a chisel.

"How much farther?" the exhausted wagon folks cried with each passing minute. "Aren't we close now?"

Children sobbed, and their elders coughed and moaned. I began to lose the feeling in my toes, and old wounds made themselves felt. The wind swept down on us mercilessly, blowing snow into our eyes and biting through the thin clothing of the freed captives. Oh, one or two had managed to tear themselves a length of the lodgeskin, and James Collard had brought his brother a thick elk hide taken off one of the dead Sioux. One or two of the younger children were in rags though, and I knew the cold must be striking hard and deep.

I felt my way through the country more by instinct than by direction, and I used my nostrils to sniff out the smoke of the wagon people's fires. Soon we glimpsed the pinpricks of light on a faraway ridge and covered the final quarter-mile. When the company was reunited, there was a good deal of celebrating.

"Thought you'd never get back," Laurence observed when I fell out of the saddle. "Where's Tom?"

"Tom stayed," I said, my lip quivering.

"Stayed?" Laurence cried. "In this cold?"

"He doesn't feel it anymore," I explained. "He had half a mountain fall on him."

"He's dead?"

"Gone to greater glory, Mama used to say," I recounted. "We put him up high so he can watch the Platte River road. But I think he'd rather be riding along home with us."

"Darby, you all right?" Laurence asked.

"Always am, aren't I?"

The soldiers hurriedly hitched the best of the horses to the strongest wagons, and I helped Conwell assign the families to one wagon or another. I was preparing to mount a piebald mare and guide the way to the fort, when Laurence objected.

"The soldiers and I know the way," he argued. "We'll get you there. Your eyes are near shut, and you've had no rest."

"Take a spot in the second wagon," Conwell instructed. And so I did, sandwiching myself between the Collard boys and the cold barrel of my Sharps.

"Gather close," Conwell urged as the soldiers put out the fires. "We've a long ride yet, and it's sure to get colder."

We were closer now than some would have deemed respectable, but as the cold grew worse, the few gaps between people disappeared The little Green boy sat staring at his bandaged wrist, moaning and groaning each time the wagon jolted us. The lead wagon up ahead threw up a cloud of powdery snow that fell relentlessly on our exposed chins and ears, and some of the smaller children retaliated by hurling snowballs at the cruel perpetrators. Most of the frozen spheres landed on the necks of our team, and the horses responded by finding even bigger rocks to slam our wheels against.

Meanwhile the moon hung in the bleak sky, its bright circle of light veiled by a thick mist.

It's a weeping moon, I told myself. The world itself's crying over Tom . . . and over the killing and the injustice that brought it about.

I did my best to cheer the folks. Sometimes I'd blow a tune on my mouth organ. The wind stole the notes though, and my lips couldn't tolerate the taste of cold steel for more than a moment or two. Ahead and behind us, women took up the singing of hymns, but our wagon was fearfully shy of churchgoers. Someone would start in on a story, but cold and exhaustion too often overpowered the teller.

For close to three hours we rumbled along. Then James Collard turned to me and sighed.

"Why'd he do it?" the boy asked.

"Tom, you mean?" I asked.

"Yes," he said. "Why'd he hurry to save us, when he knew he'd be killed?"

"I don't guess there's any way to know for certain," I explained, "but I knew him fairly well."

"And?"

"Ever notice the two fingers cut off his left hand?"

"Lots o' times," Jacob said. "He told James and me at the fort how a big wolf nibbled 'em."

"Wasn't that way at all," I said. "It's a Crow ritual to cut fingers when you lose a loved one."

"Hard on hands," James observed.

"It is. But you see they believe that by undergoing pain, you purify yourself and allow the loss to pass."

"Who died?" James asked.

"Tom's wife and son. It happened when he was away, and I don't think he ever forgave himself. Was a lifetime's sorrow, you could say. I suppose he was forever trying to make it up to that boy, by doing for others left on their own."

"Like for me and Jacob?"

220

And others, I added silently as I nodded.

"It's a hard thing, losin' folks," James said sourly. "We had a sister die, then our ma and pa. Now all we've got left's Uncle Cy out in Oregon. And we won't get there till next year."

"You'll get there though," I said, nodding somberly. "It's a hard trail, Tom always said, but you hold on tight and you'll get to the end of it."

One or two of the others voiced their agreement.

"Trust in the Lord to get you through your trials," one of the women said.

I gazed at the freezing faces as they fought to find that faith or belief that would offer warmth and encouragement. It was a rare thing, faith. Rare as Tom Shea.

I passed in and out of a troubled sleep those last few hours. When I next became aware of what was going on around me, I saw Laurence and the soldiers approaching the parade ground.

"We made it back to the fort," young James said.

"Most of us," Jacob added, frowning as he gazed across the way at an old woman who'd breathed her last.

There were other grim reminders of the cruel cold. Capt. Powers's wife and a detachment of women took charge of the threadbare wagon people and soon had them bathing in hot water and wrapped in warm blankets and buffalo hides. Many suffered frostbite, and even the lucky few who didn't had a time rubbing life back into blue toes and chafed fingers.

Three women and a baby had died. I considered it a miracle the whole batch weren't gone, for even with the sun rising, the shrill wind continued to whine. Laurence helped me stumble along to the trading post. He opened the door, dragged me to a chair, and drew Laveda aside to pass on the grim news of Tom's death.

"Oh, Darby, I'm so sorry," she said. "He was a good man, and I know you looked on him like an uncle."

"A second father," I muttered, fighting to keep my composure.

"I guess we've both of us lost a father this winter."

"More'n that, Laveda," I told her. "The best partner a wayfarer ever had, and a friend who could pass the winter without quarreling or bringing on the melancholy."

Capt. Powers arrived then, and our conversation was cut short while the officer spoke to Laveda and Laurence about the needs of the wagon folk.

"I'll do what I can," Laveda promised, "but you understand I've a business to operate, Captain. I can't simply give my supplies away."

"Some will pay what they can," the captain said. "Others promise to work off their debts."

"There's little work to be done that the three of us can't manage," she replied. "They're welcome to spread out in the storeroom, these six families you ask me to house, Captain. I can spare some flour and some elk meat. Later, when the weather breaks, Darby may shoot some more meat. They're free to buy some of it off him."

"I was hoping perhaps you'd be more generous," Powers said, shaking his head sourly.

"Don't know I'd talk generosity," I barked. "You had a stranded train, and you managed to send two soldiers to rescue 'em. Laurence and I got 'em here, and Tom sacrificed his life."

"I heard about that," Captain Powers said, nodding sadly. "Fine man, Shea. He'll be missed."

"Yes, he will," I agreed.

The captain departed, and I walked outside with Laveda to the storehouse. We managed to locate buffalo hides or blankets for those in need, and we sold a bit of this and that to the ones who had money. The emigrants filed inside when we finished, and for a short while Laveda and I sat there, too, joining in the singing and thanksgiving.

"We'll leave you to yourselves now," Laveda finally declared. "Darby?"

I nodded and limped out after her. We then walked

back to the store.

"Have you made any plans?" she asked, as we sat together beside a small fire.

"I thought to ride out when the snows thaw and have a look."

"You can't spend your whole life as a wayfarer," she grumbled. "It's time you sink roots. I know before you were reluctant on account of Tom, but he's gone now."

"Wasn't just Tom," I argued. "I've got wayfarer's feet. They'll get the itch to move on."

"But you'll stay through winter?"

"Got no other place to go, especially now you've turned over the storehouse to those wagon folks."

"And past that?"

"I always figured to take a wagon train west to Oregon. Like Tom'd do."

"You can't be forever following another's footsteps," she scolded.

"They're good footprints," I objected. "And it's a fine path."

"A lonely one. Some might prefer company."

"Some," I said, letting her burrow in under my arm. "Most even."

I slept half the day on a pallet beside the fireplace. That night after supper I sat at the window with Laveda, watching snowflakes dance their way across the heaven's and pile in drifts against the porch. The moon was breaking out of its haze, and light glimmered on the snow-covered plain below.

The weeping moon was, as all things did, passing into memory. Snows thawed. Pain subsided. And memories, well, they provided a measure of comfort as the years rolled on.

I found myself recalling a hundred things, mostly little words of wisdom or comfort Tom had spoken over our years together. It seemed impossible those times were at an end. And yet at the same time, they laid the foundation for something new and different. Perhaps something even better.

"Darby, you there?" Laveda whispered.

"Yeah, I'm here," I said, pulling her close. I thought back to the three fingers on Tom's left hand, to the pain and grief he'd so seldom shared. And I thought, feeling Laveda close to me, what a blessing it was to belong, to love, to weep.

The first tear flowed out of my eye, and I let it wind its way across my cheek and fall on my chin. Tears were a cleansing of sorts, the washing away of grief and sadness.

"It's only natural you should cry some," Tom had said after Mama died. "Wasn't she worth cryin' for, if ever a woman was?"

"Yes," I agreed then. And I wept for the same reason now.

"You all right, Darby?" Laveda asked again.

"Maybe not," I confessed. "Maybe I won't be tomorrow, either. But I will be by and by."

She held me tighter, and I gave her a kiss. It warmed me, and I knew it was true. The pain would pass. Love would bloom anew.